MISSING MAYBE DEAD

TOM MITCHELTREE

For the Ashland Library

Tom Mitchl

2006

INTRIGUE
PRESS

MADISON | WISCONSIN

Published by Intrigue Press,
an imprint of Big Earth Publishing
923 Williamson St.
Madison, WI 53703

This is a work of fiction. Any similarities to people or places,
living or dead, is purely coincidental.

ISBN: 1-890768-67-7
LOC: 2006921919

FOR MY CHILDREN: TOBY, PATRICK, JENNY AND KATY. FLORENCE HAS GIVEN US LOTS OF GOOD MEMORIES.

[1]

PAUL FISCHER LEANED back in his chair and stared out the window. It was a small window in a small room, one of two upstairs bedrooms in the cottage. Pam Livingston, prominent lawyer, wealthy woman, and his mate, had the larger one. But, he thought, he had the better view.

On his desk was a stack of final examination papers that still needed grading. His mind was far away from them. Over the last few months he had watched the orchard that bordered the house on two sides bloom into gorgeous pink, and then he had watched that pink drop away, to be replaced by the light green of newborn leaves. With each change that led closer to summer, Paul felt restless. Something inside of him was blossoming and growing, too, but he didn't know what it was.

He needed something in his life. He couldn't imagine what it was. The teaching job he had taken at Southern Oregon University proved to be more interesting than he thought it would be. A new administration wanted standards raised and curriculum tougher. The university's reputation as a party school still lingered. The president wanted the course of study to grow to match the recent change of status from college to university. Paul had accepted the challenge, but then he learned quickly that he was just one voice, and, being the new kid on the block, one of the least likely voices to be heard. That in itself, disappointing as it was, didn't explain the restlessness he felt. He had played politics in academics long enough to expect no less.

He didn't think that his life with Pam was at the heart of his restlessness, either. They shared both the house and a bed in an easy, familiar comfort. Both were so busy that they were never alone long enough to get on each other's nerves, and when they did need a break together, they flew down to San Francisco or up to Victoria for a few days. They seemed to have a good time together, he thought, although the lawyer in Pam was never far below the surface. Often he felt he did not have her complete attention.

He heard the soft tinkle of a cellular phone. Shortly afterward, Pam's office door opened, and she padded down the hall in what she called her Saturday-morning slippers. When she reached his open door, she thrust an arm into the room with the phone dangling from her hand, saying, "It's your lovely ex-wife hoping she can make your life miserable one more time."

Paul took the phone from Pam. He didn't understand the dynamics between ex-wives and new women. He knew Pam and Beth disliked each other. Both used every opportunity they could to insult the other, through him, of course, and never face to face.

When he put the phone to his ear, Beth said, "I heard that."

Pam remained standing in the doorway, and he made a face at her. "I'm sure she meant it only in the kindest sense." That caused Pam to roll her eyes, pivot on her heels, and head back to her office.

"We need to talk about the boys and plans for summer."

Not again, he thought. They had this conversation every summer. He wanted his two sons here, with him. She maneuvered behind his back to get them tied up in summer sports programs, classes, and activities so that either they could not get away to visit him, or they could only stay a short time when they did get away.

"I'm supposed to have the boys for the summer this time," he said.

"Please don't get mad," she rushed to say, an unusual starting point for her. Normally she tried to get him mad. "I'd like to keep them for the first three weeks of summer, and then you get them for the rest of the summer."

Now he was suspicious. She was offering nine weeks while the best he could usually hope for was four to six. "What's up?" he asked.

"Denise and I need some time together."

Denise was a dark shadow that had crossed his path several years ago, a shadow that remained even on cloudy days. She was Beth's "domestic partner," as Beth preferred to call her, and the reason for their initial separation and later divorce.

Paul never had been able to get right exactly what he was to feel about Denise. If she'd been a man, he would have known what to do. But she wasn't a man. She was a gruff voice that quickly sought out Beth when he called. She could only occasionally be glimpsed when he visited the boys at their mother's house.

According to his sons, Denise was okay. She was into sports. She liked hiking and camping. She was good at fishing. She was a decent cook. She was a taskmaster when it came to schoolwork. In other words, she wasn't a bad father. All of which, of course, left Paul even more confused.

"That will give you and that lawyer woman a chance to do something before the boys arrive."

That would be true, except Pam had taken on her first big criminal case, defending a man accused of killing two lesbians. The irony didn't escape Paul. The man was guilty. Pam was determined to keep him off death row.

"Pam's tied up with a case," he said. "But I suppose I can find something to do."

"I'll owe you."

"Gosh, and I thought I was always going to be the one owing you."

"Don't be nasty."

"When can I expect them?"

"Early in July. I don't know the date yet."

"Let me know as soon as you do, so I can make some plans." He couldn't resist adding, "And send my best to Denise."

"Of course I will. And she sends her love."

"How come it never gets here?"

"She says she addresses it to Hell. You'll get it in good time."

"Lovely woman," he said. "She just confirms how mentally unstable you were when you left me." He pushed the button to kill the phone call before she had time to respond. He knew she wouldn't call back, but he also knew in time that she would get even.

He took the phone back to Pam's office, the room he called "control central." Not only did the room have several phone lines, multiple computers, a fax, a copier, and a scanner, but it also had a desk for Pam's secretary in case work needed to get done on the weekends.

Pam rolled her chair away from a computer and swiveled around. "What did she want this time?"

He placed the phone on her desk. "She wants to keep the boys until the first of July, and then we've got them for the rest of the summer."

"Oh, Paul!" she moaned. "I was hoping we could get away in August, after the trial."

Paul knew that at this moment in time, nothing he said would matter. It would be the wrong thing to say. It didn't matter that the trial wouldn't be over until the end of August. It didn't matter that, as far as temperatures were concerned, right here in the Rogue River Valley was a great place to be in August. It didn't even matter that they hadn't talked about a vacation in August. It only mattered that Beth wanted something, and he had agreed to it. To Pam that was as good as losing a round in the imaginary bout she was having with his ex-wife.

"Hey," he said, backing toward the door. "I've got to get those exams graded. We'll talk about this later." He didn't retreat fast enough to miss the glare she sent his way.

Without the boys around, and with Pam working sixteen hours a day on the trial and for her other clients, the only thing he was concerned about was what he would do for those three weeks.

[2]

"DAMN IT, PAUL, I asked you not to move anything!"

Paul was standing at the kitchen sink, washing the breakfast dishes. The mistake he had made, he realized from the anger in Pam's voice, was to move a stack of papers on the dining room table so he could have room for a bowl of cereal and a cup of coffee.

"I'm sorry," he said, "I should have put back the papers."

"Wrong!" she said. "You should never have moved them in the first place."

As the pressure of Pam's approaching trial began to build, her tolerance of even the trivial had declined proportionately. Together two years now, he felt he knew her about as well as he would. Often when she was with him, she was a roller coaster ride of emotions, all seemingly directed by forces outside of herself. In a courtroom she was as cool as a lawyer could be, but with him she was a reactionary.

"I should never have moved them," he said.

She moved into the kitchen and leaned her back against the doorframe. "Don't be condescending, please."

He'd learned it was best to control his own temper because in verbal battles, the college professor was no match for the trial lawyer. He had the luxury of passive audiences in his business. Pam could not afford to let her audiences be passive. She had polished the art of verbal thrust to a lethal level.

He turned slowly to her, taking time to fold the dishtowel and put it back on its rack. Finally, smiling and holding his hands out as if to assure Pam he hadn't grabbed a carving knife, he said, "The dining room table is covered, the dinette table is covered, the coffee table is covered. I'm kind of getting tired of eating my meals standing up."

She gestured toward the kitchen window, "Eat on the patio."

"Yes," he said, "but it is late spring. It is southern Oregon. And it is still fifty-five degrees out there when I am ready to eat breakfast."

She sagged a bit. As brilliant and as beautiful as she was, she hadn't needed anyone else in her life until Paul came along. She had always had the edge, because she knew she could walk away from any relationship and not look back. What had worked so well for her before had not worked with Paul. He had walked away from her once. To get him back she had to admit—to herself and to him—that she did care for him. She had been fighting that revelation ever since.

"You're too damned handsome," she muttered.

"What's that got to do with anything?" he asked.

"That's the only thing that keeps me from going for the kill."

He walked over and pulled her into a hug. "Does that mean I'm dead meat when my looks start to fade?"

"It means I'm a bitch, and I've been a bitch for months, and you've been a saint and I don't deserve you." She paused, waiting for him to say something. "This is where you step in and say reassuring thoughts."

"You were on a roll, and so right on, I didn't want to interrupt you."

She pinched the skin above his waist. As he squirmed, trying to get free, she said, "You need to get away until the boys come. I'm not going to be much fun to live with, and it's only going to get worse until the trial is over. I'm already afraid the boys are going to see me as the wicked witch of the west when they come out."

Although he wouldn't say it to Pam, he also was worried about that. The boys liked Pam when she was at her best, but when she was busy, they only got passing attention from her. The relationship between them was solid enough, but no one pretended that it came close to love. Respect, maybe. Fondness, certainly. But not love.

Paul had to admit that bothered him. He still held out a dream of having a family again, one without all the awkwardness that sometimes went with an extended family. He also knew that he would have to settle for this. Pam had made it clear that she wasn't interested in having kids of her own. Beautiful Pam—with her blonde hair and blue eyes, with her near perfect figure, with her intelligence and success—drove men to mad thoughts of procreation. But Pam was God's little joke on the male species. She left, and men could only dream of having her babies.

Pam had pulled him back to her and was holding him again. "What do you think?" she asked.

"About getting away?"

"Isn't there some place you'd like to go?"

Without Pam? Not back east. Having Beth on the other side of the country still wasn't far enough away. He dreamed of going to the Caribbean someday, but this wasn't the season for it. It was probably too late to make arrangements for a trip to Europe. Besides, what would he do there? "I'll have to think about it," he said.

On his way back to his office upstairs, he thought that he might go up the coast, stopping in Portland for a few days, and then in Seattle, and finally in Vancouver. He might even cross over to Victoria. The ferry rides alone would be worth the trip. Would he enjoy the trip without Pam? Probably more than he would if he stayed here, with her in the mood she was in now. The idea of a trip suddenly seemed reasonable. He would drive. He'd have the best of both worlds: leisurely pace and interesting destinations.

Back in his office, he finished grading the finals. Now he only needed to record the grades and get the grade sheets back to the university before his summer vacation officially began. Tonight he would sit down with a map and plan his trip.

He had just reached that decision when the phone on his desk rang. This was his line. Pam had the lines in her office, and they shared the cell phone number. Most of the calls that came to him on this line were from school.

He picked up the phone and said, "Paul."

"Paul Fischer?"

"Yes."

"The school gave me your number. This is Bill Drexler."

From the sound of the man's voice, he expected Paul to recognize the name. And then suddenly Paul did. "Professor William Drexler?" Paul asked.

"Yes."

"It's been a while." This wasn't the voice Paul remembered. Drexler's voice had been vibrant, full of life and energy. This voice was slow and tired.

"Five or six years."

"It's good to hear from you," Paul said. "I take it you are still retired." Paul and Drexler had taught together for two years before Paul was first drawn out west. He remembered the man as being brilliant and acclaimed, an expert in American essays. He was always being called upon to help judge for a variety of awards, including twice for Pulitzers.

"Very much so. And not too far from where you are. I'm in Florence, Oregon."

Paul and Pam had driven through Florence once on a trip up the coast. It was located about seventy miles west of Eugene. He had been impressed by Honeyman State Park, with its towering white sand dunes.

"I thought that you would have retired to New York City or some place like that."

"No. I've returned to my roots. My wife and I lived here when I taught at the University of Oregon."

Paul didn't remember Drexler's having a wife, but he vaguely remembered something about a daughter. "Are you calling to catch up?"

"That's what I liked about you when we taught together. You weren't afraid to get to the point. I called because I've read about your exploits."

"Certain not those connected with my teaching. I'm so far down the seniority list that I'm listed as: to be exploited."

Drexler chuckled. "I remember those days," he said. "What I am actually interested in are your exploits solving mysteries that defy being solved."

"I've had some luck in that area," Paul said.

"I've called because I have a mystery for you."

"I'm a teacher, Professor Drexler, not a sleuth."

"I'd like you to help me find my wife."

"Professor, that's certainly something for the police."

"Yes. The police were involved, and they couldn't solve the mystery when my wife disappeared thirty years ago."

[3]

PAUL STOPPED IN Eugene for lunch, and then he found the cutoff that took him to Florence. The drive was pleasant, a road that quickly left farm land behind and wove its way through first woods and then forests. He crossed over the Siuslaw River at Mapleton and then followed the river as it grew in width as he neared Florence.

The tide was out. Large mudflats stretched wide on each side of the river. Seagulls hopped along the banks, scavenging in the mud. In the distance, Paul could see a bank of clouds that seemed to have flattened against the coastline, as if a sheet of glass extended from shore to sky. On this side of the glass, the sky was blue and clear.

On the coast, in summer, a continual battle existed between the clouds and the sunshine, some thermal confrontation that would be won out by one side or the other. One day it would stay sunny; the next day, for no apparent reason, the clouds would batter down the glass barrier and tumble onto the land. The sunshine would retreat ten miles inland to wait for the next day.

The directions to Drexler's house were simple enough. When he reached the coast highway, Paul turned left. Just before he reached the bridge back over the Siuslaw River, he turned right. That took him down to the road that cut one way back under the bridge to Old Town, or the other way along the river and eventually to the ocean. Drexler's house was a short distance, located on a side street.

The house was on the corner on the opposite side of the street from the river. Although houses lined the other side of the street, Drexler's still offered a good view because it sat on a rise bordered by an eight-foot retaining wall around the front yard.

Paul sat in his car and took in the house. Three flights of steps led to a porch. The porch itself was enclosed in glass and filled with wicker furniture. Above the porch, on the second floor, were rooms fronted with tall windows. From either spot the professor would be able to sit and look out over his neighbor's houses to the river beyond and the trees and dunes of Honeyman Park on the other side. This was, Paul thought, despite the modesty of the house, a million-dollar view.

Paul had tried his best to get out of this. After discussing it with Pam, he had decided he would take a trip through Oregon and Washington and into Canada. He hadn't planned an itinerary. He would just follow whatever interested him. With that kind of an agenda, he found it almost impossible to decline Dr. Drexler's request to stop to see him and hear his story.

He got out of his car—actually Pam's Mercedes—and began the climb up the flights of steps. As he neared the front door, a young woman stepped out on the porch to open the door for him. Paul paused at the open door and took her in. She wasn't a Pam Livingston. She was lovely in a different way. She had large, green eyes that curved down at the outside edges and turned into cheeks that curved up again. The effect was unusual, creating a face that radiated both good cheer and pleasantness. He knew absolutely nothing about her, but the attractiveness of her features made him want to like her immediately. Then she smiled, and he did like her.

She offered a hand to him. "I'm Terri Drexler. You have to be Paul Fischer." As she led him into the house, he couldn't help but notice that she was taller than most women, perhaps five-nine, and that she was full-bodied, with a beautiful shape.

It didn't help that he had to follow her up another flight of stairs. She was wearing a snug-fitting pair of jeans, and she filled them to perfection. At the top of the stairs, she led him into one of the front rooms, one with the tall windows he had noticed from the outside. In a wheelchair, near a window, sat William Drexler. Paul would never have recognized him if Terri hadn't said, "Dad, Paul Fischer is here."

Paul felt a moment of panic. On one side of him was this lovely creature with such an interesting face, with auburn hair that curled in at her neck and bounced off her shoulders as she walked—broad shoulders seemingly made to carry her large, shapely breasts. On the other side of him was a man so shriveled that Paul had to search to find anything of the man he remembered from just a few years ago.

"Cancer," the man said. The voice was Drexler's.

"I'm sorry," Paul said, the only thing he could think to say.

Bright blue eyes, eyes that Paul remembered, stared intently at him. "I haven't got a whole lot of time left."

No, Paul thought. It was Emily Dickinson who said that death was all that man needed to know about heaven, and all he needed to know about hell. Drexler looked like he stood on the edge, between heaven and hell.

Terri interrupted the awkward silence by asking, "Would you like some coffee, Paul?"

"I'd love coffee," he said.

"Cream, sugar?"

"No, just black and caffeinated."

She smiled at him, a cheerful smile that showed straight, white teeth, as she left the two of them alone. That's when he noticed that she wasn't wearing makeup. Her skin was so smooth and healthy that she didn't need it. The dark eyebrows and the natural shadows of her features gave her face all the highlights it needed.

He had to force himself to turn away from her and back to Drexler. In that instant, Paul wondered what was going on in his own head. He had a beautiful woman back home waiting for him, even if she was preoccupied at the moment, and didn't want a family with kids. The thought startled him, and he had to shake his head and tell himself not to go there. He returned his attention to the professor.

"Paul, take a seat there." Drexler gestured to a chair nearby with a limp flap of his hand.

Paul moved the chair a little closer to the wheelchair and sat down. Drexler wouldn't be with this world much longer, he thought. "I don't think I can help you, Dr. Drexler," Paul began, already sensing that he needed to get away from here quickly. The nearness of death made him nervous. And the daughter. She had done absolutely nothing provocative, but she was, in all her attractiveness and richness of features and fullness of body, mother earth, and he was, despite himself, feeling himself respond to her.

Drexler said, "It's not much of a story. One summer evening thirty years ago, my wife went out the door to go to the store for milk and to take a walk. She was working hard to get her shape back after Terri was born. Terri was three months old then. My wife never came back."

Paul was waiting for more, but Drexler stopped. His eyes held Paul's. "The police?" Paul asked.

"They did what they could back then. Florence wasn't a big town; still isn't. The police department was small. They investigated the best they could, but when they didn't find anything, they quickly lost interest."

"The FBI?"

"The few agents in the state we had then were busy with war protestors. They never took an interest in the case."

"And that was it? All that was done?"

"Of course not. Twice I hired people. I spent most of what I had paying these investigators. They couldn't find a thing. Not one thing. They too gave up quickly."

"And you expect me to do better, thirty years later?"

The professor's arm slowly closed the gap between them, and his cold, bony fingers wrapped around Paul's wrist with surprising strength. Tears began to gather on the rims of his eyes. "I don't want to die without knowing what happened to her."

"I wouldn't know where to start—"

Drexler interrupted him. "Terri will help you."

That was just what he needed, Paul thought, a cold case and a hot woman. He'd have to find a way out of this, and fast. He'd call Pam on the cell phone and have her give the Drexlers a call, telling them that he was needed at home. Anything.

Terri came into the room, carrying a tray with a coffeepot, cups, and cookies arranged on it. She put the tray down on a small table in the room and poured coffee into decorated china cups with matching saucers. She placed several cookies on the saucer next to the cup and carried it to Paul. "Butterscotch chip," she said. "One of my favorites. I hope you like them."

He took the cup from her and asked, "Did you make them?"

She smiled that smile again. "My daughter loves them."

Paul felt—What was it? He wanted to feel relieved, assuming the woman must have a husband. Instead, he felt a little disappointed.

"How old is your daughter?" he asked.

"Four. She's taking a nap. You'll get to meet her later."

Terri was thirty now, he figured. She didn't look it. That smooth skin of hers would defy age for years to come. He wondered what she thought about this desire of her father's to find out what happened to her mother. Would she share it? Her mother was a woman whom she had never known.

"Paul so far hasn't shown much enthusiasm for this project," Drexler said, with little emotion in his voice.

Terri pulled a chair from the table and placed it so that she could face both of them. "Can you blame him? You just told him he had a riddle to solve, one that hadn't been cracked in thirty years, and you told him he had a short time to do it. I can understand his lack of enthusiasm." She returned to the table for her own coffee and cookies, and then came back and sat down.

Drexler wasn't eating or drinking. "I thought maybe you could put it in a way that would make it important to him."

"No, Dad, it will never be as important to him as it is to you, but I will do what I can to prevail on him to help us out." She looked at Paul and smiled, saying, "Please."

Paul laughed. He could see that she had gotten a lot with just that smile. "Don't get me wrong. I'm not trying to tell you that you have to try harder, but this seems like so little to go on."

"I have copies of all the reports that have been written on the disappearance. Would you at least look through them before you decide anything?"

"My daughter is a wonderful cook. You can stay for dinner, and then we have a guestroom downstairs. You wouldn't get very far up the coast today before you'd be worrying about dinner and a place to sleep."

True, Paul thought. And after tasting the cookies, he suspected that dinner might not be bad, either. He'd appreciate a good, home-cooked meal. The truth was that Pam took great pride in her lack of domestication. She had a housekeeper. She had another woman who came in once a week, cooked all day, and then froze the dinners for them to warm up as needed. The woman was good and the meals were delicious, but they had that frozen food feel.

Paul gave in. "The least I can do is look at the reports."

Drexler nodded his head, as if he was sure all along that Paul would help. Terri gave Paul a look that said, simply, thank you.

"Are you ready to go back to the bedroom, Dad?" Terri asked.

Drexler seemed to sag in the chair, as if a sudden weight had been placed on him. "Yes," he said. "It's been a little too much excitement for me."

Terri put her cup on the tray and then took up a position behind the wheelchair. "Dad's been waiting at that window half the day. He was pretty sure you'd come. Unfortunately, he usually only gets out of bed now for a few minutes at a time."

"Can I help?" Paul asked.

"No," she said. "There's a bedroom with a bath down on the first floor, to the left of the stairs as you come down. Why don't you get your things from the car and put them in there? When I have Dad comfortable, I'll come down." As she wheeled him from the room, Drexler's hand fluttered in farewell.

Paul was surprised when he opened the door to the bedroom. It wasn't a bedroom at all, but a small study complete with a desk. On the desk were a computer, telephone, and fax. The sofa in the room obviously pulled out into a bed, but with it folded up, the room was compact and comfortable, a work area not unlike the one he had in Medford.

He brought his suitcases in from the car and stuck them in the den closet. It was spacious, with built-in drawers on one side and a long rack on the other to hang clothes. He didn't bother to unpack. He did not intend to stay for more than one night.

Across from the closet, on the opposite wall, was another door. He opened it to find a full bath tucked into an area not more than six feet by eight feet. He put his shaving kit on the bathroom counter and returned to the den.

"The sofa folds out," Terri said as she stuck her head into the room. "I'll make it up for you later this evening."

"Yes, I saw the bedding in the closet. I wasn't expecting this," he said, gesturing toward the room.

She came into the room and sat on the arm of the sofa. "Dad's determined to find out what happened to Mom before he dies. Unfortunately, time is running out and he hasn't gotten very far."

"How much time has he got left?"

She smiled, but the sadness showed through. She wasn't beautiful in some classical sense, he thought, but quite pretty with an interesting mix of olive skin and brown hair to go with those green eyes. She could pass for Italian. She had the kind of face that would hold this prettiness no matter how old she was. It came from a blending of features that were near perfect, creating a collective pleasantness. He saw her face and he liked her. He couldn't imagine anyone feeling anything different.

"A few weeks," she said, "at the least, maybe. Three months at the most."

"You can still smile."

"Mr. Fischer, I read about the things that happened to you in Medford. You've been in situations far worse than mine, and I've seen you smile once or twice since you've been here."

"You're about to lose your only remaining parent. I can't think of anything worse."

"Are your parents alive?"

"No," he said.

"And you still smile. Besides, who is to say that I don't have a mother alive out there?"

"After all this time, can you believe that?"

"No," she said, "He says she would have never left of her own will, and she would have found a way back if she was alive. I have to believe him because I was only a few months old when she left. Unlike my father, though, I can live with the not knowing."

"He's not likely to find out before he dies."

"That's called for desperate measures."

"Which are?"

"You're it. You're the desperate measure."

Paul sighed. "I can't possibly. . ."

She held up a hand to stop him. "I don't expect you to, but as long as he thinks something is being done, I think he can die in peace."

He started to say something, but she stopped him again. "I need to get my daughter. She has a bedroom next to Dad's upstairs."

She crossed to the doorway, and as she opened the door, he found himself blurting out a question. "Your husband?"

She turned, the look curious. "My husband? I thought father would have told you. He died in a traffic accident four years ago. We had been married for five years. We lived in this house while dad was away."

"I'm sorry," Paul said.

"Your wife?"

"Divorced."

"I know," she said. "But you have Pam Livingston."

He surprised himself by saying, "I'm with Pam Livingston, but no one has her."

"I've read a bit about her, too, and I've seen her on the news. She truly is a beautiful woman. You must feel very fortunate." The smile again, gracious and sincere, illuminating.

"Yes, that's one of the things I feel," he said. As she walked from the room, he wondered what he'd meant by that. He and Pam had a good relationship. Yes, she was preoccupied at the moment, but that was no reason to suggest to someone that all was not well. Pam was successful, rich, beautiful, and, with the growth of her law firm, more powerful in the valley day by day.

Kate Baker, Pam's grandmother, was all those things, too, yet she had only fleetingly found happiness in her life. Paul suddenly felt tired. He did not want to make comparisons. He did not want to think about the man upstairs. He did not want to think of the woman upstairs. He particularly didn't want to think about what a headache it would be to try to track someone who disappeared thirty years before.

He sat down on the sofa, slipped his shoes off, and leaned back as he lifted his feet to the coffee table. The weariness of a long drive slipped in, and he closed his eyes. The door opened again, causing him to open his eyes. In the doorway was Terri, and in her arms was a lovely little girl with blonde, blonde hair and bright blue eyes. The child looked at him and smiled shyly.

Paul could see only a little of the mother in the daughter's features. Her face did not have the same shape or quite the same appeal because of it. Instead, she had a strong face. He guessed that she had her daddy's features, and that daddy had been a very handsome man.

"This is Miranda," Terri said.

"Miranda is a beautiful name, and Miranda is a beautiful child."

"Thank you. Can you say thank you to Paul?"

Miranda lifted her head from her mother's shoulder and said in a clear, tiny voice, "Thank you."

"If you would like to take a nap, I'll wake you at dinnertime."

"I think I will only need a few minutes to rest my eyes."

"A few minutes, then," she said, and that was the last thing that Paul heard for the next three hours.

[4]

HE WOKE TO the smell of fried chicken. Half-grog-gy and not at all ready to get up from the sofa, he stayed where he was and took in the smell. Yes, it was fried chicken, and, yes, he was sure he smelled gravy as well. He tried to remember the last time he had eaten fried chicken. He couldn't. Pam made sure that the cook prepared mostly pastas, but never with fried foods. Pam wasn't exactly a health nut, but she did work out in a gym several times a week, and she watched food for both of them.

Pam was one of those women who knew how beautiful she was, and one who knew what advantages that afforded. She intend-ed to hold on to her beauty as long as she could, and by the time it faded, it would be replaced with power and wealth. She was a woman never to be at a disadvantage. She admitted once that Paul was the only man she could remember who ever had the upper hand on her. She also reminded him that she had gotten it back.

The door to the study opened and Miranda poked her head in to see if he was awake. When he turned to look at her, she pushed the door open the rest of the way and walked in. "Mama says to tell you that dinner will be ready in ten minutes."

Paul could not help but smile at the child. She was all elbows and knobby knees in a dress that floated on her. Her hair, which had been loose when he was first introduced to her, was now in pigtails. Miranda shared one feature with her mother: when she smiled, he could not help but like her.

"Tell your mama that I'll be there."

Miranda left the room, carefully closing the door behind her. Paul stared at the empty space she left behind and felt that same tug of regret he'd always felt when he saw a cute little girl. He'd never trade his boys for a thing on earth, but he did regret not having a daughter. He couldn't imagine a man not wanting one. He had cried when his boys were born. He probably would have bawled if one of them had been a girl.

Paul freshened up in the bathroom and then stepped from the den. The front door of the house opened into a hallway. Off to the left side of the hallway was the formal dining room. Off to the right was the living room. The stairs were set back in the hallway and climbed in a U to the second floor. To the right of the staircase was the hall that led to the den. To the left was a short hallway that led to the kitchen.

He walked up the hallway and peeked into the dining room to see if dinner would be served there. The dining room was spotlessly clean and tidy, a place for show, not for eating. He walked back down the hall and into the kitchen. Terri was at the stove with her back to him. He paused in the doorway for a moment to take her in. He admired her figure from behind.

"Can I help you with anything?" he asked as he stepped into the kitchen.

"Grab those hot pads and see if the biscuits are done," she said, nodding her head toward the oven. Miranda was standing on a chair next to her mother, stirring something in a saucepan.

As he grabbed the pads, he said, "Two cooks in the kitchen. Isn't that a recipe for disaster?"

"That's the message I get from Miranda. She keeps telling me that she wants to do it herself." Miranda twisted her head around to give him another smile, this time with a twinkle in the eyes that said her mother knew what she was talking about.

After Terri slid Miranda and her chair out of the way, Paul moved to the oven and pulled it open, stepping back from the blast of heat. "Do you mean to tell me that Miss Miranda is a willful child?" The biscuits looked done to him so he pulled them from the oven.

"My daughter is a willful child and proud of it. Don't forget to turn off the heat."

He set the pan on a hot plate that was centered between the burners. Once he was out of the way, Terri and then Miranda, who slid the chair back into place herself, returned to their cooking. Terri was smoothing some mashed potatoes by hand, and Miranda was stirring the gravy.

"I hope I'm not putting you out," he said.

This time Terri turned her head to him and smiled. "You're a blessing," she said. "I rarely have time to cook, and rarely a reason. Dad's down to liquids now. He's so depressed by it that he no longer eats during normal times. I fed him earlier. He's asleep now."

"Will I get a chance to talk to him tonight, about your mother?"

"After I put Miranda to bed, I'll join you in the den and go over the things we have. It will be morning again before Dad has the strength to go over the files with you. He can put in maybe two good hours in the mornings, and, if he has a good enough nap, maybe another hour in the afternoon."

Miranda turned her head again, this time without a smile on her face, and said in a serious, sad voice, "Grandpa is going to die." Tears rose up and flooded the gates, cascading down her cheeks. She didn't make a sound, though, and turned back to stir the gravy.

Her mother offered the little girl no comfort, explaining, "Both mother and daughter are working very hard to get ready for Dad's death."

To change the subject, Paul asked, "Did I ever meet you when your father and I taught together?"

"No, it's funny to think about it now, but I never went east to see him. He always flew back here for Christmas and spring breaks, and then, of course, he spent his summers here." She finally had the potatoes to her liking and moved the pot to the counter next to the stove. She began to put the food on serving dishes: the chicken from a pan to a platter, the potatoes from their pot to a large bowl, string beans to a small bowl. She pulled a gravy boat from the cupboard, took Miranda's pan from the stove, and poured the gravy.

"If your Dad wanted to be out here so much, why did he take a job back east?"

"I'm sure you know that Dad is very good at what he does. The University of Oregon did not want to lose him, but after twenty years of trying to track down leads on mother and getting nowhere, he finally decided he had to do something drastic or go crazy." She began to transfer the food to a small dining table at the other end of the kitchen. "I was engaged to Jerry. Dad decided we should have the house when we married. He would work back east. I only agreed on the condition that he come back as often as he could, and he kept a room here."

The food was almost all on the table. Miranda finished the job by removing the biscuits from the stove, of her own initiative, using the hot pads to bring the pan to the table. Paul took the pan from the girl and put it on a hot plate in the middle of the round table.

"Where would you like me to sit?" he asked.

Terri pointed to a chair. Only three chairs were positioned around the table. He found himself with a female on either side of him, and he had to admit that he liked the feeling.

"In our house, we say a prayer before meals," Terri said. He wasn't sure if it was the look on his face or something else, but she followed with, "unless that's a problem, Paul."

"No, not at all. I was raised a religious boy."

"Something that didn't carry over into manhood?"

"Life leads you to the right hand of God, or it beats religion out of you."

"And, in your case?"

"On my left is a lovely little girl."

Terri laughed. "We're not fanatics when it comes to religion. We're strong people weakened by circumstance. Sometimes we need a little help to shore us up. Could you reach back into that religious youth and remember a prayer?"

"No," Paul said, "but to preserve the traditions of the house, may I offer this prayer." He crossed himself. "Lord, thank you for the food that is about to satisfy our hunger. We ask, too, that you ease the pain in this home and help all to make those painful transitions that life offers. Perhaps some of us here haven't put our faith in you the way we should have, but please don't take that out on the others. Amen."

Miranda, who at first had bowed her head and clasped her hands together, now had her head tilted to one side with one eye open, staring up at him. "Was that prayer okay, mama?" she asked with a hint of suspicion in her voice.

Terri laughed. "That was a wonderful prayer that not only gets us to dinner, but it also protects us from other people's sins."

"You won't ask me to say a prayer again, will you?"

She placed her arms on the edge of the table and leaned forward so she could see his face. "Paul, I certainly will. I don't know if I've met a man who needs more practice than you do."

"I'd think of a good reply to that," he said, "but it would take too much time away from this dinner. I do know two things: I'm starved and this looks and smells delicious."

It was, too, he told himself half an hour later, as he stared down at the homemade cherry pie with the scoop of vanilla ice cream off to its side that sat in front of him. He didn't think he could eat another bite. He was soon surprised to find the pie gone and the plate empty.

"Tell me you have a big dog that has been sneaking food off my plate. I never eat like this."

"No, it was you," Terri said. "You were just a pig about the whole thing."

"I don't apologize. It was all so simple but so good. I couldn't help myself."

Terri rose from the table and began to clear the dishes. He got up to help her. Between the two of them, they quickly put food away, cleaned plates, and readied the dishes for the sink. While she went into the front room to put a video in the VCR for Miranda, Paul filled the sink with hot water and soapsuds. He had already started on the dishes when Terri returned.

"What are you doing?" she asked.

"Demanding equality," he said. "I'm getting tired of you women getting to do all the dishes."

"Anti-chauvinist pig," she said. "Let me at least save some female pride and rinse and dry."

"You can take them to the city, but you can't get the farm out of them," Paul said.

She leaned in and shoved him with a shoulder. He staggered a bit. He wasn't a small man, but she was easily able to rock him on his feet. He liked the strength in her. He liked her. He didn't want to take the thought any further.

To change the directions of his thoughts, he asked Terri, "Do you work as well as take care of your father?"

"I'm a teacher," she said, "at the high school level."

"What do you teach?"

"Like yourself, English."

"I'm impressed," Paul said. "You have many talents and a lovely daughter."

"It's funny how life seems only to be able to give and take, instead of just give. Despite my talents, I also have a dying father, a dead husband, and a presumably dead mother."

She said this with no sense of rancor. If Paul were in her place, he'd probably be railing at the wind, a modern day King Lear. "Before I read through these documents," Paul said, "I would like to know what you think about all of this."

She had finished drying the last of dishes, and took a towel to dry her hands before handing it to Paul. "Why don't you sit back down at the table and I'll get us a cup of coffee."

She poured the coffee and brought the two cups to the table, sliding a chair around so she could sit across from him. That was when he noticed for the first time the weariness that showed through her features. She had shadows under her eyes, and her skin was a bit blanched and stretched tight.

"This must be very hard on you."

Her smile didn't come quickly this time. For just an instant, he felt the urge to take her into his arms and hold her. She closed her eyes and rolled her head around on her shoulders. "Who would have thought that I would have so easily learned to live with stress? Sometimes I think my life has been a nightmare, long-running and with sequels. Miranda is the only thing that can keep me grounded in reality."

"Will you be okay when your father dies?"

"Are you okay with your parents dead?"

"No," he said, "I don't know how many thousands of times that I've thought of them alive only to be jerked back to the truth. I've never stopped missing them."

"I miss my father and he's not even gone yet. I miss the vital man who used to rampage like a bull, determined to give order to life. He'd find Mom and bring her back, or he'd find who took her away. He'd know what happened. But no matter what he did, the answers never came, and the bull slowed to a trot and then to a standstill, until finally he was left to cock his head to one side and stare blankly into the distance. The not knowing is what is killing him. It's eaten away at his insides; the ulcers, the indigestion, the constant heartburn finally turning to cancer."

"And your insides?"

She laughed. "You don't know me well enough to ask about my insides."

"No," he said, "I don't even know you well enough to ask you about your outsides. You still haven't answered my question. What do you think about all this?"

"Which all this? My husband, my father, or my mother?"

"All of them."

She folded the fingers of her hands together to make a bridge, and then she rested her chin on it. "My husband worked for the state park service. He went to work early one morning, driving his pickup around a sweeping bend suddenly to be confronted by two logging trucks, one trying to pass the other. My husband died; the loggers lived. I never saw him again. The casket was closed. I was seven months pregnant with Miranda and nearly went into premature labor. I had to spend the last two months in bed. God was kind, though. He let it happen at the beginning of the summer so I didn't have to miss any work. Still, Jerry and I had been raised together since we were kids. Then he was gone. I had to work hard to keep my wits about me when I went back to work."

Paul was forced to reassess the woman. Now, with the smile gone from both her face and her eyes, she wasn't quite as attractive. On the other hand, he saw no sign of hardness in either her features or her voice. Life had obviously pounded her like the waves, but it had not yet beaten her down.

She continued. "Dad thought I was strong enough to survive. He was there for the birth of Miranda, to get me back on my feet, and to see that I got back to work, and then went back east. He thought he was doing best for me. Two years later I was on the verge of a crackup. Jerry's mother died of cancer. His father died shortly after of a heart attack. A broken heart more like it. My dad saw the crackup coming before I did and retired from teaching, coming back to take care of me."

"Did you crack up?"

"How could I? Dad wasn't home very long before the doctors discovered the cancer. Suddenly he needed me more than I needed him, and the perpetual caretaker in me rose from the mire." She took a pose of heroic saintliness, and then she laughed at herself.

"And your mother?"

"My daughter and I share something in common. I never knew my mother. Miranda's never known her father. Although that is tragic for both of us, I can say in my case that I don't think I would have ever had the relationship with my father that I do if my mother had been around. My daughter and I have a special bond, too."

"What am I going to learn from the papers about the night your mother disappeared?"

"Milk."

He waited for more. When it didn't come, he asked, "Milk?"

"She realized that we did not have enough milk for breakfast. She liked to go for walks in the evening, after Dad got home, so she could have a little time away from me. I hear that I was a cranky child. Up on the highway, on the other side of the road, was a small grocery store. She told my father that she would swing by there on her walk and get milk on the way back."

"On the way back from where?"

"She would walk under the bridge, through Old Town, to the docks where the boats were tied up at night. All of that is pretty much as it was thirty years ago, only Old Town has become touristy, packed with restaurants and souvenir shops."

"Did anyone see her?"

"I was more than cranky that night. It was nearly 9:00 before she could get me settled. The store closed at 10:00. She left about 9:15 and was never seen again."

"She didn't arrive at the store?"

"No, the husband and wife who ran it never saw her."

"And in Old Town?"

"It was still early spring, before the tourist season. Old Town folded up the sidewalks at 6:00 then."

"She wasn't afraid to walk alone through Old Town at night?"

"This was 1970 in Florence, Oregon. The Vietnam War was far away. The hippies and the protesters were in Eugene, not here. Crime then couldn't have kept a weekly newspaper in Florence in business." She glanced at the watch on her wrist. "I've got to give Miranda a bath and get her ready for bed. Why don't you pour yourself another cup of coffee and I'll meet you in the den."

"Sure," he said.

She paused at the door. "Would you do me a favor?"

"What's that?"

"Could I send Miranda in to give you a hug before she goes to bed? Father hasn't been able to do that for some time, and I try to get for Miranda the bonding with a male that she can't get from a father whenever I can."

"It will be tough, but I think I can manage it," he said, smiling. It was strange, he thought, how little children made him miss so much the time his boys were small. He had always thought that would be a mother thing. Not in his case, though.

He got the coffee and then moved to the den. He would need to call Pam before he went to bed, but he wasn't too worried about waking her. For the last few months she had rarely gotten to bed before midnight.

When Terri returned to the room, she stood in the open doorway and leaned against its frame. "I'm sorry," she said. "I'm really tired. Could this wait until morning?"

"I'd like to read the files, if I could," he said.

She nodded toward the desk. "In the filing cabinet next to the desk. All the information is there in folders kept by years."

He looked at her standing there, her hair mussed from the activities of the afternoon and evening. She still looked attractive, even with the obvious weariness. "How do you do it during the school year?" he asked.

"You mean Dad and my daughter? Neither is an issue of choice. I have to do it."

"When do you find time for you?"

"Me?" She smiled to herself. "I got buried a long time ago. I had a horrible time trying to get over my husband's death. I think it was that I never got to see him after he died, and I didn't want to believe he was dead. You know," she added, "I haven't even had a date since my husband died. I may as well have been buried with him."

"Doesn't all of that make you mad?"

"I'll get mad just as soon as I find a complaint department that will listen. For now, I'm too busy to be mad."

"I want you to know that I'm impressed," Paul said.

"That's just the chicken dinner talking." As she turned to walk from the room, she said, "I'll see you in the morning."

He stared at the empty doorway for a long time before he finally turned his attention the files. Most of the reading was from the first five years after Irene Drexler disappeared, first police reports and then reports by private investigators hired by Terri's father. After that the files were mostly empty. He ran across a couple of newspaper clippings, one about Terri hired to teach at the high school, several about the death of her husband and then the birth of the baby. Each mentioned the disappearance of her mother.

Whatever work Professor Drexler had done on the case in the last two years showed up as empty folders. Paul guessed that all Drexler could do was review the material on hand and search his brain for an idea.

A light tap at the door caught his attention. "Yes," he said.

The door opened a crack, and a tiny face pushed through it. "Mama says I'm to give you a hug before I go to bed." The expression on Miranda's face was quite serious, as if this was indeed very important business.

"I think that would be okay with me, if it is okay with you," he said.

She pushed the door open and stepped in the room. She stared at him for a moment, looking for what, Paul did not know. The serious expression began to fade, replaced by a shy smile. She came over to the sofa and climbed up on it so that she was standing next to him, her face level with his. She carefully placed her arms around his neck and squeezed as hard as her little body would let her.

Paul took in her smell: fresh, as she was just out of a bath. He closed his eyes and wrapped his arms around her. So this was what he had missed, he thought, and for a second he was overcome by the loss. It had all been too short, the youth of his children, the length of his marriage. When he opened his eyes, he saw Terri standing in the doorway, watching the two of them with a smile on her face. She mouthed the word "thanks," then said, "Come on, babe. Time for bed." In a flash they were both gone.

Paul had just gone back to the first folder when his cell phone rang. He answered the call. "Paul Fischer," he said.

"How's the weather on the coast?" Pam asked.

"I haven't been out in it yet to find out. How are things going for you?"

"I'm going to pull off a miracle."

"You mean you're going to keep your client off death row?"

"No, I mean I think I can get him off."

"Pam, you and I both know he killed two women. Why on earth would you want to get him off?"

"You talk like an English teacher, not a lawyer. My job is to try to get him off, regardless. The state has to prove he did it, I have to argue he didn't. But I like your attitude. You are just the kind of doubter who will appreciate my miracle the most once I pull it off. I've found the fatal weakness in the prosecution's case."

"You're right. I'm thinking like an English teacher. If I had found the flaw, I would have called the prosecutor and told him about it."

"That's why I'm not going to tell you what it is. How long will you be in Florence?"

"I'm not sure." He said it before he realized what he had said. Just a few hours ago he was determined to leave by morning. And now? "I may have to stay a couple of days." He filled her in on the information about Drexler's wife. He concluded with, "I'm pretty sure there's nothing I can do here, but, to be polite, I feel I need to make the appearance of an effort. The professor doesn't have much more than that to hold onto at the moment."

"Whatever," she said. "I really don't want to see you for three weeks. All my time will be wrapped up in this case."

"Yes, I've noticed that."

"Don't be judgmental, Paul. You knew what you were getting when you moved in with me."

"Yes, I did," he said. A place to live he couldn't have afforded alone, a beautiful woman, and a sudden sense of dissatisfaction.

"I'll call you in a couple of days. Until then, don't call me. I need every minute I can get for this case."

"I love you," he said out of habit, but she had already disconnected.

Due to his lengthy nap, he was too awake to think about sleep. He rummaged around in his suitcase, found a sweatshirt, and put it on. Then he walked to the front porch and slipped outside. He stood on the steps and surveyed the neighborhood. He tried to see it as Terri's mother had seen it that last night.

He walked down the flights of steps to the sidewalk, and turned left to begin the trip into Old Town. A mist had rolled in that evening, thick like fog. He started down the street that led under the bridge, still no better lighted than it had been thirty years ago.

[5]

HE AWOKE BEFORE dawn and stayed in bed with his hands behind his head, staring through the dark to the ceiling. The eerie walk through Old Town late in the evening must have closely matched the last walk that Irene Drexler had taken. Where her walk had ended was a mystery. The couple that ran the store said Irene had not been in. No fishermen were on their boats that late, so none had been around to spot her. The stores and restaurants in Old Town were closed up tight by then, and all the workers had gone home.

Her walk might have ended just around the corner. It may have ended when she reached the isolated field next to the docks. It may have ended just before she got to the store. According to Drexler's files, no one had seen anything, and no one had heard anything.

With so little to work on, Paul could only guess what might have happened to her. If she had been killed and her body tossed in the river, the constant action of the ocean's tide would have tossed her up to be found. If she had been buried in Old Town, the bloodhounds brought in to track her would have found the body.

The bloodhounds had tracked her scent through the normal path she took when she went on walks, including to the store. Investigators discredited the hounds' significance, figuring that she took the same route most nights. Adding to the confusion was the fact that she sometimes walked to Old Town during the day with the baby to window shop. All in all, Paul got the feeling that not a whole lot was done to find her because no one knew for sure that a crime was involved.

From what Paul had learned so far, it was more than likely she was abducted, and she was taken far from Florence. With lakes, rivers, the ocean, and miles and miles of forest, her body could have been easily disposed of anywhere, never to be found again. He couldn't believe that Professor Drexler, having been over this material a thousand times, could think for a minute that Paul might find something previously overlooked. Not enough material existed to overlook anything. He continued to mull over how little he had learned well after the sun had come up.

Paul heard a small rapping at his door, followed by the tiny voice of Miranda, asking, "Are you awake, Mr. Fischer?"

"Yes I am," he said.

"May I come in?"

"Sure," he said.

The door opened part way and Miranda stuck her head through the opening. "Mama says to tell you that breakfast is ready."

"Thank you, honey," he said. "I'll be there in a few minutes."

Miranda pulled her head back and shut the door. Paul climbed out of bed and headed straight to the shower. Fifteen minutes later, he appeared for breakfast, showered and shaved. He dressed for the coast in comfortable slacks and a shirt with a button-down collar, sleeves rolled up.

Terri was at the stove, looking very attractive in a pair of tan slacks and an off-white blouse. As he walked into the kitchen, she said, "I lied. Breakfast is just now ready. I thought you might want to shower before you got here."

"I'm sorry if I'm keeping everyone waiting." He glanced at the kitchen clock. It was only 7:00 in the morning. She noticed his glance. "We're morning people. Have to be. During the school year, I've had to get up early to get Miranda ready for daycare before going to school. I hate to break the habit during the summer because it makes it so hard to get back in the routine in the fall."

"I teach, too, remember. I don't need to be to the university until 8:00, but we live a good half-hour away. I'm usually up by 6:30. Pam is already out the door by 7:00."

Paul walked to the coffeepot and poured himself a cup, not realizing until he had taken a seat at the table that he had just assumed he could get coffee without asking. Terri didn't notice. He looked around the small, comfortable kitchen and realized how relaxed he felt in it. The kitchen at Pam's was simply a pass-through point: a place to get coffee, a spot to put a frozen meal in the microwave, the repository for food. No one gathered there to visit, to talk. Usually meals were carried off to a place where one or the other of them had work piled up that couldn't wait a leisurely meal.

"She sounds like a very busy woman."

It took Paul a second to realize that Terri was talking about Pam. "Yes, all the time. She's determined to have the largest law firm in southern Oregon, and she is already developing ideas to make the firm a regional powerhouse."

"I have to admire that kind of ambition in a woman."

Paul admired it, too, but he wasn't sure that he felt entirely comfortable with Pam's ambition. "I don't think there are very many things that Pam couldn't do if she set her mind to it."

Terri brought a platter to the table overflowing with scrambled eggs, hash browns, and sausages. "Do you plan to marry?"

Paul disguised the fact that he didn't have an immediate answer by taking the platter, putting it in the middle of the table, and asking Miranda what she wanted before serving. Terri came back with a stack of toast and a pitcher of orange juice.

Once they were all settled and Paul had served himself, he had what he thought was a safe answer. "We've both been too busy to make plans, but I think it is understood between us that we will marry." In fact, Paul didn't know if they had such plans. He could not remember Pam saying anything about marriage even once. He'd moved in with her. He'd stayed in a spare bedroom at first, and then she had asked him to move into her bedroom. That's where he had remained. The spare bedroom became his office. He became involved with his teaching. She started her plans to build a legal empire. They had both slipped into this life very easily, but neither of them had said a word about marriage.

"I miss being married," Terri said. "Jerry and I grew up together, went to school together, and then went off to college together. I think we decided we were right for each other when we were in the sixth grade. From that time on, I never imagined myself being with anyone else. I suppose that's why I still haven't looked at another man. I still feel like I belong to Jerry."

Miranda interrupted. "Can I have some strawberry jam on my toast?" Terri pulled a piece of toast from the center of the stack, one that was still warm, and spooned jam on it from a small bowl on the table. After she had spread it on the toast, she carefully handed it to her daughter. Within two seconds, Miranda had jam dripping on her clothes and the tablecloth. Terri simply shook her head and smiled.

"As strange as it seems, because we are about as estranged as we can be, I have those same feelings sometimes about my ex-wife. I suppose that when you have kids with someone, you are forever linked to that person, no matter what."

"You have two boys?"

"Yes. They'll be visiting in a couple of weeks. Unfortunately—or fortunately, depending how you look at it— their mother and I are on opposite sides of the continent. She has custody. I get them for part of the summers, and I fly out for Christmas and spring break to be with them."

"That must be hard," she said, "having to be reunited several times a year with your ex-wife."

"She has," he paused, as he always did when describing Beth's relationship, "a female companion who makes sure my trips are just a little bit more difficult than they need to be."

"Oh," she said.

He laughed. "Only 'Oh'?"

"Florence is not particularly worldly. Yes, we do have our tourists go through, but a good part of our population works for the forest service, or logs, or fishes. They tend to be a pretty conservative lot. A polite way of saying that there is not much tolerance for diversity here."

"I'm surprised. I noticed a few shops in Old Town that looked like they might be habitats of the diverse."

"Yes, we do have a coffee shop that attracts some aging hippies. And, yes, we do have some used clothing stores that are run by some interesting people. That's considered local color, but even the local color plays by the local rule."

"Which is?"

"You may do it, but you don't flaunt it."

"That's not a bad rule anyplace."

They finished the meal with pleasant chatter, and then Terri insisted that Paul move to the front room with a cup of coffee and the morning newspaper while she and Miranda cleaned up. When he started to object, she reminded him he was a guest in the house and playing hostesses was their pleasure.

A little later Terri joined him in the living room with her own cup of coffee. "Miranda is up straightening her room, and then is going to play with the neighbor's children this morning. The mothers in our neighborhood have worked out a play schedule that allows each of us some free time during the week. I live in a wonderful neighborhood." She paused for a moment, and then she asked, "Are you ready to tell me what your plans will be?"

He was trying to think of the best way to phrase it so she wouldn't be too disappointed, but before he could find the words, his own voice betrayed him. "I'll give it a few days and see where it goes," he said.

She slumped back in the chair a bit and laughed. "I would have sworn you would have been out the door and gone this morning."

"I would have sworn the same thing," he said, still amazed at his choice.

"What made you change your mind?"

"You, Miranda," he said. "You're good company." And he again he couldn't believe what he had just said.

"Don't do it for us. Do it for Dad."

"Yes, for him, too," Paul added.

"He's up now and in the wheelchair. He's waiting for you. You might get an hour with him before he starts to drift or repeat himself. He really is only down to a couple of good hours a day. It's hard seeing him like that."

"Are you coming up?" Paul asked.

"No, I don't think so. I'm going to take Miranda next door, and then I'm going to walk down to Old Town and join those old hippies for a cup of coffee. That will be pure luxury for me. I don't get many chances to get out."

As Paul climbed the stairs, he braced himself for the sight of the professor. Yesterday he had not only been shocked by how pale and gaunt Drexler was, but also by how dry and brittle his hair had been. He looked like a man dying from the outside in.

Terri had placed the files on the table in the professor's room. She had also left a tray laden with coffee and cookies. The professor was wheeled up to the table and was looking through one of the files from the stack. With that feeble wave of the hand, he directed Paul to a chair across from him. Paul took a seat.

Drexler closed the file and shook his head, sagging with a sadness heavy with years. "Not much to go on, is there?"

"No, it's not," Paul said, but as he spoke he remembered that not long ago he had discovered most of the secrets of the three Baker women, and his starting point had been nothing more than a portrait hanging in a museum.

"What do you think?"

"I'm sure you have thought of all the possibilities yourself. I will need to go over those with you when the time comes, and then we will compare notes."

"When the time comes?"

"Yes. First I want go to city hall and look up some records. I want to know the buildings that stood between here and the store on the night she walked out of the house, I want to know who lived or worked in those buildings, and I want to know how many of those people are still around."

"I can give you all of that information."

"I know you can, Dr. Drexler, but I also know if your memory is just a little faulty, I'll be missing a piece that might keep me from finding an answer. I'll find out what I can find out, and then you can tell me if I'm missing any pieces of this puzzle."

Drexler nodded. "That makes good sense."

"I've learned a bit about research over the years. I will also need some Internet access. I assume the computer in the den will do that for me."

"You'll have to talk to Terri about that. I never was much with computers. By the way, what do you think of Terri?" Drexler's bright eyes shone from his ravaged features as he watched Paul's face for a reaction.

The sly, old dog, Paul thought. Perhaps there was another motive for getting Paul Fischer to come to Florence. Like finding a man for Terri? Unfortunately, Paul was taken, regardless of how nice Drexler's daughter might be.

"You've done a wonderful job raising her. She really seems to have her act together."

"Pooh! If she had her act together, she would have been remarried by now. She's a good-looking woman who doesn't look twice at a man. Life doesn't make sense at all. A beautiful woman sits back and lets the world pass her by. A child raised without a mother has a child to be raised without a father. A good woman disappears into the night never to be heard of again. It kind of makes a mockery of all the things that churches and schools teach us about life, doesn't it?"

"Terri seems to have a good head on her shoulders. I'm sure she will be okay."

"What she needs is for me to die. Once I'm gone, she can get her grieving done and move ahead with her life. By the way, how's life between you and the lawyer?"

Again, Paul was treated to the sparkling, dancing eyes. Drexler did have a hidden agenda. "Pam and I have a good relationship."

"I hear about so few. Tell me about it."

"She's an intelligent woman, intellectual and complicated. She knows what she likes and what she wants. She's a good companion. Trips with her are a joy because she's so good at organizing them."

The professor straightened himself in his wheelchair and used his arms to hold himself up. "And sex?"

Paul smiled. "She is a beautiful woman."

"Which doesn't answer a damned thing."

"Which is what I intended," Paul said with a laugh. What he could have said was that Pam's beauty certainly helped him get beyond the fact that a certain abandonment was missing from their sex life. Pam never lost control, even in her most passionate moments.

"Do you plan to marry her?"

"What does this have to do with your missing wife?"

"Not a damned thing. It has to do with my present daughter. She's ripe for a man, and I don't want you walking in and taking advantage of her."

Paul was left with his mouth open and a half a smile on his face. Finally he said, "I don't remember having the reputation of being a womanizer when we taught together. I really don't know where all of this is coming from."

"Heat." Drexler said.

"Heat?"

"That's right. When the two of you were in this room together yesterday, I felt the temperature rise. You were both throwing off heat."

Paul thought to protest the comment, but he let it ride. He had felt the heat, too. "First, let me assure you that I am not going to take advantage of your daughter. Second, and getting back to your missing wife, you need to give me a rundown on all that you have done to date. I only want an overview. I'll find out the details for myself. Then, you'll need to tell me how to get to the city hall and the police department so I can check on some things myself."

Paul listened as Drexler narrated the story of the thirty-year search. He didn't hear anything that he hadn't learned from reading the files, but he felt it was important for Drexler to have his say. More than likely, the only satisfaction the professor would have before he died would be to know that he had tried his best to find out what happened. Paul was sure he wasn't going to be able to do any more than Drexler had done.

The professor was already becoming visibly weaker by the time Paul spotted Terri walking up the steps to the front porch. He had jotted down some notes as Drexler talked, but he hadn't heard one thing he felt would do him any good. The one thing that had caught his attention was when Drexler said that Irene hadn't been in the best of moods when she left the house that night. Paul asked the professor to explain, but Drexler waved it off, saying, "Oh, it was nothing."

[6]

BY THE END of his second day in Florence, Paul knew much more about the town and its history. After Terri returned to care for her father, Paul spent the day traveling from the police station to city hall, and from city hall to the public library. Along the way, he collected information: first about the disappearance of Irene Drexler, then about the Florence of 1970, and finally about the evolution of the town itself.

In 1970 Florence was still a pretty sleepy place, with tourists coming in the summer, but not in hordes. Most came for the fishing on any one of the half dozen or more coastal lakes or on the Siuslaw River. Some came for the salmon fishing on the charter boats. Others came to camp at Honeyman Park. Others simply came for the day to walk on the beach.

Tourists came in limited numbers, and the town grew slowly but steadily. Bay Street recycled old buildings. A boat-engine repair shop became a kite shop. A bookstore became a pizza parlor. A candy store became a bookstore. Most people who catered to the tourists hoped to make enough money during the season to hang on for the next.

That changed in the seventies. Fairly mild weather year-round attracted retirees. Retirement communities like Green Trees sprang up close to the channel that led the Siuslaw to a long jetty and out to the Pacific. These began as mobile home communities, but were made permanent by regulations that required homes be built on solid foundations.

With an influx of year-long residents, the town was able to flex its muscles a bit with a steady flow of income. Tourists, logging, and fishing industries were now joined by stores, shops, and restaurants to give the retired folks places to go. Some upscaling took place, a lot of which Paul had witnessed as he walked through Old Town. Somewhere along the line someone had had a vision, because even the newer buildings were built in the tradition of the old, helping to maintain the quaint quality of this section of town.

Unlike so many other towns along the coast, Florence had grown more east to west than north to south. Part of that was due to its location. To the north, the coast highway dropped down from steep bluffs that hemmed in the coastline. Below the bluffs were a series of lakes that stunted growth for miles more. To the south, Florence butted up against the Siuslaw River. A small portion of the town bridged the river, but was quickly stopped by the state park. Now the area between Highway 101 and the ocean was filling in fast, much of it with retirement or vacation homes. To the east, the town was bordered again by the Siuslaw and the coast range of mountains pushing in near the ocean.

Paul studied maps and photographs of the area from 1970 to now, and was surprised by how little had changed. As the librarian had said to him, "The big things are still here: the mountains, the river, the ocean, and the dunes. They so dominate the landscape that it leaves little territory for the rest of us to play with."

Paul's last stop was the newspaper office, on a side street in Old Town. He went through all the back issues of the paper, from 1965 on, to see what he could find out about Florence, about the Drexlers, and about Irene's disappearance. He didn't expect to find anything that wasn't already back at the professor's house, but also he wanted to make sure that not one scrap of information went overlooked. He wanted to be satisfied that he had done everything he could for Drexler and his daughter. It was after 5:00 when he left the newspaper office. In his briefcase he carried close to a hundred photocopied pages—from the newspaper, library, and public records. Paul knew most of his pages were duplicates of what Drexler had, but he hadn't tried to sort it, instead simply copying everything he could find that he thought might be valuable.

Terri had told him that dinner would be ready at 6:00. He was looking forward to sitting down with Terri and Miranda for another meal. Something so simple reminded him of how much he missed his boys, and, more, how much he missed the family life he had shared with his sons and wife before the divorce.

Since he had time, he stopped his car at a coffee shop on the first block of Old Town. From his research he knew that the coffee shop had been there when Irene disappeared. It was, in the beginning, frequented by the counter culture who drifted to the coast at the end of the sixties and through the seventies to escape a society in upheaval because of race riots and war protests. Many had camped in the hills. Some had taken up permanent residence, finding the mild weather a few miles inland fair conditions for growing an outstanding crop of marijuana.

The coffee shop had survived, even after the hippies had grown into responsible adults with children, jobs, and ties to the community. It was a social hub, a place where the natives congregated, especially in the off-season when there were no tourists.

Paul looked around as he walked in. The front of the shop was a filled with a collection of odd shaped tables, surrounded by mismatched chairs. It was as if someone went on a buying spree at the closeout sale of an antique store. Everything about it was informal, from the assortment of tablecloths to the newspapers left scattered on the table. The message was simple: have a cup of coffee and stay as long as you want. With a view out the front windows of the Siuslaw perhaps a hundred feet or so away and the bridge that crossed it farther down river, sitting at a table near the front on a rainy day might be one of the best spots in Florence.

Paul was also surprised, because tucked into one of the back corners of the shop was a computer with a sign that said it was available for Internet access. Old worlds and new worlds colliding? Paul didn't think so. He thought of the Internet as being a kind of new world exploration, an adventure not unlike a journey taken by Lewis and Clark.

Paul ordered a mocha from a dark-haired woman behind the counter, moved to the front of the shop, and took one of the tables by the window. He had been seated for only a few minutes, looking through the latest issue of the local paper, when he sensed someone nearby, someone huge. He glanced up to see a tall man with very broad shoulders and a very flat stomach standing over him. The man was handsome in a cold sort of way. The coldness came from a face that did not smile and eyes that were not friendly.

Paul felt like standing up to show his own size and fit physique, but he recognized the foolishness of the idea. Yes, Paul was six foot, and, yes, he had bulked up to two hundred pounds, most of it muscle held in check with a good diet and lots of exercise. But the man had him by at least four inches and sixty pounds. Paul sat and waited.

A hand thrust out at him. "I'm Dave Crane. I own this place."

Paul took the hand and shook it. "Paul Fischer."

"I know who you are. Terri was in this morning. She talked about you." Crane lowered himself into a chair across from Paul. "She told me a little about what you were doing."

"I'm probably not going to be able to do much."

"That's probably best."

Paul stared at the man for a moment, trying to decide what Crane might mean by that. The face remained the same. It was a good face with strong features; the focus of it was sharp blue eyes. Crane had a head of rich, thick, curly, dark hair, and a five o'clock shadow that looked uncontrollable. Paul could imagine a smile on the lips, but he couldn't see the eyes warming to match.

"That's a curious statement. Why might it be better if I don't do much?"

"Because I suspect that if you find anything at all, someone is going to be hurt by it. Whatever happened, happened. Thirty years have passed. Nothing you do will change anything."

"Terri's father wants an answer. Thirty years of not knowing have taken their toll on him. He wants to die in peace."

Dave snorted, something that was meant to be a laugh, Paul guessed. "Once he's dead, it won't make much difference whether or not he knows the truth about his wife."

"Do you know the truth?"

"I'm Terri's age. I don't know anything about her mother. I do know that we've some folks who don't feel comfortable with someone digging into the past, and that has nothing to do with Irene Drexler."

"I'll try to keep my research to the point," Paul said. "By the way, this is great coffee."

Dave was not to be redirected, as Paul had hoped. "The sixties and seventies were pretty wild times. Some folks did some things they ain't too proud of now. They certainly wouldn't want those things aired today."

"Like I said, I'm only interested in Irene Drexler."

Dave shoved back the chair and rose up slowly, giving Paul a second chance to see just how big he was. "Make sure you keep it to Irene Drexler. I know how you hung a whole bunch of people out to dry down south with your research."

"Those folks were dead," Paul said.

"Well, these folks ain't dead. Don't forget it."

He walked behind the counter and disappeared through a door into the kitchen. Paul was left to stare after him, wondering what the hell that was all about.

Paul finished his coffee, took his empty cup and placed it on the counter, and left. He did not see Dave Crane again. He drove the short distance to the Drexler's house. As he pulled to a stop in the front, he caught a glimpse of Miranda in the living room window. He'd barely lifted a hand to wave hello when she suddenly disappeared. As he climbed the steps to the porch, he wondered if she was off to tell her mother that he was back. He got an immediate answer as the door swung open. Miranda was there to greet him.

"You are awfully nice to come home to," he said.

"Mama has dinner almost ready. She said you didn't dare be late."

He entered the house. Miranda followed behind him as he took his briefcase to the den before taking off his coat and heading to the kitchen. She then deserted him for the television in the front room. Tonight, he guessed from the aroma in the kitchen, they would be having stew.

"You know," he said, "I'm not much of a cook, but I do know how to use a credit card and take people out to dinner."

Terri turned and gave him a smile. "I will take you up on that before you go."

He looked over her shoulder and confirmed that it was stew. "That smells great. On the other hand, I remember helping you put away quite a bit of leftovers last night. Why aren't we having those?"

"Don't worry. We will. And you'll see this stew again before you go. Cooking isn't one of my favorite things."

"I think it would be," he said, "considering how good you are at it."

"You know how to protect your stomach, don't you? Flattery. What did you get accomplished today?"

He poured himself a cup of coffee and took a seat at the kitchen table. "I made visits to the city hall, the police department, the library, and the newspaper office. I was able to gather most of the information I wanted, although I expect I will be going back to the newspaper office quite a few more times to search their dead files."

She pulled a wooden ladle from the pan on the stove and set it aside before putting the lid back on the stew. "This needs about ten more minutes. I've made biscuits, too."

"Can't wait," he said.

She wiped her hands on her apron and then came over to sit across from him. She had a few strands of hair hanging down on her forehead, and he thought she looked totally domesticated. But Terri struck him as the housewife of television commercials: far too pretty to be in a kitchen cooking dinner.

"Did you find anything interesting?"

"I haven't had a chance to look at the material yet. By the way, who is Dave Crane?" he asked.

A half-smile came to her face, before it faded into a roll of the eyes. "What did he do now?"

"He warned me about sticking my nose in places it shouldn't be in a way I suppose he may consider friendly."

"That figures."

"A friend?"

"Dave had a crush on me in high school. I actually dated him a few times when Jerry and I were having a spat. Dave was the king of the school. He was big from an early age. He was the star basketball player and the star football player. He was homecoming king. He was the guy the girls lusted after."

"Pouring coffee seems a bit of a comedown from all that."

"He was the one the girls lusted after, but he wasn't the one any would set out to marry. As talented as he was, you'd think he would have gone to college on a sports scholarship. Not Dave. When it came to academics, he couldn't keep up. His girlfriend-of-the-moment was responsible for making him academically eligible for sports. That meant doing his homework for him and helping him cram for tests. He's not a stupid man, but his SAT scores were so low that no college would touch him, and he didn't have the money to make it to college any other way."

"I did see a wedding ring on his finger," Paul said. "Someone must have found him worth the effort."

"Did Sherry serve you?"

"Sherry?"

"A dark-haired woman, short and a little stocky?"

"Yes."

"That's Dave's wife. She was pregnant when she got out of high school, and she pretty well made sure that everyone knew about it and knew that it was Dave's."

Paul sipped his coffee before saying, "So Dave let himself get caught."

"Oh, I'm pretty sure he would have made a break for it if he could, but Sherry's dad was the police chief and Dave's dad was a minister."

Paul laughed. "I suppose I shouldn't laugh, but Dave doesn't sound like the cleverest man alive."

"Don't sell him short. He's big and he knows how to use his size to get what he wants. And he doesn't have a sense of humor. Whatever message he intended to give you wasn't meant to be friendly."

"Does he still think he has some kind of a claim to you?"

"He's made it clear more than once that he'd like to take care of my interests."

"Could his threatening me be tied to that? Maybe he sees me as competition for your attentions."

She laughed. "In my mind, you're both taken. So there's no competition."

Why did those words have a bite to them? Paul could almost feel himself flinch. Silly, he thought. He was taken. Nothing to argue there. "Are there any folks in town who might feel my probing could turn up something they don't want turned up?"

"I wouldn't be surprised. We've got a few folks left over from the sixties: folks with problems with drugs, the draft, and radical behavior. You never can be sure if Tim and Dorris, a couple who never uses their last name, and who come in from the hills every week or so to have dinner at Mo's, do some shopping, and take in a movie, are really Tim and Dorris, if you know what I mean." She got up to check on the stew.

The television clicked off in the other room, and shortly afterward Miranda appeared in the kitchen doorway. "Is dinner ready? I'm really, really hungry."

"It's just done," Terri said.

Once they were seated at the table, the prayer said this time by Miranda, Paul asked, "How's your Dad today?"

She handed him the plate with biscuits. "He was pretty cheerful this afternoon. He has his hopes up that you will find out something."

Paul took two biscuits and then held the plate so Miranda could help herself. That taken care of, he said, "That's what I was afraid of. I feel like I'm caught between a rock and hard spot. I want to do something because I know how desperately he wants closure. On the other hand, I know how unlikely it is that I will find an answer in such a short time, if at all. I may just end up depressing him even more than he already is depressed."

"Dad's not like that. He'll remember the offer to help but not the failure to produce. Do you really think it is unlikely that you will find anything new?"

"I honestly don't know. First I'm going to focus on strangers. Your mother's disappearance happened well before the tourist season began, so there weren't many strangers in town. I have copies of police reports for the two weeks leading up to the disappearance, and I'm going to look for contacts between the police and hitchhikers, vagrants, that kind of thing. I'm also collecting the names of the people who worked in the area at the time. If they are still around, I'll be asking them if they remember anything unusual about that time besides the disappearance. Did they notice any strangers? Did someone get stranded for a few days because of a car breaking down? Maybe someone new came in to work for a few days and then took off again. Anything that might connect the disappearance to a stranger."

"And if no one remembers anything like that?"

"I'd like to be able to say I can eliminate a stranger as a possibility, but we both know I won't be able to. After thirty years, memories will be faulty or nonexistent. The police reports may be the only reliable data, and even that may not be complete. Maybe a cop rousted a bum and didn't feel like doing the paperwork. And none of that even addresses the thousands of other possibilities. Maybe Irene decided to walk down by the river; maybe she tripped and fell in. Maybe her body was washed out to sea never to be seen again. Or maybe it washed up in a remote spot down the coast and was never found. Or maybe a trucker pulled off the highway that night looking for a cup of coffee, saw Irene, and took advantage of the moment. Maybe he dumped her body a hundred miles from here, deep in the forest."

Paul stopped. Terri had a funny look on her face. She nodded her head toward Miranda. Her daughter was staring at him with eyes huge. "She may have little ears," Terri said, "but she has a big imagination."

"Ah, yes. I wasn't thinking. Maybe we should save this conversation for later."

"I think the conversation is okay, but I do think you might tone down the details."

He nodded, and then he smiled at Miranda. "And how was your day today?"

She continued her wide-eyed stare. "Not as scary as yours," she said.

By the time Paul and Terri had stopped laughing, Miranda was once again totally involved with her stew and biscuits.

Terri asked, "What happens if you can't find anything that indicates a stranger?"

"The obvious answer to that is it had been someone she knew or someone who knew her. Back then, Old Town before tourist season wasn't exactly a bustle of activity. We will have X number of names, and we start trying to eliminate those names as possible suspects."

"So although you may not know who did it, you might be able to give Dad a short list of names of people who might have done it?"

"Yes, and not very happily, yes. Yes, I most likely won't know who did it. And yes, I will have a list compiled from totally circumstantial evidence, and therefore a list that is almost totally useless. The odds are much greater that the murderer, if there is one, won't have his name on the list at all. We don't even know if a crime was committed, and even if we did, we don't know if it was a premeditated or random act."

Terri began to scoop more stew onto his plate without asking him if he wanted more. The fact that he had left his plate clean suggested he had liked the stew. "But a list of names. That would be so much more than Dad has had up to this point. That might well be enough to satisfy him."

Paul watched her put more food on his plate. He thought again about how different Terri was from Pam. When it came to Paul, Pam was inattentive. If his clothes clashed, she wouldn't have noticed. If he had a stain on his tie, she'd be the last to see it. If his shirt needed ironing, Pam would not spot it. If his plate was cleaned and he still looked hungry, she would have never thought to ask him if he wanted more, nor would she have assumed he did and dished it up without being asked.

He knew it was unfair to think of Pam in those terms, but he also knew that he often felt taken for granted. She was so busy with her own career—one that invaded their home and took over most of their spare time together—that she had no time to worry about his. She just assumed that he was happy.

She just assumed that his job was going well if he didn't talk about it. She just assumed that he couldn't ever want anyone more than he wanted her.

For the most part he was happy. He liked his teaching job, and he like the way the college was pushing for higher standards now that it had been named a university. And, he knew, to have made love to a naked Pam Livingston was about as close to nirvana as a man could get.

That didn't keep him from wishing, though, that she would pay a little more attention to him.

[7]

IN THE EVENING, Terri and Paul sat shoulder to shoulder on the sofa, their feet up on the coffee table, stacks of papers on their laps. They were looking through the material that Paul had gathered to see if any of it was different from what was already in Drexler's files.

"According to these reports, no police officer made contact with an unknown person during the weeks before and after the disappearance. No hitchhikers stopped. No hobos. No bums. No stalled travelers. No truckers sleeping in their trucks along the highway."

"That doesn't negate the possibility of a lazy officer failing to write up a report."

"No, no," Terri said, leaning in to him, her left breast heavy on his arm. "Dad discovered that the police chief asked his men if any contacts had gone unreported, making it clear that he didn't give a damn if they hadn't written it up. He was looking for any lead he could get into the disappearance of my mother."

Paul decided he could move a drifter to the back of the suspect list, but at the moment his thoughts were not on the investigation at hand but on the breast, which still rested on his arm. He glanced at the reports she held and tried his best not to move his arm.

"Everything I've seen so far seems to discredit the theory of a stranger passing through being responsible for the disappearance."

She moved back. "What next, then?" she asked.

"Tomorrow I'm going to review the county coroner records to see what I can find out about people who have drowned in this area, especially along the coast or in the river. I want to know what happens to their bodies."

"So you think she might have fallen into the river?"

"Not really. But I want to be able to discredit that theory as well. The fewer possibilities that remain, the less I have to research, and the better I can maximize my time."

Terri turned her head to look at him, and for a moment they stared into each other's eyes. Paul smiled.

Pam was a beautiful woman. He often found himself admiring that beauty. Terri wasn't beautiful at all in the same way. In fact, while most people would agree that Pam was a lovely woman, far fewer would say the same of Terri. She had features that appealed to a certain taste. Unfortunately, Paul thought, he had that taste.

"I love the way your mind is so orderly. My father is a brilliant man, but he can be overwhelmed by too much detail. He could take one of his files and analyze it to the infinite, but when it came to making sense of all the files together, he was in over his head. I'm actually the one who suggested he contact you. I was fascinated by the stories in the newspaper that I read."

"I would have preferred a different route to publicity. It took months for me to get beyond the psychological trauma that comes with someone trying to kill you and damned near making good on the try."

"They say you saved Pam's life."

"I was given too much credit," he said.

"You must love her very much."

He didn't know how to respond to that. He and Pam had moved into a comfortable life together. They enjoyed each other's company, and they had a good sexual relationship when she wasn't too busy. When the word love came up, he was usually the one to use it. He couldn't remember Pam ever saying spontaneously that she loved him.

He settled for saying, "We seem to be a good match."

She caught his eyes again, and literally read the features on his face, holding his look until he began to feel uncomfortable but unable to turn his eyes away. Finally she said, "You have an interesting face. You're actually very handsome. Nice features. Beautiful blue eyes. Straight nose. Full lips, a little unusual for a man. You also have a face that radiates your emotions."

He smiled at her. "Do you read tea leaves, too?"

"No," she said, "but I've made it a practice as a teacher to examine the faces of my students each day I see them to learn what I can from their expressions. You'd be surprised how much I've learned. I've been able to tell a bad day from more serious problems. I've been able to identify serious problems before they had a chance to get worse. Twice I've reported child abuse from what I saw there. Faces tell stories if you learn to read them."

"I see that I may have to wear a mask when I'm around you."

"Be careful of the mask you chose. It can tell a story about you, too."

Before he could reply, he was rescued by his cell phone. As he reached for it, he said, "This can only be Pam."

"Would you like me to leave?" she asked.

"No, we still have lots to cover." That was true, too. Paul wanted to ask Terri some questions before she went to bed. Her father had hinted that maybe all wasn't well between himself and his wife when she left that night. Paul wanted to know if Terri knew anything about that.

"Paul?"

He was surprised by the voice. It wasn't Pam. It was Beth. He glanced at his watch. It was after midnight back east. "Is there a problem with the boys?"

"No. They're fine," she hurried to reassure him. "I wasn't exactly honest with you when I told you why I needed time away from the boys. I think it's better you hear it from me than from them."

What, he wondered, could she possibly tell him that could top learning that she was leaving him for another woman? "What is it?"

"Denise and I are not doing very well. When the boys leave, she and I are going to separate. I'll need the time to myself to sort some things."

Paul eased himself back on the sofa and glanced at Terri. She was reading through a file, apparently paying little attention to his conversation. "Do you have someone else?" he asked. That caused Terri to glance quickly his way.

"No, this isn't about anyone else. You know that I've been in therapy. And you know Denise; your doctor needs to be a lesbian, your lawyer needs to be a lesbian, your therapist needs to be a lesbian: they are the only ones who will understand. A year ago I switched to a straight therapist."

"And?"

"I now think that Denise is my transition person, the one I needed to get me out of the relationship with you. Transition people rarely last once they've served their purpose. I think Denise has served her purpose. I need time alone now to make sure."

"Then what?"

Her voice softened. Suddenly it reminded him of those endless, late-night calls they shared with each other before they married. It was an integral part of their courtship, and it was also a part of their lovemaking. It was a verbal seduction of sorts. He remembered how both of their voices would soften and slow as they reconnected emotionally with each other on the phone.

"Do you mean, like in another woman?"

"That is a thought that comes to mind."

"I don't know. My relationship with Denise was not about sex. Beyond Denise, I've never had the same kinds of feelings toward another woman. Right now I need time to think, to process."

"What brought this on?"

"You."

"Me?"

"I know you've gone through some terrible things, and I haven't been there for you. I feel guilty about that."

"I thought all of that was behind us."

"Is it behind you?"

He glanced at Terri. What exactly was her appeal? He knew. Her appeal was that she took him back to a time with Beth when he was happier than he had ever been. "I haven't thought about it," he said. "You made it so clear that everything was over that I saw no reason to keep thinking about it."

"Would you think about it? Leaving you might well have been the stupidest thing I've ever done in life. Or maybe it was the right thing after all, but for reasons I've yet to understand. I'm going to need your help to find out the answers."

"I'll do what I can to help," he said, adding, "within reason."

"You don't love Pam Livingston, and she doesn't love you. You've just forged a good contract together."

"I'll think about that, too," he said.

"That's all I ask. Can I call you if I need someone to talk to?"

The easy answer to that was no, but with an ex-wife with whom he'd had children, no easy answers existed. She would always be the mother of his children. She would always be the only one so far with whom he had experienced domestic bliss. Besides being his wife, she had also been his best friend. Losing one was painful; losing both had been devastating. Saying no would be easy. Coming to terms with the past would be incredibly difficult, but it also might be the one act he needed to complete that would free him to have the kind of love he had with Beth again.

"Sure," he said. "I may be doing some traveling around during the next few weeks, but my cell phone is going with me."

"Thanks, Paul. When all of this came crashing down on me, I knew I needed a good friend to talk to. And you know what?"

"My name was the first to pop into your head."

"I'd forgotten what good friends we had been. Good night, Paul."

He closed the cover on the phone to turn it off, and he held it in his hand, staring at the simple piece of plastic that could hold so many surprises.

"Was that Pam?"

He turned to look at Terri. He could read her face, too, at least a little. This was a woman who was very curious. He could imagine, from the part of the conversation she had heard, that she would be curious. "No," he said. "That was Beth, my ex-wife. She called to tell me that she and her lover were separating."

"My, you do have a complicated life. It sounds to me like Beth is still connected to you, and I can tell by the expression on your face that you're still connected to her."

"It seems," he said, "that we should be able to put our pasts to rest at some point."

Terri smiled and giggled. The giggle broke into rich, deep laughter. With her hand over her mouth and tears welling up in her eyes, she waved the other hand around to indicate the sheets of paper and stacks of folders. When she could finally catch a breath, she asked, "And just what is all of this?"

He stared for a moment and then he understood. He started to laugh, too. They were wading through an event that happened thirty years before because it, too, had never been put to rest. When his own laughter finally slowed, he realized that he still had a lot to work on if he was ever going to have another relationship of any meaning, be it with Pam Livingston, or another woman such as Terri, or, even, with Beth. He forced himself away from those thoughts and back to the papers.

This was a good time to ask the question, he decided. "Terri, what was the relationship like between your father and mother when she left that night?"

This time when Terri turned to him, she drew away a bit to get a better look. "I would guess, for a man who has an ex-wife, that a question like that must have some relevance. But just because you may not have always been on the best of terms with your wife doesn't mean that my father and mother were the same. Everything I know about Dad and everything I know about my mother tells me that they loved each other and that my father was devastated when she turned up missing."

"Please don't read things into my questions. When I asked your father the same question, he hesitated before answering. I also know from the police files that they questioned your father extensively about the relationship, because when a spouse goes missing, the partner is usually the first suspect. The police found nothing suspicious, and I would like to take everyone at his or her word, but I did notice the pause."

"The only thing that father has ever said was that Mom was depressed for a while after I was born. Having suffered the blues myself after having Miranda, I can understand that."

Paul accepted that for the moment, although he knew that her blues were probably more a reaction to the death of her husband than to the birth of their child. They went back to work on the files, taking the photocopies Paul had made and then putting them in the appropriate folders that her father had accumulated. Once that was done, they each went through a folder, comparing what was in it originally to what Paul had added.

Nothing jumped out at Paul from this exercise. Instead of finding new information, what he discovered was a wealth of detail that was missing in Drexler's research. As Terri had suggested, Drexler was a man who could get overwhelmed with detail, so maybe he left out some things intentionally. Paul would have to go through it all again, from beginning to end, before he knew for sure if he had anything new to go on.

Terri had evidently forgiven him his question. Within a short time, she was once again shoulder-to-shoulder with him, leaning occasionally to point out something in a file on his lap, and once again resting a breast on his arm. She seemed so guileless that he couldn't imagine her doing this consciously.

They were almost through the files when his cell phone rang again. This time he knew it would be Pam. As he answered the phone, Terri got up and excused herself, saying good night to him quietly so as not to interrupt his call.

"Did Beth get through to you?" Pam asked as soon as he answered.

"Yes, she did."

"I'm sure she told you I was a little abrupt with her."

"She didn't mention it."

"Really? Then it must have been an important call."

Sometimes Paul felt that Pam simply could not ask him directly about anything relating to Beth. She had to work around to what she wanted to know, and she had to put the whole thing in a confrontational light, to continue the epic battle between herself and his ex-wife. The only trouble with this was Paul saw no battle. They didn't like each other, that he understood. But Beth was not at war with Pam. Only Pam seemed to see it that way.

"How were you abrupt?"

"I told her not to call here again."

"Yes, that does qualify as abrupt, but I'm sure Beth saw it as just another typical communication between the two of you."

"What is that supposed to mean?"

"You don't like each other. The secret is out. Suspend hostilities and accept the dislike for what it is."

"I have no reason to be hostile."

"Exactly! I rest my case."

"Being cute doesn't become you. What did she want?"

"She and Denise are going through hard times. They are about to separate, perhaps permanently."

"And you're supposed to rush to her rescue?"

"I wasn't invited to the rescue. She wanted me to know this before I heard it from the boys."

"And you don't think she wants you to come to her rescue?"

"Beth and I haven't been together for nearly four years. We've been divorced for over two. Never once during that time did Beth ever suggest that the solution to her problems was to get back together with me."

"Maybe she's just now beginning to realize it."

"Well, as long as I'm here and she's there, I don't think either one of us has much to worry about."

"I do worry, though. She keeps a hold on you, using the boys as the tie."

"She's their mother. I'm their father. It's in everyone's best interest if we try to parent them together, despite the distance."

Her tone softened. "I know I'm being a bitch, but she has that one connection with you I don't, and there are times I feel it."

"We could have children of our own, you know. I've made that clear. We're not talking a sacrifice here on my part. I love being a father."

The softness was gone. "Maybe, some day, but not until I have this firm where I want it to be. It's all the child I have room for right now. Listen, I have a ton of work to do before I go to bed. I'll call you in a few days." She hung up.

End of conversation, Paul thought. This was how all discussions of children ended. Discussions of marriage would end in the same way. They would talk about it just as soon as she had the firm where she wanted it. Unfortunately, he had overheard her discussion with one of her partners about the plan to open offices in Eugene, Salem, and Portland eventually. Once that happened, he was sure that she would want more offices in both Washington State and California. Her child might never finish growing.

But what could he expect? Pam never knew her real father. She kept her stepfather at arm's length despite the fact that he had been a good surrogate father. In her thirties now, she had never been married, and she had shown no interest in having children. He doubted that Pam would ever have room for children, and if she did, he doubted that they would mean any more to her than his own children.

When his boys were with them, she was good about signing them up for golf, tennis, and swimming lessons at the club. And she made sure that they ate meals together whenever possible. Before the visit was up, Pam would see to it that they made a memorable trip together, although usually a fairly short one.

He also knew that his boys liked her. She was simply too beautiful, too intelligent, and too nice for them to think otherwise. But he also noticed it was either to him or to their mother that they turned when something important came up. Pam made no pretense of being a surrogate mother, and they had figured that out quickly.

Paul felt that he and his boys had something in common. He was attracted to Pam because she was so lovely. Why, now, he wondered, did that no longer seem enough?

[8]

PAUL SAT AT a table in Mo's Restaurant, about to partake of clam chowder, a dish that had made Mo's legendary, spawning a chain of restaurants. Across from him sat Max Leiber, the sheriff deputy responsible for river patrols. He covered the Siuslaw from the jetty to above Mapleton. The Coast Guard had the jetty to the sea. The coroner had directed Paul to Leiber. The deputy was a short, heavyset man, with dark, curly hair and no other distinguishing features. His features were such that he could have faded into the background of almost any setting.

Paul found it ironic that the cost of finding out what happened to bodies that ended up in the Siuslaw would be a lunch at Mo's. He tried to eat fast before they got to any gory details.

"As I said on the phone," Paul said, "Professor Drexler would like to have some idea of what might have happened to his wife before he dies. One of the theories is that she might have somehow ended up in the Siuslaw River. My questions is, if that had been the case, is it possible that the body would never have been found?"

Leiber was piling onions on his hamburger. Paul looked at the lettuce, tomatoes, and onions, with very little else to go with them, and decided he wouldn't get his hamburgers here. Once his creation was complete, Leiber took a big bite, causing a small shower of vegetable bits to land on his plate and the table as well. Having satisfied his hunger, he answered the question, still chewing his food. "It all depends."

Paul waited, but no further pronouncements spilled out. Finally he asked, "Depends on what?"

Waving his hamburger toward the river, Leiber said, "That."

Struggling with patience, Paul managed to get out, a smile still on his face, "What about that?"

"The river," he said, stabbing his hamburger toward the window. "High tide, low tide, water temperature, location of where she might have gone in, whether or not she was conscious in the water, what she was wearing. Whether or not she was weighted down with something."

"Let's take this one step at a time. High and low tide?"

"Easy," Leiber said. If the tide is coming in, chances are good the body isn't going to end up far from where it went in. In fact, under the right conditions it might even be pushed up stream and end up on one of the mudflats when the tide went out. If the tide was going out, you'd find the body on one of the riverbanks, more than likely on the dunes side back then because of the way the channel was. They've since dredged it."

"What you are saying, then, is the body would more than likely be found."

Leiber looked at Paul like maybe he was slow learner. "Yeah, exactly, unless the body got snagged on something."

"What about water temperature?" Paul asked.

Still chewing while talking, Leiber said, "That has more to do with decomposition than anything else. The warmer the water, the quicker the body pops to the surface; the colder the longer it takes. In the coldest water, the body might go in and out with the tide through quite a few cycles before we got it."

"Conscious or unconscious?"

"She might have stayed afloat quite a while before she went under. If that's the case, depending on the tide, her body would have been found higher up the river or lower down."

"But found."

"That river's not a black hole. It spits out what it swallows eventually."

"What if the body were weighted down with something or snagged?"

"I'll just assume here that you haven't had much experience plucking bodies from water." He waited for Paul to reply.

Paul nodded. He wasn't ashamed to admit it. That experience had slipped by him. Funny, he didn't feel a bit of regret. "No, none."

"Yeah, I could see that." Leiber started on his fries before he continued. Paul observed that the man seemed to be the most talkative only when he had something in his mouth. "A body's going to decompose in time. We've got enough crabs and fish down there to help it along. Whatever is holding on to the body to keep it under is going to run out of body to hold onto. Most of the remains are going to wash up somewhere, and by then it will only take a slight breeze and a fair nose to figure out where it is."

Poetic, Paul thought. The man is pure poetry. "So you are saying that if a body went in this river at night in the spring, it would have been found."

"Yup. Anything from here to the mouth of the jetty is likely to get spit up and found eventually."

"I appreciate that information," Paul said. "It seems to discount the notion of her ending up the river one way or another."

Waving a fry first in one direction and then another, Leiber said, "Of course, if she had ended up in a lake, she might still be down there. We've got Siltcoos, Mercer, Wohink. . ."

Paul interrupted him. "She wasn't walking anywhere near one of the lakes."

"You're the one who said she might have been weighted down. That would mean someone was out to get rid of her body for good. Anyone from around here would know how to do that in a lake. We've got a couple with some deep spots. Drop a body in one of those, in the cold of spring, and weight it down good, chances are it will stay put. Crappy, bluegill, bass: most are bottom feeders in the spring. The fish would have a feast, the water wouldn't have currents to push the remains around, and chances are, even if it did break free, the cold would slow the decomposition so much it would never reach the surface. That's what I'd do if I wanted to get rid of a body."

That's what Paul would like to do to Leiber, he thought, for throwing that wrench into the theory. Paul didn't want to think about lakes, at least for now.

Paul rose from the table and picked up the ticket, checking the price, and then placing a two-dollar tip on the table. "I need to do some more research. Thanks for the help. I'll pay for this on the way out."

"No problem," Leiber said, a French fry dangling from his mouth. "I'm open to a free lunch any day."

After he paid, Paul left, walking across the footbridge that tied Mo's on its pilings with the bank of the river. He glanced down into the water, almost expecting to see a body floating beneath the surface.

He had walked to Mo's from Drexler's house. He now started the walk back on the sidewalk, past dress shops and souvenir shops, thinking about lakes as he went. If someone had killed Irene Drexler and had the means to dump her in the middle of a lake, then the person had to be a resident at the time with a boat. The resorts weren't open, and a boat tied on the river wouldn't have a way to get to a lake.

Someone that established, Paul thought, would have had a connection to Irene Drexler. Since no one had found such a trail, the theory didn't make much sense. For now he would rule out the idea of a lake as being too wild, at least until something showed up to point him in that direction again.

He reached the block across from the coffee shop and veered off to his left. Just behind the kite shop, a favorite tourist stop, was an open stretch of land that went right down to the water's edge. Looking up and down the block at all the other developments in the area, Paul wondered why this one stretch of beach hadn't been developed.

Standing next to the water, he looked down river to the double arches of the bridge over the Siuslaw. Staring, still thinking about lakes, he hadn't heard anyone approach. Suddenly he sensed someone nearby and turned to find an old man standing next to him, a man with a huge, thick, straggly beard that was still black but heavily streaked with white. An equal amount of black and white hair on his head flowed down his neck and over his shoulders. In the middle of all this hair was a nose and two dark, almost black eyes that stared out under thick and bushy brows.

"I expect you'll be looking for me," the man said to Paul.

"I don't believe we've met," Paul said.

The man nodded his head toward the new coffee shop next to the river, down the street from Crane's shop. "Used to be my engine repair shop. Had it there for forty years."

Now Paul knew who the man was. He was Ernie Crawford. He was someone that Paul did want to talk to. Irene Drexler would have walked past his repair shop the night she disappeared, and the police reports were not completely clear as to whether or not Ernie had still been at work when she walked by.

"Can I buy you a cup of coffee?" Paul asked.

Ernie spit on the ground. "Not a good idea to look too social with you."

That was a curious thing to say, Paul thought. "I want to know what you remember about the night Irene Drexler disappeared."

"Long time ago. Who'd remember?"

Paul watched the man. He wasn't paying attention to Paul; instead he was looking out across the river. The black eyes stared without blinking. "It was also big news at the time. Usually things that are traumatic are remembered, often quite clearly."

"Weren't no trauma for me."

"So you didn't see Irene Drexler that night?"

"Gone before she went by."

"But you had seen her walk by before?"

"Knew who she was." He spit again.

"Ever talk to her?"

"No reason. She didn't have a motor."

"What time did you leave work that night?"

"How am I supposed to remember that?"

"You seem to be pretty sure you didn't see the woman go by. I'm just assuming that you had left work before she went by."

"Might have been up to my ass in an engine. Might never have seen her."

"So you still might have been at work?"

"Might have, but didn't see anything."

Paul stood, too, staring off, trying to appear completely relaxed. He wasn't relaxed. He'd seen the police reports. Ernie had insisted at the time that he had left work before the woman passed. But no one saw him until after Irene Drexler had disappeared. Under pressure from the police, he had claimed that he had gone home and taken a nap before heading to a bar for a beer. Was this now faulty memory, or was Ernie actually trying to tell Paul the truth? And just what was the truth?

"It sounds like you might have still been at work when Irene walked by?

"Like I said, might have been."

"And maybe now you remember that you noticed she went by?"

"That might be the case," he said, still staring across the river.

"But that's not what you told the police."

"It's not what I will tell them if they ask again. Never thought it was much in a man's interests to be cozy with the police."

"So why are you telling me this?"

"I don't know what happened to the woman, but I know it weren't me who had anything to do with her."

"That's what you're trying to tell me."

"Yes, sir." He glanced sideways at Paul.

"Anything else I should know?" Paul asked.

"Friendly warning," Ernie said. "Poke too much and there's a few folks here who wouldn't like it much. Not like it so much it might not be healthy for you."

"Does that mean you think the person responsible for Irene's disappearance might still be around?" Paul asked.

"I don't know what everybody's got to hide. I just know a few folks want the past to stay buried."

"Did someone send you to talk to me?"

"Someone? More like a committee. Whatever happened to Drexler's wife, he's better off not knowing." Ernie spit one more time and then turned and walked away.

Paul watched him walk back up the block toward the docks, but he couldn't help glancing over to the coffee shop across the street. He could see people inside, sitting around a table. He knew that if he walked in there right now, he'd get a good look at some people who might have sent Ernie over with a message, or he might have a confrontation he didn't need right now. A confrontation might make it less likely to get cooperation later.

As he walked back to the Drexlers', he was surprised to find himself respond to the threat. He wasn't easily intimidated and he'd rarely felt fear in the past, but he had gone through a lot since then. He realized now that he wasn't emotionally as strong as he had once been. Not when it came to threats.

When he finally stood in front of Drexler's house again, he saw Miranda's face appear in the window, and when she saw him she smiled and waved. He smiled and waved back.

Miranda disappeared long enough to get to the door and open it for him when he reached the last flight of steps.

Inside, she shut the door behind them, and then she took his hand and dragged him to the kitchen where her mother was. Mumbling more to himself than Miranda, he said, "Kid, you are nice to come home to."

Terri was at the sink, finishing up the dishes. She glanced back at him and smiled, and then the smile turned to a frown. "The food couldn't have been that bad at Mo's," she said.

"The food was fine; the clam chowder lived up to its reputation."

She turned her back to the sink and wiped her hands on the apron wrapped around her waist. "So what was it that put such a strain on your features?"

She was good at reading faces, he thought. If he were married to her, he'd never be able to hide a lie. Then he realized what he was thinking. He had Pam. How could he think about being married to another woman?

"I met Ernie Crawford."

"He's a little off the wall, but he's not likely to leave a man looking as pale as you do."

"He passed on some friendly advice. He let me know that some good folks here weren't very happy with me poking around."

"I wouldn't doubt that," she said, smiling. "Rumors have a few people around here with pasts they don't want stirred up."

"He also told me that a few wouldn't think twice about putting me in harm's way if I didn't back off."

"Sounds like Ernie knows which one of your buttons to push," she said, stepping into him and wrapping her arms around him. She pulled him tight to her. He cautiously wrapped his arms around her, and then she reached up and pulled his head down so that the sides of their faces touched. She held him like that for several minutes. She felt so good, smelled so good he finally had to pull back. She easily let go of him and stepped back. "That brought some color back," she said.

"Yes," he said.

To cover the embarrassment he was beginning to feel, he asked, "Is your dad up?"

"He's waiting for you upstairs. Before you go, tell me what you learned." She didn't turn back to him but kept on with the dishes. He wondered if she, too, was feeling embarrassment.

"Unless we find out something for sure that tells us otherwise, I'm going to assume two facts from what I learned today. First, your mother didn't end up in the river. Second, she was beyond the boat repair shop before whatever happened to her happened to her."

This time Terri turned back around. She stood very still, and she searched his face again. Finally she said, "Damn. You are good. Thirty years of nothing new, and already in only a day you've found out more than the police and investigators did."

He wondered if she was being sarcastic. "The sheriff who patrols the river convinced me that if your mother had gone into it, her body would have been found. Ernie, without admitting it directly, said he'd seen your mother walk by, and he hadn't said anything at the time because he didn't want the police poking into his life."

"I'm not doubting you at all," she said. "I'm in awe of what you have done in such a short time."

He relaxed his defenses. He wondered if it was her words he was trying to protect himself from, or if it was her physical presence. Her body had felt incredibly good next to his. "Thanks," he said. "I'm not sure what it means, if anything."

"Don't tell Dad about the river. The river is the one thing he can understand that could have taken Mom's life. If you can't find out what happened to her, that's about the only explanation we have that will allow him to die with some peace of spirit."

"Okay," he said.

She reached out a hand and touched him on the arm. "Did my hugging you make you feel uncomfortable?"

"No," he said. "That it felt so good made me feel uncomfortable."

She reached her hand up from his arm and very gently stroked his cheek. "Both your face and your heart are far, far too honest for your own good. I have this uncontrollable need to mother. I won't do it again."

He turned to walk away, throwing back over his shoulder, "It wasn't my mother I was thinking about when you had me in your arms." He headed to the stairs quickly, not wanting to hear how she might respond to that.

Drexler sat slumped in his wheelchair, a pale balloon with the life gone out of it. His skin was loose and wrinkled, and it had already taken on the tint of the dead. His hair was now pure white, thin, and brittle. Paul felt that if he swept his hand over the professor's head, the hair would be wiped away. Paul moved a chair next to the professor and sat down.

"I watched you walk back from town," Drexler said. "You seemed to be dragging a bit. I'm sure you're not that out of shape."

"No, it wasn't that," Paul said. "The folks down in Old Town don't like me poking around."

"I'm . . ." The words caught in his throat and then he coughed. It took him nearly a minute to rein in the coughing. "That's good," he said. "It means they're taking you seriously. They stopped taking me seriously years ago. I can't wait for you to tell me what you found out."

Paul filled him in, struggling with the information about the river. He understood what Terri told him, but Drexler wanted the truth. He compromised, softened it, finishing with, "And, from what I've learned so far, I don't see the river as the answer to this."

Drexler nodded, absorbing all of what Paul had said. "Terri probably told you that I hoped it was the river that took her," Drexler murmured.

"She said that, yes."

Drexler stared out the window through the narrow gap that still allowed him to see the river from his house. "I came to the same conclusion long ago. The river here always gives back what it takes. The river would have been an answer I could have lived with, though."

Or died with, Paul thought. "I have to ask you a question, and I need an honest answer. I know what time and our minds can do to the truth. The two can take it out of focus enough so we can live with it. I need to know what happened between your wife and yourself on the night she walked out the door for the last time."

Drexler continued to stare out the window. He seemed to slump even more in his wheelchair, and then he licked his lips, but nothing came from them. Paul thought for a moment that he might have faded out. Terri said he had bouts of semi-consciousness now. To his relief, Drexler eventually raised his head and turned to look at Paul. He had tears running down his cheeks.

"As I said," he whispered, "she left to go to the market before it closed. We only had one car at the time. She asked me in the morning to get some things at the store on my way back from Eugene. I'd forgotten them."

Paul knew that the trip to Eugene took over an hour. For Drexler to get to the University of Oregon in time for his classes, he would have to leave at least an hour and a half early each day. If he had a 7:30 class, that meant he had to leave by 6:00 and be up not long after 5:00.

Paul also knew that office hours for professors usually extended to at least four. He doubted that Drexler made it home much before 6:00 each night. That was probably hard on a new, young mother who needed the support of her husband through those tough months after a child was born.

He knew it for sure. This was when he had first failed Beth as a husband. He, too, had been wrapped up in his academic career. Being a father and a family man wasn't half as interesting to him at the time. Beth had endured it through two children and a lot more years of marriage before she broke. He wondered if Irene, perhaps more frail than Beth, might have broken much earlier.

Drexler continued. "She was pretty mad at me that night. No, she was pretty mad at me for most of that year. I was gone from home too much. I was never there when she needed help. I'd come home exhausted, and I'd be impatient with her and the pregnancy, and then, after the baby, I'd be impatient with the baby. She kept telling me that I needed to get my priorities straight or she'd get them straight for me."

"What do you think she meant by that?"

"I don't know. She grew pretty distant there in the end. I thought at the time she was just trying to punish me for not making the kind of changes she wanted me to make for her."

"What kind of changes?"

"A teaching position was opening up at the high school. She wanted me to take it." His rough, bent fingers brushed away at the tears on his face.

"You said no."

"You shouldn't even have to ask. We didn't go through the torture of graduate schools, master's comps, and Ph.D. theses to end up teaching in a high school. Where was the prestige in that?"

Or the money, Paul thought. Such a move would have cost Drexler not only standing but also financial security. "She didn't understand?"

"She refused to understand. The birth had been hard on her. She had to work hard to get the weight off after the baby was born. Terri was a fussy baby. Irene never got enough sleep. She was so determined to get her figure back, not only did she take those long walks, but she ate like a bird. None of it was healthy, and she wouldn't hear any of it. She had her mind made up."

"Any idea about what?"

Drexler shook his head slowly side to side. "I've racked my brains on that one. The only thing I can say for sure is I think she planned to punish me."

"When she left that night?"

"She screamed at me when she went out the door. She said, 'You're pushing me over the edge!' She might have said more, but she slammed the door first and I didn't catch it. At the time I remember thinking, all this over some milk I had forgotten to get." The tears again flowed down his cheeks. "I didn't understand it until much later. I didn't know until then how much I'd let her down." He reached a hand out and patted Paul on the arm. "Promise you'll never tell any of this to Terri. I've tried to paint the best picture of her mother that I could for her."

"I won't," Paul said.

Drexler's hand slipped off Paul's arm and dropped down over the edge of the chair. The man slumped to the side and his head slowly sank to his chest. Paul was worried for a moment, but he was reassured by the even breathing. It appeared that Professor Drexler, emotionally taxed, had simply run out of gas. Still, to be cautious, he hurried down the stairs to get Terri.

A half an hour later, while Paul sat on the sofa in the study and went through another file for the third time, Terri stuck her head in the doorway. "He's okay," she said. "He just wears out. In some ways it's good when he slips off like that. He doesn't have to think about anything."

"I was afraid that I overtaxed him."

"You did, but that's what he wants. He doesn't just want to slip away. He wants to go out with all his emotions being pulled at."

"Yes, well the pulling may be harder on me than him."

She had that motherly look on her face again. "You're a very interesting man," she said at last.

And you are a very interesting woman, he thought. He said, instead, "I'm a man, not a superman. I don't know if I can keep doing this with the pressure that's being put on me and with what it is doing to your father."

"I don't see you as a man who would give up."

No, he thought, he couldn't see him as man who would give up, either. He could handle the pressure that came from the research. What really caused the pressure was Terri. She was much too close to what Paul always dreamed he wanted in a woman.

"I haven't given up yet."

She continued to let her eyes wander over him, still with that look on her face. Apparently satisfied by something she saw, she said, "I've only been with one man in my life."

He lifted his eyes to hers and said, "I haven't been with that many women."

She nodded her head, and then she left the room. He stared after her, not quite sure what it was that had passed back and forth between them, but whatever it was, he knew it had been electric.

[9]

HE HAD TO get out of the house. He wasn't sure what he was running from, either Terri or her father. He made an excuse, saying to Terri that he wanted to see for himself how far it was from Old Town to the ocean. She assumed it had to do with bodies in rivers, but it didn't. He needed to get away.

As he followed Terri's directions to the North Jetty, he kept reminding himself that he had a job he liked in southern Oregon, he was living with a beautiful, intelligent, successful woman, and he hadn't been happier in years. By the time he followed the twisting road down to the beach, he was even more muddled than before. Although the logic stood clear in his mind, it kept getting erased by the feeling of Terri's body next to his.

This wasn't one of those postcard days at the beach in Oregon. The sky was overcast, the winds were up, and the tide was running in. As he parked the car in the lot near a lookout tower manned by the Coast Guard during stormy weather, he could see below the clouds the sea for miles in the distance, all of it cold, dull, and gray. A rock jetty extended well out into the foaming surf, and at this moment it had plumes of spray shooting over it on the channel side.

Getting onto the jetty was easy. He simply walked along the sand and up onto the rocks. Near the beach the gaps between the big boulders had been filled in with small rocks and sand. He strolled out on the jetty, the walking smooth for the first part, the only hazard the spray shooting up around him. He stopped long enough to look back up the channel, where the rocks of the North and South Jetties ended and the Siuslaw began. The water was rough, with troughs that dropped five feet or more and waves that crested another five in the opposite direction. The thought of a body in that sent a chill down his spine.

Walking got rough about two-thirds of the way down the jetty. Here an extension had been added more than a decade ago, and no one had bothered to fill in the gaps between the boulders. Paul had to work his way out to the end, hopping from one rock to the next, and then pausing to plan his next path.

He made it as close to the end as he dared. Here, where the jetty's point met the ocean head on, huge sheets of spray flew into the air and landed a few feet from him, although he was a good thirty feet from the end of the jetty. He was so taken by the sight that he didn't notice the two men who came up behind him.

When he finally noticed the first one, Paul was amused. The man was definitely dressed for the jetty. He had on a parka with the hood laced tightly around his face so that only nose stood out. Above that was a pair of dark glasses. Paul glanced to his other side. Another man stood next to the first, dressed in the same way. Paul was no longer amused.

This would be a good time for a retreat, Paul thought. When he started to turn, one of the men grabbed Paul by the upper arm and turned him back. The second man took hold of his other arm.

"Mr. Fischer," the one on the right said, his voice barely audible over the sound of the wind and waves, "we need to have a talk."

"I've already talked with Ernie Crawford and Dave Crane," Paul said.

"That may be so," the second man said, "but you haven't had a talk with us."

All right, Paul told himself, so this wasn't either Crawford or Crane. "But let me guess, the message is going to be the same?"

"I don't know what their message was," said the first man, "but our message is very simple. Get in your car and go home. Buy a few postcards. Tell everyone how nice Florence is. Then never come back."

The message was the same, but these men apparently were not connected with Crawford or Crane. Great, thought Paul, I've got groups competing with each other to run me out of town. He wondered if there might be a prize for the ones who finally succeeded. "I'm simply here doing some research for an old friend."

The second man gripped Paul's arm tightly, until it hurt. "You take your research and shove it up your butt and shit it out some place far from here. Do you understand?"

Paul lurched into the first man, throwing all three of them off balance. Both men had to let go of him to avoid falling. Paul broke away and stepped back. Unfortunately, he had turned the wrong way. The two men were still between him and the path back to safety.

"I don't know what you're afraid of," Paul said, "but both of you appear to be too young to have had anything to do with Irene Drexler's disappearance, so why don't you just back off and let me do what I've been asked to do? It doesn't have anything to do with you."

"You're not getting the message," one of them said.

"No," Paul snapped back, "you're not getting the message. I'm not backing off. I came here to do something, and I'm going to try my damnedest to do it."

Before he could even brace himself, the two men charged Paul and hit him so hard that he went flying backward. He twisted in the air just enough to see the boulder rushing up at him. His body glanced off it and then tumbled down to the next one, and then slid off that onto a third. He was wedged in the rocks so the falling had stopped, but suddenly he was drenched in a huge spray of water, and a surge from a wave nearly floated him up from the rocks. He was only a few feet from being in the ocean.

One of the men leaned over the rocks and shouted down to him, "Next time we'll make sure you end up in the water. They'll be dragging the river for your body."

The second man shouted down, "Now you just stay put for about ten minutes. Try to come up before then, and we'll finish the job."

Paul gave them two minutes and then he climbed up the rocks to the top of the jetty. The two were leaping from rock to rock, quickly moving back toward the beach. He'd never catch them, nor did he want to. He could protect himself, but he wasn't brought up to fight. He started after the two, keeping his distance. He'd gone maybe twenty yards, when one of the men glanced back. He reached out and stopped the second man, and then the two turned to stare at Paul. He kept coming.

For about one more yard. That was when one of the men pulled something from his parka pocket and pointed it in Paul's direction. Paul didn't hear it. But when the bullet splintered a rock no more than a foot from him, he knew enough to hit the ground. Fortunately he was still on the new part of the jetty, so he could drop down out of sight. He heard three more bullets plow into the rocks around him.

He started to look for anything he could use as a weapon. He found some small hunks of rock and began pulling them to him, but even these must have weighed ten pounds or more. He wasn't going to be able to throw them very far or very hard. He wiggled a little toward the ocean side of the jetty so that he could peek between a couple of the boulders. To his relief the men had continued back toward the beach.

Paul stood up. He watched as the two crossed the lot and then disappeared behind some dunes. They had parked in a spot out of view of the jetty. Paul would not be able to see what they were driving. Although the road twisted through dunes and then climbed up a windy part to the highway above, Paul knew he wouldn't get a glimpse of the vehicle.

He walked slowly back toward the beach, keeping an eye on the dunes to make sure the men hadn't simply hidden from view and were waiting for him again. He became less concerned as he got to the end of the jetty. By then half a dozen cars had arrived at what had previously been a deserted beach. People were showing up to enjoy a walk on the beach or a hike on the jetty. He hoped they would have more fun than he had had.

When Paul reached his car, he saw that he would still have a wait to get into dry clothes. The air had been let out of one of his tires. They were nice enough about it, though. They left the valve stem where he could find it, and they had only flattened one tire. Or, he realized, not nice at all. If they had done more damage, Paul would have had to call for help, and that would have left some kind of a record of what happened out here. The men weren't dumb. They followed him. They got him alone. They put a good scare in him. They convinced him the next time would be worse.

They did one more thing, too. They confirmed his resolve. Paul didn't like to be pushed around. He didn't like to be threatened. And he didn't give up because someone said to. More than ever he wanted to know what it was that happened here thirty years ago that had so many people nervous about his presence. He changed the tire and drove back to Drexler's house.

Miranda was in the window again when he dragged himself out of his car, but this time it wasn't the little girl who opened the door for him but Terri. Paul didn't know what Miranda had said, but the look on Terri's face suggested it caused a panic. She grabbed him under and arm and helped him in the house.

He tried to pull away. "I'm OK.," he said. "I'm OK."

"You're not OK." She helped him onto a bench in the hallway.

"It's nothing but water." He reached up and touched the side of his face to confirm that it was water. When he looked at his fingers, they were covered with blood. While Terri rushed to the bathroom, Paul raised himself up enough to look in the hall mirror. The left side of his head and face were covered by a sheet of blood. As he lowered his body back down, he said, "That explains why the other folks in the parking lot gave me such a wide berth while I was changing my tire."

Terri rushed back, loaded down with a pan of warm water, towels, and a first aid kit. She washed the blood away and located the gash in his scalp. "You should get stitches for this."

"I don't need them."

"Are you this stubborn by nature, or is it just for my benefit?"

"Don't give yourself too much credit. This is all by nature."

It took her awhile to stop the bleeding. Then she had him keep pressure on the wound with a piece of gauze while she awkwardly pulled off his soggy jacket and removed his shirt and T-shirt, forcing him to move the gauze from one hand to the other. If it weren't for the lump on his head, Paul thought, this truly would have been a wonderful experience. She wiped him dry and then checked him for other cuts or bruises.

"You've got two nasty scrapes, one on your side and another on your back. I suspect you're going to be black and blue, too. Are you going to tell me what happened?"

He gave her a short version of what happened.

"Did you call the police?" she asked.

"No."

She stood back, her hands on her hips. "But you do plan to call them."

"No."

She whirled away, saying, "Then I'm going to call them."

He managed to grab an arm before she could get to the phone. "I don't want the police involved just yet."

"Someone tried to kill you," she said, a flare of anger showing.

"If they had wanted to kill me, they would have picked me off the rocks and finished tossing me in the ocean. Or they would have walked back and put a bullet in my head. They just wanted to scare me."

"How can you be so sure?"

"Unlike a lot of people, I've been scared by some of the best."

Her mouth opened but nothing came out. Finally she closed it, and then, as if enlightened, said, "So you think you're an expert on criminal behavior."

"No, but I do know when someone is trying to kill me. Trust me on that one."

She carefully cleaned the blood from his hair, and she dabbed at the gash with a thick cream. "This should keep the blood from oozing if you keep your hands away from it." She played with his hair until she had it covering the wound. She stepped back. "No one will notice," she said, with some satisfaction. She put her hands on either side of his face and tilted his head up to look into his eyes. "Now, tell me so I will understand why you are not going to the police."

"If the police get involved, then these folks will probably back off, and chances are good that I will never know what is happening here. If I encourage these people to keep coming at me, I might just find an answer to what is going on."

"I'm not going to keep putting you back together again. You just remember this. People who would shove you off a ten foot drop onto boulders or who would fire a gun at you from a distance, don't really care if they kill you or not. They could have just as easily killed you by accident."

"But they didn't."

"This time."

"I thought you wanted an answer for your father."

"I don't want you dead," she said, slowly twisting his head back and forth.

He could see that he hadn't done much for her anger at him. "I'll be careful," he said.

She dropped her hands to her side. "I'm going to write down everything that you have told me so far. I want you to describe the men to me. I want you to tell me everything you remember."

"I'm not going to do that if you plan to go to the police."

"I won't take it to the police," she said, "unless next time you don't come back. You go get out of those wet pants and soak in a hot bath."

He rose to his feet slowly, awkwardly, his body already stiffening up on him.

[10]

HE DIDN'T MAKE it out of the house again until 10:00 the next morning, and that was only after he had soaked in a hot bath for half an hour. He had some nasty black and blue marks, scrapes that were painful when his clothing brushed against them, and a head that still throbbed.

He hadn't considered the possibility of a concussion. Terri had done that for him. She kept an eye on him throughout the evening, although she still was not talking to him beyond monosyllabic answers. He was awakened in the middle of the night when the lights in the den came on. Groggy, he was aware that Terri had come in and sat on the bed to pry open his eyelids, examining the size of his pupils. Apparently satisfied that he hadn't suffered brain damage, she slipped out again, turning off the lights behind her. He did not get back to sleep right away.

He walked back to Old Town, loose enough by the time he reached the business district to hide the discomfort that he felt. If the two men who had accosted him were watching, they would not get the satisfaction of seeing the damage they had done.

He had a destination. Halfway down the second block, on the riverside, was a bookstore. The store was owned by Walter

Higgins, a man who had remodeled and updated the shop several times over, keeping up with the changing times in Florence so that he had made the business prosper year in and year out. Now he carried an extensive collection of new paperbacks for the vacationers as well as an assortment of other goods that would appeal to tourists. Unlike most of the shops in the area, he emphasized quality: original oil seascapes by local artists, hand-carved sea birds, intricate model fishing boats, plus dozens of other temptations.

Paul wasn't interested in local artwork. What interested him was the fact that Higgins had owned the shop for thirty years, and, according to police reports, he had been in the store updating his books the night that Irene Drexler disappeared.

Paul walked through the open door of the Old Town Book Nook. A young girl, a teenager, stood behind the counter and greeted him with a smile and a nod of her head. Paul walked back to her. She was pretty, the cheerleader type, with blonde hair and blue eyes, and she had a shape that would take the boys' minds off their game.

Paul stopped at the counter and casually leaned against it, mostly to take weight off some sore spots in his body. He was sure his smile was more grimace than anything, but he did the best he could and asked nicely, "Is Mr. Higgins in?"

The girl didn't seem the least bit surprised by the question, as if it was one asked often by strangers who walked in the shop. "Dad's out on the deck." She nodded toward a pair of French doors in the back that were covered in a sheer white curtain.

"Do you think he would mind if I interrupted him?"

"No, Mr. Fischer, I think he's expecting you."

"Only in town two days, and I'm already well known," he said, laughing.

"I recognized you from the pictures in the papers. That was a pretty big story a couple of years ago."

"A couple of years ago you wouldn't have been old enough to read the papers." He was still amazed when he realized how a simple research project had turned into headline news in southern Oregon and a story of interest in a variety of other newspapers.

She reached across the counter and patted his arm. "Thanks, gramps, but I know we all look like kids to you. Actually, I'm twenty-two, and I'm starting graduate school in journalism at the University of Oregon in the fall. We studied the story in one of my classes."

"My apologies," Paul said. "And, by the way, I'm not old enough to be your father, let alone your grandfather."

"Sensitive about your age?"

"No more than you. Is your Dad expecting me?"

"Everyone knows why you are here. Dad said you'd be around to ask him about that night."

Paul nodded and then started walking toward the doors. "Thanks," he said.

"By the way," she called after him. "You're a lot cuter than your pictures."

"I love it when pretty young things give me compliments."

"Does that happen often?"

He turned back so she could see his smile. "You're the first today."

He opened the doors and found himself on a narrow deck that ran the width of the building. A railing surrounded the deck, and the deck was cantilevered from the back of the store so that the Siuslaw ran under it. To his left sat Water Higgins at a small, wrought iron table. He was drinking a cup of coffee while reading a newspaper. He glanced up at Paul and nodded his head in much the same way his daughter had.

As Paul walked toward the table, he took in Higgins' features. His hair was thick and brown, with just a hint of gray in it. His face was tanned and lightly lined. Brown eyes blended in with the features. Higgins was handsome in the same way his daughter was handsome, but he was a bit bland, all shades of brown so that nothing stood out; not like the blue of his daughter's eyes.

Higgins stood and reached out to shake hands with Paul. "I thought it wouldn't be long before I showed up on your short list of people to see."

Paul's hand was taken in a firm grip and then quickly dropped. "Real short. Only a few names." In truth, Paul thought, no names if it came to suspects. He was interested in Higgins and the Markses because he understood that they were working that night. And, of course, he couldn't forget about Ernie Crawford.

"Have a seat. Coffee?"

"Sure."

Paul sat while Higgins poured him a cup of coffee from a carafe on the table. "Cream and sugar," he said, gesturing to a pitcher and bowl on the table.

"Great service, great view," Paul said. "If I had this to look forward to, I think I'd love to go to work each day."

"Today we have sunshine and no clouds. The river's beautiful. In about an hour, the wind will come up and put a chill in the air that will drive me inside. God gave us some spectacular weather down here, and then with a perverse sense of humor, made it damned near impossible to enjoy it."

Paul sipped his coffee. It was fresh ground and strong, just the way he liked it. He looked up at Higgins and watched the man's eyes as he said, "I need to know about that night."

The eyes gave away nothing. "You read the reports."

"I'm learning that reports may not hold the whole story."

Higgins returned the favor by watching Paul's eyes. "Just how good are you at finding out things? According to the papers, damned good. Is that a fair assessment?"

"Maybe a shade more credit than I deserve, but I'd say if I have a chance at finding out something, I'll find it out."

Higgins nodded. "Then maybe I'd better tell you about the night instead of the report."

"The two might not be the same?"

"The people in Old Town were a pretty closed group back then. The cops weren't a part of it. We often told them what they wanted to hear to get them off our backs, and we told them nothing that might make them curious enough to come back."

"Late sixties, early seventies."

"Pigs versus us."

"I wasn't old enough to be a part of that," Paul said. If he had been, he thought, he probably would have had the same attitude. "In fact, you don't look old enough, either."

"Twenty-two at the time."

"I hope I look as good as you do when I'm fifty-two."

"Clean living."

"I'm glad to hear that. I'm all for clean living."

"Let me tell you about that night," Walter Higgins began. "The store's been redone a couple of times since then, of course. The counter was up front near the door. I was there doing my books when Irene walked by. When she saw me, she stopped and tapped on the window."

"Do you know what time that was?"

"Do you mean could she have been someplace else before she got to my store?"

"Yes."

"I'd say she had walked non-stop to my shop."

"Did you talk?"

"According to the police report, I didn't even see her that night."

"Which was obviously wrong."

Higgins nodded. "Yes, we did talk. She indicated that she wanted in. When I let her inside, she said she needed someone with an open ear and a closed mouth."

Paul watched Higgins carefully. "She wanted to tell you that she was unhappy with her husband."

Higgins raised his cup of coffee to Paul in a salute. "You are good."

"It's not so hard when everyone suddenly wants to tell the truth."

"You're right, she did want to complain about Bill. I listened, but I didn't give it much thought at the time. Women bitch; men fight."

"What exactly were her complaints?"

"The usual. Bill was gone too much. He had the car so she was pretty much stranded with the baby. The baby didn't give her much rest. Terri still wasn't sleeping through the night then."

"Did you get any sense that these complaints were more serious than they sounded to you at the time?"

Higgins shook his head no. "Not really. Bill was building his reputation back then. He was working hard to move up the ladder where the good pay would be. I always thought of him as being a good husband who understood that the success of his career was at the heart of the security of his family. He also turned out to be a hell of a good father. Too bad Irene wasn't around to see it."

"Then what happened?"

"She seemed to feel better, having had her bitch, and she left. She walked on up the street. I really didn't pay any attention to her after that. I wanted to get the books done and go home."

"What do you think happened to her?"

"You know," Higgins said, "it was kind of like that Patty Hearst thing around here for a long time. We talked it to death, and we said we hoped we didn't die before we found out what happened to her." He paused and looked out over the river, a sad smile on his lips. "In time it just sort of faded away. I couldn't say what happened. The police did a thorough job of searching Old Town. If her body had been here or on one of the boats, they would have found it."

"And you didn't see her come back this way?"

Higgins was still staring across the river. "No. I gave that a lot of thought. The books took longer than I thought they would. If anyone had gone down the street again that night, either way, I would have noticed. Besides, if she had gone to the store, she would have come back up the next block over. For a long time I sort of blamed myself. It was a real quiet night. If she'd made any kind of a noise, I would have heard it. I worried a lot that I'd missed something."

"You still haven't answered my question. What do you think happened?"

Higgins turned and looked Paul square in the eyes. "I think Bill killed her."

Paul slowly leaned back in his chair, keeping the eye contact with Higgins. "Why do you think that?" he asked making sure to keep his voice level. He didn't want to react in any way that might make the man think again about telling him something that was this damning.

"She wasn't happy. She hadn't been happy through the pregnancy. Bill was off to the university days and evenings, it seemed. When he was home on the weekends, he was usually buried in paperwork. She resented the hell out of that. She pretty well let everyone know. I could imagine the arguments they must have had. I think maybe she got back late from her walk, and that started them at it. I think he killed her." He nodded his head several times. "Yes, I think he killed her."

"So where did he put the body?" Paul asked.

Higgins turned to look at him, a hint of doubt in his eyes. "The body?"

"Yes, what did he do with the body?"

"Buried it in the cellar?"

"As you said, the police were thorough. They searched every inch of Bill's property. So where'd he put the body?"

"Hid it and moved it later?"

"He called half an hour after she didn't get back when she should have. The police stopped at the house, did a preliminary look around, and cruised through Old Town. The big search didn't start until the next morning, but between the first call and then, they had officers both at Bill's house and in Old Town. One officer even thought to check the hood of Bill's car to see if it was warm. It wasn't. So where'd he put the body?"

"That's a good question," Higgins said.

Yes, Paul thought. That was a hell of a question. If the body was still in Old Town when the police conducted their search, then somebody had to have a hell of hiding place. Chances were much better that the body was gone before the search.

"If we get the answer to where the body went, then we'll get the answer to what happened to her. Have you ever considered that she might have run off?"

Higgins laughed. "I don't think if she were running off, she'd have taken time to stop and bitch to me."

"You didn't get that feeling, then?"

"That she was off to meet someone?"

"Yes."

"This is a small town now. It was even smaller then. If folks were having an affair, someone would have known about it."

"Which means everyone would have known about it?"

"Pretty much."

"So you don't remember any rumors?"

"Not one about Irene, other than she was pissed at Bill."

The French doors opened and Julia stuck her head out. "Hey, Dad," she said, "You promised me a break."

"I'd better be going," Paul said, starting to push his chair back from the table.

"No, no," Higgins said, motioning him to stay put. "She plans to take her break out here with you. She's at that age when any man without a wedding ring is fair game."

Paul started to protest, ""I think I'm a little old for her, and I am involved."

As he got up, Higgins patted Paul on the shoulder and whispered, "She talks the talk, but she doesn't walk the walk."

As Julia swayed toward him in skin-tight jeans, Paul hoped that was an accurate assessment of the man's daughter. She squeezed between Paul and her father as he passed, turning so that her backside brushed against Paul's shoulder. She then turned back to the table, pouring more coffee into Paul's cup without asking him if he wanted any, and then pouring coffee in her own. She sat down at the table and leaned her elbows on it, resting her chin in her hands and staring into Paul's eyes. She held the stare without a hint of self-consciousness.

Paul felt like squirming, but he wouldn't give her the satisfaction of knowing she was making him feel uncomfortable. To break the impasse, he asked, "Print media?"

She continued to hold the gaze, saying, "Broadcast. I plan to be on-the-air talent."

"So you are not necessarily interested in journalism per se."

"Don't get me wrong," she said, her eyes examining each of the features on his face, first one eye and then the other, the nose, the mouth, and then a sweep from ear to ear. "I plan to be a damned fine journalist. I also plan to be one of those attractive anchor people on a news show in a major market that makes a hell of a lot of money."

"Don't you worry that your career might fade with your looks?"

She grinned, the smile turning lopsided by the weight of her cheeks on her hands. "I plan to invest wisely and retire early. Besides, does this face look like its going to fade quickly?" She lifted her head from her hands, tilted it to one side, and smiled sweetly for his benefit.

What could he say? Straight nose. Big, blue eyes. Great bone structure. Hair without a strand out of place. White, white teeth, even as could be. She had Miss America written all over her. "Very nice," he said. "You might have trouble with a face like that, though. People might not believe that bad news could come from those lips."

"With the right makeup job, I can look as hard as nails."

He was tempted to laugh, but he realized that she believed it. He looked at her features again, and then he saw it, too. It wouldn't take much to add a touch of cruelty to her face. "I think I see it," he said.

She smiled again, this time a hundred watts. "This is not an 'if' thing," she said. "It is a 'when' thing. I'm going to make it big. Your little story here might not be a bad way for me to get a step up in the direction I'm heading."

And a mercenary, as well, he thought. "Here I thought it was my good looks that had you so interested in me."

"Oh, yes, that, too," she said, rolling her eyes.

"So far, I don't have enough of a story to make a weekly newspaper, let alone national headlines. I don't think you will launch your career on this one."

"Don't you think that I'm the one who should decide that? After all, it is my career we're talking about."

"Yes, but it's my story."

"And you don't intend to share."

"No, actually, I would like to share it with you. You can have all the intimidations and threats. I'll keep all the information."

She picked up a spoon and played with it while she talked, twirling it in her fingers. "Getting a lot of information?"

"Nothing that would impress anyone."

"More intimidations and threats than information?"

"Seems some folks don't want me looking into the past."

She nodded her head, and Paul thought he saw something cross her face, like a shadow, that gave the strong impression of a hardness that could be there if she wanted it to be. "Any idea why not?"

"I'm only twenty-two."

Good answer, he thought. Prehistory for her. "Any guesses?"

"By the time I knew about the sixties and seventies, they were ancient history." She carefully set the spoon down on the table and asked, "Are you still with Pam Livingston?"

"We've been involved for a while, yes," he said.

"Cool," she said.

Paul wondered just what it was that could be classified as 'cool.' "Anything else I can help you with?"

"I'll let you know," she said. With that she stood up and headed back to the doors. "Break's over."

The break was over for Paul, too. Higgins was right. The wind was starting to come up, sweeping across the river and picking up the chill from the water. He followed Julia into the store, said his good-byes to both of them, and left the shop.

He walked back toward Drexler's house, aware of how much his body had stiffened while he sat in the chill next to the river. He had to struggle to keep from showing the pain he felt as he walked. On the way, he reviewed what he knew. So far two people who had said they had seen nothing on the night Irene disappeared, now said they had seen something. That, he thought, was more than curious. Neither had a reason suddenly to change his story. No one would have been able to prove that they lied, unless . . . unless both knew the other had seen the woman that night. If that were the case, one telling the truth might put the other in a bad light.

Without noticing it, Paul had started to limp by the time he was out of sight of the coffee shop. Was it possible that both men might have been involved in the disappearance of Irene? Two men working in tandem might have been able to shuffle a body around while the police searched the area. But why would they do that? Why would one or both kill the woman? That made no sense.

What Higgins had said made more sense. They too wanted to know what had happened to a woman who had disappeared. Maybe both men saw this as an opportunity to find out, and that was the reason for them to tell the truth. Paul began to shake his head as the house came into view. If they were telling the truth now, Paul thought.

As he stiffly worked his way up the steps to the house, he wondered again what he had gotten himself into. With so little information to go on, he did not have much of a base against which to measure what he had learned. He paused at the front door, his hand reaching for the knob, when it opened to the smiling face of Miranda. He smiled back at her. As he walked in the house, now aware of both his limp and his aches, he put all those questions to rest. He hadn't gotten slammed against the rocks on the jetty because he was moving away from the truth. He was getting warm, and somebody didn't like that at all.

Terri came to the doorway of the kitchen and leaned against it, wiping her hands on an apron. "I'm making a cherry pie, but don't think I'm making it for you, or that you deserve it." She had made it clear the night before that she was mad at him for refusing to go to the police. Apparently she was still mad.

She was wearing a simple cotton dress, belted at the waist with short sleeves. On her it looked elegant, he thought. "You're pretty, even when you're mad," he said. This time he didn't question whether he should have said it.

[11]

PAUL SAT ON the sofa in the den with a children's book on his lap. Miranda was snuggled up next to him as he read to her from the book, taking time to match words to pictures. His arm was wrapped around the child, and for the first time in years, he remembered what had been so great about being a father of little children. He realized it wasn't the innocence of children he missed, but being accepted by them.

Terri came into the room and stood for a moment to take in the scene. Finally, she said, "I guess you will get pie after all."

Paul looked up from the book. "Miranda can already recognize a lot of words. She'll be reading in no time."

"Her mother's a teacher. What do you expect?"

"You've done a wonderful job with her," he said.

"Dad has helped. He's provided the male influence in her life."

The sadness in her statement wasn't missed by either of them. "Yes," he said. That was all he could say. Yes, Drexler would be dead soon. Yes, Miranda needed a male in her life. Yes, Paul was not likely to be that male, despite the comfort he felt with the child nestled in beside him. "Dinner was wonderful," he said.

"Thanks for doing the dishes."

"That's the best I can do. I can't cook."

"My lovely little daughter needs to take a bath. I thought I'd put her in the tub down here, if you don't mind."

"Not at all. As soon as I finish the marvelous story of a bear, a squirrel, and a raccoon, I need to get back to work."

Terri moved to the sofa and sat down next to Miranda, leaning so she, too, could see the book. Her shoulder touched Paul's. Paul finished reading the story while Terri reached across to point out things on the pages to Miranda. More than once Paul and Terri's heads came together. Neither, Paul noticed, tried to draw them away when they did.

When the story was done, Paul put the book away while Miranda and Terri disappeared into the bathroom. Paul returned to the sofa with another folder, this one thicker than all the others.

Ira Marks had owned the small market that was Irene Drexler's destination on the night she disappeared. According to all the reports from that night, Irene had never made it to the store. Paul would normally have accepted that and skipped an interview with Marks, but after two stories had changed, he was curious to see if this one would change, too.

Getting in to see Marks wasn't as easy as he thought it would be. Marks had, Paul smiled to himself, made his mark. He had built the first supermarket in Florence, and when that had been a big success, he started building them in every major town on the coast. Those, too, took off, so he headed inland. He now owned forty-two stores in Washington and Oregon, Marks Markets. He'd become a wealthy man.

He hadn't been a man to forget his roots. The corporate headquarters for the stores was still in Florence, and Marks was one of the community's wealthiest and most influential citizens. He had been mayor. He had served on city council. He had served on the school board. Marks had been on every committee in the last twenty years that had accomplished anything worth doing.

Paul would get exactly fifteen minutes in the afternoon between 2:30 and 2:45. Marks's secretary had made it clear that if Paul were late by even a minute, the meeting would be cancelled. That didn't sound to Paul like a man who was going to have a lot to add to the story.

Paul couldn't find any information on Beverly, Ira's wife. He knew that they were still married and had been back when Terri's mother disappeared. Unlike her husband, she was not involved in the community, and, according to accounts that Paul read from social events attended by Ira, Beverly's name was rarely mentioned.

Paul's cell phone rang. He picked up the phone from the coffee table and answered it. "Paul."

"Good, you're there," Pam said. "Something's come up."

How many times had he heard that in the last two years? Pam was stretched in so many directions that something was always coming up. With his own time boxed in by classes and his set of professional responsibilities, this usually meant that something the two had planned together needed to be cancelled.

"Hi, how are you?"

"Wiped out. Paul, the damned prosecuting attorney has managed to get a delay. It seems my client may have been involved in a case of gay bashing. The D.A. wants time to look into it. If it's true, then my job is going to be even more difficult than it already is."

Paul actually thought Pam's job should be quite simple. She should provide an adequate defense, one that was appeal-proof, for a man who was obviously guilty, and lose the case in the name of justice. He understood why lawyers got such a bad name. They were ethically charged with undermining the justice system.

"How long of a delay?" he asked.

"Two weeks."

She didn't need to tell him. The boys would now definitely be there before she went to trial. She would not want them marauding through the house with all of her papers so carefully spread out. "That's going to be a problem with the boys," he said.

"I hate to ask you this, Paul, but could you take the boys off someplace for a couple of weeks, until the trial gets done?"

Paul didn't know what to say. He could stand his ground and insist the boys come anyway, perhaps staying in the guesthouse behind Pam's house, but he knew she wouldn't go for that. Half her office staff would be staying in the guesthouse during the trial. Hold his ground? Insist? This wasn't his house; Pam owned it. He was just as much a guest in it as the boys would be.

"I suppose we could stay in a motel."

"Paul, I don't mean to cause a problem, but you know as well as I do that if the boys are within twenty miles of me, they'll want to spend time with me. You need to take them on a vacation someplace."

The whole idea, he thought, was that the boys were going to be on vacation, with the two of them, in Medford in the very house they were now being asked to vacate. He kept his temper in check because he knew it would do no good to lose it. Besides, he also knew how much this case meant to Pam.

"I'll think of something," he said.

"I knew you'd come through. How's the research going down there?"

"More twists and turns than straight lines."

"Are you going to find out what happened to the woman?"

"Maybe, but I don't know if I will find out in time."

"In time for the professor's death?"

"Yes."

"If anyone can do it, I know you can. When you figure out your plans, let me know them."

"I will," he said.

Pam clicked off, and he was left to read a disconnected message on his cell phone. This was another thing that bothered him about their relationship. When Pam was caught up with a client, it was as if they did not exist as a couple. Paul was like Pam's secretary, one more person with whom to leave a message. When she could relax, and when she could focus on him, then he once again drifted toward the center of her universe. He just never stayed there very long.

This time she didn't even say good-bye. No "I love you." No "I miss you." No "When do you think you'll be back?" He was simply an inconvenience to her plans for the moment, something that had to be dealt with, like the delay in the court proceeding.

He wondered what was going on. He'd put up with it for two years without this flood of feelings. Why was he so depressed by it all now? Before he had a chance to answer that, the bathroom door burst open and Miranda came charging in, wearing her nightgown. In a surprisingly athletic move for a four-year-old, she ran across the room, jumped in the air, landed on her knees on the sofa, and bounced right into Paul's arms. She wrapped her arms around his neck and gave him a strong hug.

"Wow," he said. "What a move. I do like the end results."

"She's been practicing that for about a half a year on me." Terri leaned in the bathroom doorway and smiled.

"And you smell good."

Miranda shoved herself back so she could see his face. "I smell just like Mama."

"I've noticed that your Mama smells good, too."

She gave him a kiss on the cheek. "Mama said I had to give you a hug and a kiss before I went to bed."

"I hope that wasn't too much trouble for you."

She giggled. "I was going to do it anyway." She hopped off his lap and grabbed Terri's hand, dragging her toward the door. "Mama said she'll read some more to me in bed."

"I'll be back in a while," Terri said.

Paul returned to the folder. He had only opened it when his phone rang again. For just an instant, he hoped it was Pam calling back to tell him that she forgot to say she loved him. This time, though, when he answered it, Beth was on the other end.

"Hi," she said. She had a voice that was deep and husky for a woman. He never had to guess who it was when she called.

"Hi. How are you doing?"

"Not very good. Denise isn't taking this very well at all. She's moving out this weekend, and, in the meantime, she's stomping all over the house, slamming doors and rattling everything that she can rattle while she packs. I've got the boys spending time with friends for a couple of days."

"You're not in any danger, are you?"

"Men don't have a monopoly on violence, no, but Denise is not one to harm anyone. She actually is a very gentle, loving, caring person. A bit noisy when she's mad, but pretty good the rest of the time."

"Any other problems?"

"Money."

Money again. Beth had come after more money from him on a number of occasions, but he learned quickly that Denise had been the one behind that. "What about money?" he asked.

"I'm not going to be able to keep the house without Denise's support."

"So you need more money from me."

"No, not now. I'm going to look around to see if I can find something cheaper. With the support I'm already getting from you, I should be okay, but it's still going to worry me until I get everything worked out."

"If you need money . . ."

"I know. I do want one thing, though. Is there a chance we could get together and talk?"

"I'm not planning to come back there this summer."

"I was thinking of coming out to Oregon at the end of the summer. Since you seem to be so established there, I thought I might come out to see what the job market is like. It would be great for the boys if we weren't so far away."

So many emotions tore at him at once that he was left with nothing to say for several seconds. Have the boys around all the time? Incredible! Having Beth around all the time would be incredible in a different way. He didn't have to imagine what Pam would say. He could hear her words clearly: "Over my dead body!"

"That would be good for the boys," he said.

"And you?"

"Me?"

"How would you feel about it?"

"I think," he said, "I will need to think about that."

"That's fair," she said. "At least you didn't reject the idea out of hand."

No, he hadn't, and that too disturbed him. "How are the boys?"

"They're fine. I told them we'd call you Saturday night, after Denise had finished her moving."

"I'm pretty sure I'll still be here," he said.

"I'll talk to you then. Good night," she said. "And thanks, Paul. You have every reason to never want to talk to me again."

"Every time I try to do that, a memory of the good times slips in and I'm left powerless."

"You can still be a sweet guy. You just need to learn to do it a little more often."

"I'll work on it."

"Good night again," she said and hung up.

He tossed the phone on the table and slumped back on the sofa, putting his feet up and his hands behind his head. That's the way that Terri found him when she came back in the room.

"Another phone call?" she asked.

"Beth."

"I heard bits of your conversation with Pam. Something about a change of plans."

She came over and sat down beside him, leaning back with her hands in her lap and putting her feet up on the coffee table. They both sat that way in silence, their thoughts rolling one over the other, but not shared.

Paul broke the silence. "If you were married to a divorced man with children, and the children's mother moved close by, what kind of a relationship do you think you would have with her?"

"Is this hypothetical or an incredibly original proposal of marriage?"

He smiled. "Let's be hypothetical for now."

"I think I would try to work with the mother so we could both do our best to raise the kids."

"Do you think that's possible?"

"I think it is possible for me, but I couldn't say for the mother. Women have jealousies that cannot be defined by the rational, and those are at their worst when it comes to children and lovers. Even if things were for the best, I suspect I'd have my hands full."

They both sat silent again, and then Paul said, "I like you. I like the way your mind works."

She smiled. "I'm still young enough to prefer compliments that refer to the turn of my ankle, but I get so few of any kind as it is, I'll take one for my mind."

Paul glanced at her and let his eyes run down to her crossed ankles. Slowly he followed the curve of her calves to the turn of her thighs. He moved more quickly past her lap, and then he slowed again when he came to her breasts. There, for just a bit too long, his eyes lingered. He finally was able to tear them away and move to her face, where two shiny eyes and a lovely smile were waiting for him.

"You got hung up there toward the top, didn't you?"

He could feel himself blush. "When it's mountainous in that area, it takes a little longer to make the climb," he said.

"You weren't climbing; you were doing a fly by."

He patted the file on his lap. "Well, now, time to go back to work."

"That's called redirecting," she said, laughing.

"Yes it is," he said. "Tell me what you know about the Marks family."

She smiled, enjoying his discomfort before she came to his rescue with, "The Marks family. Ira has been everything in this community. I don't know what I can tell you about Beverly. No one sees much of her."

"Does she do volunteer work?"

"Not that I know of."

"I thought it strange that the newspapers would be loaded with information about Ira, but his wife's name was rarely mentioned."

"I guess she's just shy," Terri said. She started to say something more, but then she stopped herself.

Paul closed the file on his lap. "I don't expect much to come out of the interview," he said. "Everyone seems to agree that your mother never made it to the market."

"So what do you think so far?"

"So far? You want the softened version or what I really think?" He glanced at her to gauge her reaction.

She didn't even blink an eye, saying, "Honesty, of course."

"Okay. Your mother was mad at your dad that night. She left in a huff because he got home late from work again and forgot to pick up milk. She stopped off to vent with Walter Higgins. She then continued her walk, taking the long way around so she would get to the store just before it closed to give her as much time out of the house as possible. At the time, an open field was next to the docks, used for parking cars and leaving boats on trailers that needed to be repaired. I suspect your mother walked across the field. I suspect that what ever happened to her, happened in the middle of it."

Terri's silence drew another glance from Paul. "Why do you say that?" she asked, quietly but with a hint of emotion in her voice.

Paul reached an arm around her shoulder and drew her to him until her head rested on his shoulder. "I'm sorry," he said.

"Your mother isn't real to me. She's history that I'm trying to put in order. I forget that you have emotions tied to her."

"I'm okay," she said. "Although I never knew her, that she might have come to a violent end still bothers me. I do want to know why you say that."

"Noise. No one heard anything. That's consistent with all the interviews of people who were anywhere near Old Town that night. The center of the field is the farthest point in any direction from stores and houses in the area. If she had been able to call out, I don't think anyone would have heard it from there."

"So what do you do next?"

"Try to find out who might have been in that field at the same time."

"Wouldn't that be impossible now?"

"Yes and no. I'm working on the premise that it was someone in the community. In the police reports there's a lot of information about the whereabouts of a couple dozen people who could have been in the area because they lived nearby or they owned a boat tied to the docks or they ran one of the businesses in Old Town. The police didn't do a bad job on this case. They actually documented alibis for these people."

She rolled her head up to look at his face. When he glanced down, he saw that their lips were only inches apart. She smelled just like Miranda, sort of a mild fragrance of both strawberries and vanilla. The two, mixed with some faint, indiscernible aroma of woman, were very appealing. He took a long, audible breath, and reluctantly moved his eyes from her lips.

"Where was I?" he asked.

"Looking at my lips."

He blushed again. "Damn, will you stop making me do that?"

"Blush?"

"It's okay not to notice."

"I think it's cute."

"Back to what I was saying. Yes, they documented alibis, which meant they could confirm that each of these people was seen at a certain place at a certain time. What I'm interested in is how far away they were from the center of that field, and if they had time to get to their alibi from that spot when whatever happened to your mother happened."

"What about—?" She struggled. "You know. Disposing of Mom?"

"John Doe, having a drink in Joe's Bar at 9:55 that evening, might well have had your mother's body in the trunk of his car."

"Where do you think all that will lead?"

"It's a process of elimination. Eventually I will get down to a few names. Then I will start looking at those names in a variety of ways. Could any of them have had a relationship with your mother we don't know about? Could any of them have had a grudge against your father? Do any of them have records? We might get two hits on one person. That person then becomes the center of attention until we can definitely remove him from the list."

"This could take you all summer."

"I may be here longer than I thought," Paul said. "Pam's trial got extended. I may have my boys come here for a couple of weeks so we can stay out of Pam's way until the trial is over."

She rolled her head back up to look at him again. "That's not a look of being pleasantly pleased on your face."

"It's an inconvenience."

"Is there a little hint of anger in that, too?"

He looked back down at her and stared into her eyes. She had lovely eyes, and he found himself unable to tear his away. "There's a lot of accommodating in our relationship."

And then their lips came together and they were wrapped in each other's arms. Terri was the first to offer resistance, slowly and feebly trying to push him away. Their bodies separated before their lips did. She drew herself away from him and stood, but her fingers were clenched in his shirt and she nearly pulled him up with her before she thought to let go. She turned and hurried to the door, pausing for a second to say, "I want you to lock this door behind you, and under no circumstance, even if I beg, are you to let me back in this room tonight." She rushed from the room, leaving the door open behind her, and he could hear her practically bounding up the stairs.

Paul flopped back on the sofa and closed his eyes. Nothing was going right, he told himself. Then, as he took in the scent that Terri had left behind, he added, almost nothing.

[12]

PAUL ARRIVED AT Marks Markets Corporate Headquarters ten minutes early. Finding the place was not much of a challenge, as it sat back from the coastal highway under a huge sign. The building was neither large nor impressive. On the outside it was mostly cedar siding, shake roof, and a few narrow, slat windows. Inside were a lot of smooth plaster walls with wood stained dark brown used around the doors and baseboards. The carpeting was industrial grade and medium blue, without a pattern.

The receptionist sat behind a set of sliding windows at the front of the building. She directed him to a hallway to his left. At the end of that hallway was a small waiting area with a secretary behind a metal desk with a fake veneer top. When he gave her his name, she told him to sit and wait. He sat and waited for exactly eight and a half minutes before the secretary walked him to a set of plain double doors, stained dark to match the other trim. She opened one door and directed him inside.

Marks sat behind his desk, not bothering to rise as Paul entered. The man had a long, weathered face. His hair was black sprayed with an overlay of gray, and his mustache was thick and roughly trimmed. Although the face was pleasant enough,

Paul found the eyes wanting. Ira Marks wasn't pleased to see Paul and he was impatient about the waste of time.

Marks threw up a hand in the direction of a chair across from his desk. Paul took that as an invitation to sit, which he did. Once comfortable, Paul decided he was the one who would have to do the talking. Marks had dropped his head back down to a stack of papers in front of him. "I'm Paul Fischer."

"What a surprise," Marks said without looking up.

Rude? Defensive? Maybe this just was the way that Marks was, Paul thought, but it didn't fit the typical description of a town's outstanding citizen. "I wanted to ask you some questions about the night Irene Drexler disappeared."

"Can you read?"

Paul did a slow burn. Pointed rudeness was unforgivable in his book. "It's one of the requirements of being a college professor."

"Good, then go back and read the police reports from that night. I didn't see a thing, I didn't hear a thing, and I don't know a thing." The head stayed down, the eyes scanning through figures on the sheet of paper in front of him.

"Then perhaps I could talk to your wife."

Mark's head snapped up. The eyes came alive, and this time they were sparking with anger. "You come near my wife and I'll personally beat the shit out of you. If I know nothing, then she knows less than nothing."

"Thanks for your time," Paul said, getting up and walking to the door. He felt that if he didn't get out the office quickly he would say something he was sure to wish he hadn't said.

"Don't rush off. You still have eight minutes."

As Paul opened the door, he threw back over his shoulder, "No thanks. My time's too precious to waste." He snapped the door closed behind him and ignored the secretary as he left the building.

Paul sat in his car, angry about what he had done. Marks obviously wanted to push Paul's buttons, and Paul had let him. If he hadn't flared up, perhaps he could have gotten something from Marks. He relaxed behind the wheel. He had gotten something. His past research had taught him that even information that did not provide him with what he wanted had value. It could tell him if he was on the right track. It could eliminate a possibility. It could raise a question he hadn't considered before.

So, what had he learned from this? Marks claimed to know nothing. On the other hand, why had Marks worked so hard to discourage Paul? If he indeed knew nothing, then all the posturing in there had been unnecessary. And, what was with Marks's wife that he didn't want Paul talking to her? That meant one thing to Paul. He would have to see what else he could find out about the wife.

Crawford and Higgins had both come forward with information, and in Paul's eyes that made them both less likely to be responsible for Irene's disappearance. Marks's resistance to helping Paul made him more suspect.

Paul pulled out of the parking lot and headed back to Drexler's house. Next he would crosscheck all the alibis with locations and times. With luck, a name would emerge that would open up the investigation. Without something breaking, Paul was feeling pretty hopeless. Investigating something that happened thirty years before was hard enough, but to try to find anything new after all that time seemed impossible.

But he had. He had found out new information.

Back at the house, he discovered Terri curled up on the sofa in the front room, reading a book. When she saw him, she lifted her head, tilted it to one side, and smiled at him. She had a nice smile, he thought for the twentieth time. "You're back early," she said.

"Mr. Marks was not very cooperative, and he made it clear that Mrs. Marks, should I dare go anywhere near her, wouldn't be very cooperative either. We seem to have a secret here involving Mrs. Marks. You wouldn't know anything about that, would you?"

She slipped her bookmark back into the book, and then she put the book on the back of the sofa. "I'm kind of in a spot here," she said. "I do know a little more than I told you, but that information comes from having heard some of the older teachers talk about the two Marks boys. I'm tied up in some confidentiality issues."

He could have taken a chair across from her, but he decided to sit on the sofa instead. Still curled up, she twisted a little more toward him until their legs touched. He could feel her warmth against him. He liked the feeling.

"Let me see if I can maybe do some guessing, and then let's see if you can tell me if I'm guessing in the right direction."

"I think that's cheating," she said.

"We know that teachers don't like cheats, but we also know that at least one teacher in this room is desperate to know what happened to her mother. And we also know that right now the other teacher in the room is running out of clues. Try to help me here."

"Let me hear what you have to say."

"You have a very prominent man."

"Very prominent."

"And this man, it would seem, has a woman who should be an asset to his stature in the community."

"But she isn't."

"Which means a reason must exist that is more compelling than the social implications of an absentee wife. It is less embarrassing to not have her around than it is to have her around."

"That could be," she offered in a neutral tone.

"What is it that might be the problem? No social graces? I would suspect that could be fixed over thirty years. Painfully shy? Still fixable. A social embarrassment? Not fixable? I would have to guess drink or drugs."

"Don't look to me to answer that."

"Back to the social prominence of the man in the community. Drugs would not do. A man in his position would probably choose divorce over getting tied up in a drug bust. That would have to make the drug legal. That would have to make it a problem with drink or prescription drugs." He looked at her, waiting for a sign of confirmation.

Terri stared back at him, smiling, but showing no other sign that she was going to give him what he wanted.

He said, "Blink once for yes, twice for no."

She smiled and did not blink.

"I'm going to assume," he said, "that I've hit the nail on the head. If I'm heading in a time-wasting, wrong direction, I think it would be in your best interest to let me know."

She smiled, but her mouth stayed closed.

"You know, you're really pretty when you're being totally obstinate. For your information, though, despite your help, I think I'm on the right track. My guess is it's alcohol because that doesn't need the cooperation of a doctor. One question I would like answered is how long Mrs. Marks has had this problem."

Terri smiled and said, "You're not bad looking yourself."

They were stuck that way, sitting next to each other on the couch, admirers, but with no place for them to go. "I didn't hear you clawing at my door last night."

"That's because I lashed myself to my bed."

"You should have told me. That sounds kind of kinky and fun."

"Not when you're by yourself." She paused for a moment to gather thoughts, and then she said, "We're kidding here, aren't we?"

"Yes," he said. "No," he added.

"That's what I thought. Listen," she said, "I don't have any sticky relationships. I've managed to survive pretty much as a teacher, a daughter, and a mother, without feeling a great compulsion to get involved with a man. Having you here, though, and having you so close, has stimulated—no, that's not a good word—has awakened in me a sense of what I've been missing. That's not good. Not for either one of us."

"I know," he said. "The trouble is that you've awakened in me a sense that maybe I'm missing something."

"Do we need to do something about that?"

"Do you mean like hop in bed?"

"No, I was thinking more in terms of you moving into a motel."

"Is that what you want me to do?"

They were now looking into each other eyes, holding the stare, searching. "No. I want us to be adults. Miranda is enjoying having you here. So am I. Dad wants you here. I do not want, though, to be in the middle of a triangle."

"That's fair," he said.

"So we are going to be adults about this?"

"Absolutely." He reached an arm out, wrapped his hand behind her neck, and pulled her to him. The kiss took a long time. They were not exactly hungry for each other, but they were more into exploration: the soft, gentle feel of their lips together, the smell of each other so close, the touch and the warmth of their skin in contact. Neither pulled away, but eventually they both needed to come up for air.

"Good," she said. "I'm glad we're going to be adults about it."

He pulled her lips back to his and then he moved his face next to hers and rubbed his cheek slowly around, feeling the smoothness of both her skin and her hair. "Are you sure you don't want me to leave?" he asked.

"That's not a fair question to ask me right at this moment, because my body is screaming for something else."

"Do you want that?"

"That's not a fair question to ask me while it's screaming."

He could feel his own breathing picking up to match hers. "What then?"

"In a calmer moment, I'm sure one I will reach in a couple of hours if I get up and leave you right now, we need to talk about what's going on here. You've got a woman back home who makes me look like a stray picked up by the dogcatcher. Before I let you touch me again, I have to know what the hell is wrong with you, chasing a mutt when you've got a purebred."

"Can we go for a walk?" he asked.

"To?"

"Talk. I don't know what's going on. Until I came down here, I thought I was pretty happy."

"Miranda's over at the neighbor's now. Mary brings the girls here and watches Dad for me when I need to go out. Let me give her a call." Before she got up, she reached over and grabbed him behind the neck, roughly pulling his lips to hers and kissing him with a passion that had been missing before. Then, quickly, she shoved him away and got up to hurry to the phone in the kitchen.

When she finally returned, she had herself back in order, although she was still a little flush in the cheeks. "She'll be here in just a few minutes."

"Are you okay?"

Slowly, articulating each word, she said, "No, I'm not okay. Thank you. You just turned on emotions I didn't even know I had."

"Are you looking for an apology?"

"No, I'm complimenting you. Just don't do it again soon or I'll explode."

The front door flew open and two little girls rushed in, followed by the neighbor, a woman about Terri's age. She was a little plump, unkempt, and frazzled. She seemed to Paul to be a perfectly contented wife and mother.

"This is Mary, my neighbor," Terri said.

Mary gave Paul a long once-over and said, "He's every bit as good looking as you said he was."

Terri blushed. "Thanks, Mary, for making me feel like an idiot."

Mary giggled, girlish, "There's nothing wrong with admiring a good-looking man. They certainly don't think twice about admiring a woman. Terri is beautiful, isn't she, Paul?"

"Positively," Paul said.

Terri grabbed him by the hand and dragged him toward the front door. "She'll have us both blushing before she's done, I promise you. She delights in it. We'll be back later," she added, as she hurried them out the door.

When they were well away from the house and walking in the direction of Old Town, Terri said, "I need to know what is going on between you and Pam."

"That's two of us," he said.

"That's no answer."

He nodded. He didn't know what the answer was. "Pam is everything the new woman should be."

"But you are having trouble with the new woman."

She said it in a way that didn't have an edge to it, not the way that Pam would have said it. Pam always challenged him when it came to his attitude toward the new, liberated woman. She wanted to know how he felt about assertiveness. Did it bother him that she made more money than he did? How did he feel about the fact that he didn't get to make decisions for the both of them?

Maybe some of that bothered him. He wasn't sure. His own mother had managed a bookstore. She worked on committees for bond issues and reelection campaigns. She was the president of the hospital auxiliary. She was respected for her activism and her opinions. She also could make flowers and vegetables bloom and grow, and she could sew and cook, and she could love her child. She was, he thought, earth mother, connected to her physical and emotional world, which always came first, before being connected to the superficial and contrived world beyond all of that. Pam was not earth mother. She was a master player in the superficial and contrived world. He didn't mind that, but it bothered him that she felt this world was the only one that was important.

The woman walking beside him was earth mother. That's what it was all about, but he didn't know if he could explain it to her without demeaning someone in the process.

Finally, he said, "I wish Pam wanted kids."

"Because you want more?" She was watching him out of the side of her eye. His answers to these questions, he knew, would decide what happened between the two of them, good or bad.

"I love being a father. I miss getting the chance to be one."

"You are great with Miranda."

"Miranda is great. I'd love to have a daughter. Pam, I'm afraid, will never want kids. Most of that comes from the fact that she never knew her own father, and part is that her own relatives rejected him and in the same sense rejected her, and finally in part because she would not allow herself to have a parent/child relationship with her stepfather. Subconsciously I think she believes that any child she brought in the world would have to go through the same empty childhood that she went through."

"Have you talked to her about these things?"

"Yes."

"And?"

"She says that I should be so lucky if she marries me, let alone has my children."

"It doesn't sound to me like having more children is much of an issue, then."

It was his turn to look at her through the corner of his eye. "Why would you say that?"

"Because you're still with her. Something else must keep you connected."

And what would that be, he wondered? Her beauty? Her wealth? Obviously Pam's beauty wasn't enough to keep Paul from being drawn to Terri. No, if anything, the connection had more to do with how hard he had to fight to get her than anything else. He couldn't throw away a prize that he came close to paying for with his life. Could he?

"But I'm not with her," he said. "I'm with you."

She turned to him with a quizzical look on her face, stopping so that he had to stop, too. "Physically, yes, but we're talking emotionally."

That was the revelation, though. He was talking emotionally. "Yes, we're talking emotionally, and, no, I don't understand it yet."

She had one hand resting on his arm as she searched his face for some clue as to the meaning of all they were saying. "I'm confused."

"Me, too."

"So, what's next?"

"We find out what happened to your mother."

The question hung there on her lips. He had made a leap she wasn't prepared for. "And after that?"

"I don't know," he said. "All of this is pretty new to me. I haven't got a clue what it means yet. I need to think about your mother and let the rest rest."

She pulled on his arm and led him on to Old Town. "Then," she said, "let's hit the coffee shop and see if we stir up any interest."

"That's fine for you to say. Are you going to let them bounce you off a jetty next time?"

"No, that's why we've got you here," she said.

They crossed the road to the other side and walked under the awning of the coffee shop.

Dave Crane had a smile for Terri when she walked in the door that faded as soon as he saw Paul behind her. Paul could actually see anger creep up the other man's face as he began a slow burn. The two of them walked to the counter.

"Hi, Dave," Terri said. "How about a couple of mochas?" Turning to Paul, she asked, "Is that okay with you?"

"Perfect," he said.

Looking at neither of them, Dave concentrated on making the two coffees, but he made just a little too much noise slamming things around to disguise his feelings. Paul noticed a slight smile on Terri's face. She was enjoying this. She asked Dave, "Anything interesting happening?"

Dave jerked his head toward a clipboard that was hanging from a nail on a post next to the counter. "Got a petition going."

Terri moved down to the clipboard and read the petition. "Skateboarders?"

"Trying to keep them off the streets and sidewalks around here. They bug the tourists."

Terri flipped through several sheets of paper, each loaded with signatures. "The kids already complain about too little to do in town. Taking the skateboarding away will just get them more upset."

"Let them get jobs and work for a living. Then maybe they'll know why I don't want my customers chased away."

"I'll have to think about it before I sign," she said.

He finished one coffee and slid it onto the counter. "You'll never sign it. Everyone knows you're a bleeding heart." He set the second next to the first, and, as he did, he glared at Paul. "I thought you'd have moved on by now."

Paul smiled at him. "Lovely town. Friendly people. I see no reason to move on."

"For some," he said, "sea air isn't healthy."

Terri paid for the coffees before Paul could pull out his wallet. As she handed the money to Dave, she asked, "Any particular reason you keep threatening Paul?"

Dave took the money, rang it up, and bounced two quarters back to her. "I only have his good health at heart."

"Anything happens to his good health and I'll make sure the police start here with their questioning," Terri said.

"And I won't have a clue about it."

"Sometimes I think you never did have a clue. You know, Paul here is only trying to find out what happened to my mother. It's pretty important to my dad. I can't imagine you not wanting us to find out the truth. Nor can I imagine you wanting to help cover up something that might lead to finding out what happened to my mother. So why are you being such a hardass?"

Dave leaned across the counter, propping himself up with his elbows. "I'm just trying to do your friend a favor. I'm the friendliest guy around here asking him to watch what he pokes his nose into."

"So, can you tell us why these less friendly people don't want Paul nosing around?"

"If they don't want him to know the reason, you can bet that they don't want anyone else to know, either."

"Maybe you could give me a clue who they are," she said.

"I only hear rumors; I don't hear names. The message is pretty clear, though. Your boyfriend needs to pack up and leave."

Paul glanced behind him. A half a dozen people were in the shop for coffee, and every one of them was listening to the conversation. He looked at each one. Three were in their early twenties. He guessed they either worked in the small fish processing plant near the docks or on one of the boats. Two men sat at a table by the window. They were a little older, either in their late twenties or early thirties. They looked a lot alike, so Paul guessed they were brothers. Something seemed familiar about them, but he couldn't put a finger on it. The last customer was Ernie Crawford, and he had a big smile on his face as he took it all in.

Paul picked up the two coffees from the counter and began to walk away with them, the move designed to make Terri follow him. She gave him a look that said she didn't appreciate him walking off. With no further reason to stay at the counter, she reluctantly followed along.

Paul didn't move to the front of the coffee shop, but to a booth off to the side that led to the restrooms. She plopped down across from him, whispering as she sat, "I wasn't done talking to him."

"I know," he said. "You still hadn't gotten him mad enough to punch one of us."

"It's obvious that he knows something."

"It's obvious that he knows enough to try to warn me off, but I'm not convinced that he knows more than that."

"Then why would he even bother to do it?"

"Loyalty. I'm the outsider here. If he hears that someone doesn't want an outsider poking around, then I'd expect a man like that to do his part to chase the outsider away."

"Okay, smart fellow, can you tell me why someone wants to chase you off if it isn't about my mom?"

Again, he was caught up in her face. When she became animated, as she was now, her eyes sparkled and she had a slight smile. This was when she was her prettiest.

"I don't know," he said. "I plan to go to the library to see what I can find out about what other things were happening when your mother disappeared. Someone has something to hide. Finding out what that is might open up all sorts of things."

"Why don't you use the computer here?" she asked, gesturing to the one behind her.

"Anyone with a little computer knowledge could trace where I went on the computer. The last thing I want is for these people to know I've expanded my research beyond your mother. Who are those two men by the window?"

"Those are Ira Marks's sons."

"That's it," he said. "I thought they looked familiar. I can see now it's because they look like their father."

"That's about where the similarity ends," she said.

"Why's that?"

"Neither has the corporate genius of their father. He has them overseeing warehouses. He's got a daughter who might take over Marks Markets when he retires, I think, but she is older, married, and has two kids of her own, so who knows.

These two couldn't operate a mom and pop market without screwing it up."

"What about those three younger men?" Paul indicated their table with a slight nod.

"Friends in high school. They're trying to make it running a charter boat. Business is so bad right now that one of them could starve from the profits. The three are quickly heading for poverty."

"You don't sound too concerned," he said.

"The quicker they figure it out, the quicker they can put their energy into something that might work for them."

Small towns, he thought. Everyone knows everyone's business. With so many people knowing so much about each other, it was a mystery to him why someone here didn't know what happened to Irene Drexler. And he was surprised that whatever other secrets were hidden in this town weren't known by enough people for him to pry them loose.

From a small pocketbook she carried with her, Terri pulled a penny and slapped it down in front of him. He got the message. "I'm just wondering what kind of a mystery we could have here, one not connected to your mother, that's worth hiding for over thirty years."

"One that comes with a high penalty," she said.

Terri was stirring her coffee with a swizzle stick she'd picked up at the counter. He could see that she didn't realize the significance of her own words. "I'd be really impressed, but I don't think you know what you just said."

"Sure I do," she said, the expression on her face belying her confidence.

"Crimes from thirty years ago that come with a big price must have no statute of limitations."

"Like the murder of my mother."

"I'm not sure all of this is about your mother. I'm pretty sure we are looking at two, maybe three different things. That's what has people upset."

She leaned a hand on her chin and sighed. "Don't tell me," she said, "that you are going to solve some long-lost mystery, and it isn't going to be my mother's disappearance."

"No," Paul said, "my plan is to solve them all."

[13]

THAT AFTERNOON PAUL had a short visit
with Drexler. The little time they had together distressed him. The
professor slumped to one side of his wheelchair and had a great deal
of difficulty concentrating on the questions that Paul asked.

Paul was trying to probe Drexler's memory about any
other events that might have taken place during the time of
his wife's disappearance; any unusual rumors that he might remember. Drexler tried his best, but he simply could not con-
centrate. This was one of those times that the pain took the best
of him, and the medication took the rest. After ten minutes,
Paul asked Terri to come upstairs. With his help she put Drexler
back to bed, where the old man quickly fell asleep.

Paul stood in the bedroom doorway as he watched Terri
tuck in her father. She stood over him for a moment to make
sure he was not in any distress. Usually strong, this time she
seemed to slump herself, the weight of her father's illness obvious. Paul moved to her side and put an arm around her waist
and let her sag against him. After a moment she turned into
him, buried her face in his chest, and shook with quiet sobs. He
held her for ten minutes, until she had cried herself out.

She pushed back from him and wiped at the tears that streaked her cheeks with the sleeve of her shirt. Finally she said, "I must look a mess."

"You're a beautiful mess."

"Don't be nice. You'll just get me crying again." She took his hand and led him from the room. In the hall, she said, "I'm afraid it's not going to be much longer."

"I know," he said. "I feel like I'm letting him down. Every time I talk to him, he has his hopes up. I can almost see him deflate when I have so little to tell him."

"Was he able to help you at all?"

"No, nothing. His work was in Eugene. This is where he came to sleep and eat. Your mother was the one tuned to the happenings here, not your father."

"What else did she have to do, with Dad away all the time?"

"I want you to do something for me," Paul said. "I want you to find out everything you can about the last year of your mother's life. I want you to talk to anyone who knew her back then. I want you to probe your dad when he has the energy."

"I'll be covering the same stuff all over again, won't I?"

"No," he said, "I don't think so. Everyone who has looked into your mother's disappearance has assumed that the abduction was sexually motivated. I'm not saying that they were mistaken, but they were running under an obvious assumption because your mother was an attractive woman. I want to do a little lateral thinking."

"Lateral thinking?"

"I want to look at this from a different direction. Someone— or several someones—don't want me probing in the past. One of them obviously has something to hide. What if your mother found out what that was? Maybe she wasn't abducted at all. Maybe she was murdered to keep her quiet."

Terri was shaking her head no, as if she did not want to believe what he was saying, but the expression on her face showed a slow dawning, as if the possibility wasn't impossible at all. "I can't imagine anyone around here with something so deep and dark in his past to want to kill my mother."

"I'm not getting anywhere pursuing an abduction. I've got to shake this up in hopes of making something happen. Your dad's condition tonight convinced me I must hurry."

"I'll see what I can do," Terri said. "I can think of maybe a half a dozen people who knew my mother fairly well who still live in the community. I'll call them after dinner."

He glanced at his watch. "Good. I've got about an hour I can spend in the library. I want to expand the scope of my research. Before I was concentrating on things that had happened in Oregon, particularly in Lane County. I think I need to see what was happening in the rest of the nation."

"You'll be back for dinner?"

"Yes," he said. "After dinner I'm going to sort whatever information I can find, and then I'm going out again tonight to walk the route your mother took at about the same time she would have taken it."

"I'll go with you," she said.

"No you won't."

"You've already been attacked once."

"And maybe I need to be attacked again. If I can identify just one of these people, then I can crack the door open a bit. I'll get an idea of where I need to go next."

"Maybe to the hospital."

"If someone wanted me dead, he could kill me anytime. He doesn't need to wait for me to walk out in the dark. We haven't much time left."

Tears pooled again in her eyes, and trickled over. "You promise you won't let anything happen to you."

"I'll be fine."

She put her hands on his chest and lifted her lips to his. The kiss was short and light. She didn't pull back from him, and Paul let his face move slowly around hers, again feeling the tickle of her hair on his cheek, smelling the slight scent of her perfume, listening to the softness of her breath. He let out the breath he had been holding, and then he kissed her, his lips pressing hers apart.

She rested her forehead on his shoulder. "This is crazy," she said.

"Insane," he whispered.

She stepped back and smiled at him. "I've got dinner to cook. You need to figure out a better way to stay away from me."

"I don't want to stay away," he said.

"I know. And I don't want you to. That's the problem."

She left him standing in the hall, confused about everything: Irene, Professor Drexler, Terri, Pam—Paul. Any man who saw him with Pam Livingston would think that Paul lived the good life. What was it about him that was so determined to undermine the foundation of that life?

The research in the local library took his mind off Terri. He needed to stop thinking about her. He had known her less than a week and already the two had a passion for each other. He could understand how vulnerable she was, with both her father dying and no other man in her life. He didn't have an excuse. Pam was a willing enough sex partner, one who never denied him her favors unless she was as busy as she was now. He had no complaints, and he certainly didn't have any justification for feeling attracted to Terri the way he was.

At the library, he took advantage of Internet access so common now that even this small library had a half a dozen computers available to the patrons. The combination of access in addition to a good selection of databases for magazines and newspapers during the whole century gave Paul everything he needed in the way of information. He ordered his research first locally, then in Oregon, next in the Northwest, and finally nationally.

He was particularly interested in criminal acts, but he found he couldn't separate those from all the violent protests that were taking place at the time against the Vietnam War and racial discrimination. Eugene had been a hotbed of protest. Outside of Portland, Eugene was one of the few pools of liberalism in the state. It didn't hurt that the senator, Wayne Morris, was a vocal opponent to the war. On campus when students weren't trying to burn down the ROTC building, they were trying to blow up the administration building.

Paul followed these stories as best he could, trying to find names and descriptions of those involved, particularly those who had not been arrested at the time. He thought that one of the troublemakers might have slipped over to the coast to hide out and Irene might have recognized him.

He didn't take the possibility too seriously. Sixty miles wasn't enough distance, especially if one was involved in a protest that carried a ten-year sentence. He was going to be thorough, though, trying to eliminate even the most unlikely scenarios.

He returned in time for dinner. He left a large stack of printouts in the study and went to the kitchen. Terri was at the stove. He came up behind her and leaned his head over her shoulder to see what she was cooking. When his cheek brushed hers, she tensed. He stepped back, a little confused.

Without turning around, Terri said, "Pam called."

Now he understood. "What did she want?"

"She asked if you would call. Apparently your cell phone is off."

"Yes, I turned it off when I was in the library."

A silence hung between them. Paul waited. He knew that she wanted to say something more. "She seems very nice," she said.

"Yes, she can be very nice, outside of a courtroom."

"She talked about my father. She was very caring and understanding."

"She never knew her father. She has this thing about fathers."

"I liked her."

"She's a very likable woman."

She turned around, tears running down her cheeks. "Then why are we doing this?"

He pulled her to him and hugged her. "We haven't done anything except maybe comfort each other. I suspect that if we are drawn to each other, if we are drawn into more of a relationship than we already have, then it won't be about Pam, it will be about us."

"I feel like I'm doing something wrong," she said.

"You haven't done anything wrong, and I haven't done anything wrong."

"Yet."

"Yet—maybe never. I'm not going to make guesses. We're doing the best we can here, under the circumstances, and I don't have anything to feel guilty about."

"Yet."

He carefully turned her back to the stove. "Cook dinner," he said. "I'm going to give Pam a call."

Miranda was in the front room, watching television. He stopped for a moment to say hi to her, and then he shut himself in the study to make the call to Pam. As soon as she answered, he could tell where she was in the house. She was in her office. In the background music played softly, but he also heard the hum of electrical goodies: fax, printer, computer, and the like.

"Hi," he said.

"She sounds nice on the phone. Is she as pretty as she sounds, too?"

"I didn't know you could tell pretty over the phone."

"Maybe not, but I can tell when a woman's voice tenses when she finds out it's me on the phone. Do I have something to worry about?"

Paul sat down on the edge of the coffee table, his feet apart and his head down, staring at the floor. The simple act added a delay to his answer that he knew Pam would read to mean yes; she did have something to worry about. "We're going to need to talk," he said.

"You've had too short a time to fall in love, so I'd guess we're talking infatuation. I don't need added stress right now, Paul."

"It's neither love nor infatuation; it is, though, an attraction. Terri asked a pretty good question. To paraphrase Paul Newman, she wanted to know why, when I had steak at home, I would be interested in hamburger."

"She's hamburger?"

"No. She just thinks she is. She's prime cut and doesn't have a clue."

"And you are interested."

This was a part of it, too, he told himself. Even when Pam was talking about a threat to their relationship, she was cool and in control. She wasn't his lover at this moment, but a lawyer cross-examining. "She's a woman in distress, she's got a wonderful little girl, she's very pretty, and she's very lonely."

"And you're a bleeding heart liberal, Paul."

"And I'm a bleeding heart liberal. How can I not care about what happens to her?"

"I wouldn't expect you not to. But let me caution you. Our relationship is more fragile than you think. I've made lots of concessions to keep us together; some of them I'd just as soon not have made. I won't take it lightly being treated unfairly."

"We have an attraction. Neither of us wants to act on it. I'm concerned, though, that I have the attraction. You are everything a man should want in life."

"And you want more?"

"I'm not sure what I want. Why did you call?"

"I was feeling bad because I basically kicked you and the kids out of the house."

"Reconsidering?"

"Not at all. I don't want you around until I have this trial in hand. But after this conversation, I won't feel guilty anymore."

"Sometime, we will need to talk about the future."

"The future is the expansion of my law practice. Your future is for you to go along for the ride or to decide to get off."

"And where do love and family and children fit into all of that?"

"If I didn't love you, you wouldn't be living with me, Paul. Family and children are your fantasy. Make do with the boys you already have. I don't want children of my own. Call it a Baker thing. We're just not very good at having them."

"As always, you leave me with lots to think about."

"Think about this. I'm rich, my career is on the rise; you've got advantages that most people can only dream about. You were a fool the first time when you walked away from the Baker story poor; don't go being a fool again. You'll never have it as good as you have it now." She disconnected, as if she had somehow said good-bye with her last statement.

He flipped shut the phone. He had lived with things the way they were because he expected them to get better. And now Pam said that this was as good as it would get. Was he asking for too much?

A tiny tap at the door meant that Miranda was outside. She opened the door enough to stick her head in and said, "Mama says to tell you that dinner is ready." She leaned her head to one side until it was almost upside down and added, "You look sad."

He found himself leaning to keep her face right side up. "I am a little sad," he said, "but if you came over here and gave me a hug, I bet I would feel a lot better."

The door flew open and she skipped into the room and threw herself into his arms, wrapping her own around his neck and squeezing her cheek against his. He wrapped his arms around her tiny body and held her to him. "You really know how to make a guy feel a lot better," he said.

"Mama says that hugs are good for you."

"Your mama is a pretty smart lady."

"Thanks."

He glanced up to see Terri standing in the doorway, a soft smile on her face and more tears trickling down her cheeks.

"I seem to be really good at making you cry."

"These are good tears."

He stood up from the coffee table, lifting Miranda with him and carrying her to the kitchen. Terri, just ahead of him, asked, "What did Pam have to say?"

"Sh—" He caught himself just in time. "Do a number two or get off the pot."

Terri laughed. "Her exact words?" she asked.

"More or less. She's a hell of a lawyer. She can read a lot in a facial expression. She's almost psychic when it comes to voices on the phone."

"Saw right through me?"

"Heard right through you. Not only could she tell from your voice that something might be happening between us, but she also figured out that you were pretty."

"I'm sorry, Paul. I'm just making things worse for you."

In the kitchen he gently sat Miranda in her chair, and then he went back to Terri to help her move the food to the table. "You're not making things worse for me," he said. "I'm the one who hasn't got his life figured out yet."

"I don't want Pam mad at you because of me."

He carried a casserole to the table and returned to the counter. "Pam is far too clever to get mad. She sees anger as an inhibitor when it comes to doing her best work. I've been warned that she will not tolerate indiscretion. No, she won't get mad, but she will close the door on me in a hurry and not open it again. Tolerance isn't one of her virtues."

"Then we need to stop all of this nonsense now."

"Human emotions are a bother, but we'd be bored stiff without them. I started out thinking that this was about you and Pam and me. Now I understand that it's about me."

"What a relief. And I was thinking that it might be about me," she said, a hint of sarcasm in her voice.

He brushed hair away from her face and kissed her on the temple. "Let's find out what happened to your mother, and then let's worry about me and you. I can only deal with one mystery at a time."

Miranda, delighted to have the attention from two adults at the dinner table, dominated the conversation, talking about everything from what she did at the neighbor's house that afternoon to her plans for the evening, which involved both of them reading to her before she went to bed.

After he had helped clear the table, Paul retreated to the study and poured over the information he had gathered at the library. War, racial unrest, and protest dominated the headlines in all parts of the country. Little of interest seemed to happen in Florence, too out of the mainstream and too conservative to be much effected by what was going on in the rest of the world.

Eugene was a beehive of politics. Several protests had required heavy police control. Violence on campus was common, from fires to small bombs. The University of Oregon was gaining a reputation for radicalism that remained three decades later.

The rest of the Northwest shared, more or less, the same fate as Eugene. The big protests were saved for other parts of the country. L.A. was sometimes ablaze. Riots sprang up across the country. Protests ranged from the peaceful to the ultra violent. Sometimes the police were at the heart of the violence. Sometimes the protesters were. Bombs were a common weapon of the protesting groups. The Weathermen set off twenty-five bombs in the late sixties and early seventies, including one at the MIT Research Center. They were lucky they didn't kill more people than they did, he thought. To look back on it from this distance, Paul thought, only made it look all the more crazy.

Terri brought Miranda in for her story a little after 8:00. After Paul had read from the collection of fairy tales to her for twenty minutes, Terri took the book and Miranda upstairs to finish the story. While she was up there, Paul decided to slip out to walk into town. He wanted to avoid another discussion about the danger.

The scene at the jetty already seemed so distant and remote that it did not feel real to Paul. The threat of danger was only something vague, not a reality. What he needed to make real was the feeling of Old Town as Irene walked through it that night. Although he was leaving early, he decided that he would walk downtown and wait there until about 9:30, then continue the route he thought Irene had taken that night.

He wasn't sure what he expected to discover. He knew from his research of the three Baker sisters that it did not all come together for him until he spent a night in their house, preserved as it had been when they still lived in it. The women had come alive to him that night, as if he shared the space with their ghosts; given through this experience special insight he did not have before. It sounded as crazy to him then as it did now, but he hoped that walking in the footsteps of Irene's ghost would give him the same kind of insight.

The night was cool and an evening fog was drifting in. A weather event stood offshore that could move at almost any time onto the coast. He did not glance back as he walked away from the house. If he had, he would have seen Terri standing in the upstairs window, watching over him for as long as she could until he disappeared from her view.

Old Town was not as quiet now as it would have been when Irene walked through that night. Now restaurants and bars stayed open until late, and the movie theater would not let out until after 10:00. Shops were closed, including the coffee shops, and few people were visible. Those he could see were moving either from car to bar or from bar to car.

It wasn't even 9:00. If he were going to get a good feel for the walk that Irene took, he would have to wait another fifteen minutes. That would have been about the time when Ernie Crawford had first seen her pass, and then she would have showed up at the window of Walter Higgins's store.

Paul walked past the coffee shops and the kitchen utensil store to a small park area that had been carved out in the middle of Old Town. Near the street was a brick courtyard lined with benches. Behind it was a grassy area with a picnic table and a gazebo. Beyond that was a small, floating platform that was surrounded by a railing and attached to the shore by a gangplank. Tourists used this for taking pictures of the river and the bridge, and it was also used by locals as a spot to fish.

Paul sat on one of the benches and listened to the night. Above, on the bridge, he could hear the eerie howl of tires over the hollow roadbed. Closer, he could hear music faintly drifting in and out of a bar as doors opened and closed. Occasionally a car would start up and drive away. With the river high and wide, the tide going out, and the ocean not that far away, it would seem that water would dominate the noise of the night, but instead it was no more than a quiet rush of water, like a hose under water that was filling a play pool.

A soft clicking of footsteps echoed up the street, increasing in volume until a young woman came into view. Tonight, Paul thought, Old Town was a much safer place for a young woman to be than it had been on the night Irene had last walked here.

The young woman slowed when she saw him, and then she moved in his direction. Julia Higgins stopped in front of him. He hadn't recognized her because she wore a baseball cap on her head, her ponytail sticking out the back, and she was wrapped up in a bulky windbreaker.

"Paul," she said. "You certainly show up at some interesting times."

He nodded to her. "I didn't recognize you at first all bundled up like that."

She sat down next to him on the bench. "I know. It's the pits. I have a body that was meant to be put on display, and it's been exiled to a climate that demands it be hidden away."

Bold, Paul thought. He wondered if she was fishing for a compliment. "Even bundled up," he said, "I'm sure you don't go unnoticed. Were you working?"

"My night to close up and restock the shelves. What are you doing?"

"Getting a feel for Old Town at night."

"I'd love to stay and visit," she said, "but I've got a friend and a sofa and a movie waiting." She stood up. "I think maybe you should walk back to Terri Mankin and do the same. You're not the most popular man with some people in this town, and I don't think you want to run into any of them in the dark."

"Why is that?" he asked.

"Secrets," she said. "Lots of secrets."

"Such as?"

She chuckled. "They don't tell me their secrets. They know I'm a journalism major."

"Then how do you know they really have them?"

"By how angry they are because you're nosing around."

"I only want to know what happened to Irene Drexler."

She started to walk away. "I warned you," she said.

He watched her walk down to the lot where the kite shop was located and then disappear from view. A few minutes later a new Honda Civic coupe pulled from the lot. It had a spoiler on the back and bright chrome wheels. It looked more like the car a young man would drive, but Julia quickly went through the gears and skillfully slipped it around a corner, demonstrating it wasn't too much car for her.

Paul did take note of her warning. He still had a few minutes to wait, so he decided he might be better off in a less prominent place. He walked from the courtyard to a path that led back to the river, one that went through the little park and down the plank that led to the floating platform.

Paul walked down the plank. It was no more than ten by twelve feet, but its far edge gave the feeling that he was out on the river. From here, if he had a camera, he could have gotten good pictures of the bridge in one direction and a small, paddle wheeler anchored upstream in the other.

He kept his ears tuned to the noises around him. He glanced back often to see if he could see anything in the shadows. What surprised him about the attack was its speed. One second he was staring out across the river, and the next he was whirling around to see two figures dressed completely in black charging down the plank directly toward him.

He had no time to move. The best he could do was brace himself against the railing and wait for the assault. Both men, wearing black ski masks, were on him before he could get set. Paul did the best he could, throwing a punch that caught one on the side of the head. That wasn't enough to keep the other from slamming into him, taking his breath away.

He wasn't quite sure what damage he might have inflicted. He kicked, kneed, elbowed, and punched every chance he got, but the other man recovered quickly and they were both on him. In seconds they had him doubled over and gasping for breath. Moments after that, they each had him by his arms and legs, and suddenly he was flying through the air, over the railing, and into the black water below. How strange, he thought, that something so quick and so violent could be carried out without a word. And then he hit the water.

He went under, twisting and turning in the current, but still managing to push himself to the surface. Struggling for breath from the beating, he could only wheeze in air, and abruptly he was slammed against something, only to bounce off and be slammed against something else. A bang to the back of his head blurred his thoughts. When he could clear them again, he was aware that the water was cold. Paul remembered that poles were sunk into the river near the shore, and he realized he was being slammed into them by the combination of current and outgoing tide.

He tried to swim out away from the shore to avoid the poles. While part of his brain registered the cold and another part registered the fear he felt, another wondered about the poles. Tie-ups for boats? Barriers to keep floating debris from pushing up against the buildings that overhung the bank?

He no longer had the luxury of random thoughts. The bridge was looming up ahead, and he was heading directly toward one of the concrete buttresses that supported the structure.

He tried to maneuver his body, already exhausted by the coldness of the water and the weight of his clothing. He bounced off the concrete once, then he hit it again and again; each impact was another blow taking strength out of him. He did not feel panic, but he was frightened by what he felt. His mind was starting to drift; life didn't seem to be that precious.

He struggled for something to pull him back. He was being dragged down the river toward the ocean. He was being dragged under by the weight of his clothes. His energy was being seeped out of him by the cold. The combination was draining his will. Could this have been Irene's fate, he wondered? He shook his head. The river gives up what it takes.

He kicked off his shoes and worked his way out of his jacket. Both helped. He could keep his head up, but removing his clothing had taken the little strength he had left. He could keep himself afloat for the time being, but he knew he was in real trouble. He'd been pushed out to the middle of the channel where the water was deepest, and the combination of current and tide was a vice that held him. It would only get worse the farther down the channel he went; eventually he would run into the combination of current, tide and wave action. What the river had yet to do to him, the ocean would finish. He had to get to shore.

It was a battle using resources grown way too soft over the last two years. As he strained against the current, he cursed the life Pam had given them, one with tennis or golf a couple of times a week, filled with rich meals in good restaurants, when they were not eating at home. Paul never had the time to stay as fit as he wanted to be, yet Pam seemed to thrive with her work schedule, needing neither much of a diet nor excessive exercise to keep her figure.

He was tiring rapidly and the shore was still too far.

The river made several turns before it reached the ocean. Paul could just make out in the distance where the bend was located, illuminated by a smattering of light along the shore. If he could angle himself to the right, he thought he might have a chance to reach the shore at the bend. If he missed it, he was a drowned man. He was nearly drained of strength. The spark that would keep him afloat at all costs, the essence of life that demanded that he hold on, the will to live: where were they? Why were they gone?

In the end, it wasn't Paul who saved himself, but the river. He saw to his left a buoy slip by. Slowly it dawned on him: he was on the danger side of the buoy. That meant it was a hazard for boats. He let himself slip under the water, sinking perhaps a foot or two when his feet touched bottom. He let himself settle into a crouch, bouncing along the bottom, and then he pushed at an angle toward the shore. He came up out of the water, took a deep breath, and did it again. He hopped his way to the shore, a life-saving technique he had learned in some distant swimming class.

He burrowed into the sand and stayed there until his body could generate enough heat to revive him. When he finally had the strength to sit up, he was a complete mess, soaked through and caked in sand. He couldn't stay here. The fog had already chilled the air and his wet clothes only added to his discomfort. He started down the beach, slowly at first, then picked up his pace as his body generated enough warmth to drive his muscles.

He followed the beach to the open area between the restaurant and the houses across from Drexler's. He stayed in the shadows, afraid that someone might be watching to see if he had survived the dip into the river. Finally, he had little choice but to cross the street in the light to get to the steps up to Drexler's front door.

He glanced up to see Terri in the window. She would be waiting, he thought, timing his trip to town, waiting impatiently for his return and ready to call the police if he was even a minute overdue.

She met him at the door with a blanket in hand. She quickly went to him, wrapping the blanket around him and helping him up the final steps into the house.

[14]

HE WAS TOO cold and too weak to protest when
Terri insisted on calling the police. He sat, miserable, on a chair
in the kitchen, blankets wrapped around him, while the two local
cops questioned him. Neither seemed particularly interested or
impressed by what had happened to Paul. They asked questions
about what he had been doing before the attack, specifically
wanting to know if he had been in the bars in Old Town.

Terri was the one who lost patience with them. She told
them about the attack on the jetty. Although this may have
gained a little ground with them, their attitude was that Paul
had been seriously remiss by not reporting that incident.

Before the police officers left, one mentioned that he thought
he had seen two men in the shadows of the trees that lined the
curve of the road leading up to the house as he was pulling up.
By the time he got out of his car, the men were gone.

So they knew he was still alive, Paul thought.

After they had taken their notes, one of them informed
Paul that they would turn it over to Max Leiber, since both at-

tacks involved the river or the jetty, and, if something ended up in the river, it was Max's job to investigate.

Terri ran a hot bath for him. He made a mess of the bathroom when he stripped off his soggy, sand-encrusted clothing. Even in the tub, he couldn't shake the chill that racked his body. When the water began to cool, he got out and dried himself off, putting on pajama bottoms and a T-shirt. Terri was waiting for him with the bed made and extra blanket on top.

He crawled under the covers while Terri went in to clean up the bathroom. He was still shivering when she took his wet clothing and towels to the laundry room. She paused for a moment, taking in Paul, who could not control the trembling under the covers. When she returned from the laundry room, she turned out the lights, slipped off her shoes, and crawled under the covers with him, warming him with her own body heat.

"The hell I had to go through to get you in bed with me," Paul said, still too weak to laugh.

"I hope that damn near getting killed was worth it to you."

"Definitely. If I see these two guys dressed in black and wearing ski masks in a crowd, I'll be able to pick them out."

"What did you accomplish, then?"

"I learned not to go swimming at night, and not to swim without a buddy."

"You're hopeless," she said. "I'm never letting you go out alone again."

"Then we might be swimming together next time."

"Paul, let's just tell Dad that it's impossible. That's twice now you could have been killed. The next time you may not be so lucky."

"Lucky? It was pure swimming ability and athleticism that save me."

"And your boxing skills. Don't forget those."

"That's why my swimming skills are so important."

"I'm convinced you shouldn't be continuing this," she said.

His shivering subsided. The warmth of her body seemed to seep into him. He could feel himself begin to react to her. "You're right," he said, "maybe we shouldn't be continuing this."

"I'm glad you agree . . ." She stopped. "Oh! I think I know what you're talking about. I'm delighted to know that all your body parts still work."

"Not half as delighted as I am."

She moved away from him. "Since you seem to be returning from the dead, I think maybe I'd better return to my bed."

"Wait for a while. I never got to have slumber parties when I was a kid. Besides, let me assure you that I'm now too tired and too sore to launch any kind of an assault."

She reached out an arm from under the covers and brushed hair back from his eyes. "You really were stupid going out there alone."

"That's easy to say after I washed up on a beach like a dead fish. I don't look at it as a wasted experience, though. Anytime you survive an attempt on your life, it's good for lots of things, like nightmares, cold sweats, irrational fears. . . . I am going to ask you to do me a favor, though. Since I don't think I'm going to be ready to leave this room for a day or two, I'd like you to go to Higgins's bookstore and see if you can talk to Julia alone."

"You don't think Julia has something to do with this?"

"Not really. She more or less told me I was stupid to be down there alone at night, too. What I want to know is if she noticed anyone hanging around, dressed in black."

"Paul, I'm serious. You need to give it up before you get killed."

He rolled on his side so they were face to face. "I'm a man who usually doesn't give up unless I have a hell of a good reason to. I'm still alive, I still don't know what happened to your mother, and now I'm beginning to get mad."

"Which will give someone a good reason to make sure you're dead next time."

"I'm not dead," he said. "And I have no intention of being dead, either. I have too many things I enjoy doing alive."

"You've got me convinced, but have you got them convinced?"

"The next time I find myself doing something foolish, I'm going to remember lying here with you, and then I'm going to be really careful because someday I think I'd like to do it again, and I won't be able to if I'm dead."

She got out from under the covers and stood up, her face flushed. "You really confuse me," she said, "but you do it in a lovely way." She bent down and kissed him lightly on the lips, and hurried from the room.

Paul smiled to himself. This wasn't like him at all. He questioned, with his life put on a fast track by both divorce and near death, if he wasn't having a premature forty's crisis. And if he was, he wondered if such a thing got any better than this. Within a minute he was sound asleep.

Sleep of the dead, sleep of the dead—the phrase kept running through his mind. Although not much daylight slipped into the den through the window covered with a heavy curtain, he could tell that he had made it through the night and into the next day. His body ached, in part from his last trauma, but also from having been in bed too long. He managed to pry open one eye. Sitting cross-legged on the edge of the bed was Miranda. She was staring at him. He worked open the other eye.

"Mama said I was to watch you," Miranda said.

"You're doing a wonderful job of it," Paul croaked, his voice warped by a dry throat, a stuffed nose, and throbbing sinuses. "What are you supposed to be watching for?"

"For you to wake up."

"I'm nearly there. Just give me a few more hours."

Miranda giggled. "It's already afternoon. You've been sleeping a long time."

"Yes, I have." He checked his wristwatch. It was nearly 3:00. "Once I wake up, what are you supposed to do next?"

"Tell Mama."

"Then I think you should go do that. And ask her if she might have a cup of coffee."

Shortly after Miranda ran off, Terri appeared at the door with a cup of coffee. She put it on the table next to the fold-out bed, and sat down near him. "You don't look good. I almost called a doctor twice today."

"I wasn't quite over my first set of aches and pains when I got these added to them. My body needs a time out. I am going to take a shower, shave, and then climb right back in this bed. Then I'm going to wade my way through all the files and papers I've collected one more time. Did you get a chance to talk to Julia?"

"I've been too worried about you."

He pulled himself up into a sitting position. "I'm perfectly okay," he said.

She stopped him before he could say more. "Don't tell me you're perfectly okay when you look like you do."

"Right now I'm tired," he said. "My body does ache, especially where I was bumped on the head and where I was slammed into a concrete buttress. I've got some bruises. I hurt. But I'm not seriously injured. After a little more rest, I'll want to get up and walk around to see if I can loosen up some muscles and work out some pains. I'm not quite ready to rush back into the world because Miranda could flatten me right now with her left hand."

"You sound like you are coming down with a cold."

"Hey. If that's the worst of it . . ."

She handed him the cup of coffee. "If you will watch Miranda, I'll go down and talk to Julia."

"Can I take my shower first?"

She nodded. She continued to sit, her eyes on him, the expression on her face not quite readable. She said, "You're only the second man in my life to share a bed with me."

"There are a lot of underprivileged men in this world, then."

"Don't treat it lightly," she said.

He nodded. "Let me assure you I'm not. I'm going through some kind of real struggle here that reaches well beyond you, but you are at its center. I don't understand it. I just know I can't wait to get you back in my bed and to be able to do it without feeling guilty."

"That would be nice, but I don't think it is something that is going to happen right away."

"No, I'm afraid not. I've got lots of business to take care of that has nothing to do with you, Florence, or your missing mother."

"Pam Livingston."

"And Beth, my former wife. So much of life is reaction; not enough of it is sorting and dealing with issues from the past. Not enough of it is packaging and putting in storage. We do that with the dead so we can go on with life, but with the living we seem to keep running from the hurt instead of trying to deal with it. Pam is my reaction to Beth; you are my reaction to Pam," he said.

"I buried Jerry. I mourned him. He's packed away."

"And don't think for a minute I don't envy you the closure."

"You sound like you have a long way to go."

He patted the bed next to him. "Move closer." When she did, he took one of her hands in his. "You're lovely. Your daughter is lovely. You wake in me longings for everything from family to incredible sex. You don't have those kinds of longings if they are being fulfilled in your life. What I need to do now, and it is something I haven't done at all, is to figure out exactly what I need. I've been so busy accommodating my boys, Beth, and Pam, that I forgot that I had a life to live, too."

"I'm afraid you'll hurt me," she said. She said it so honestly that Paul felt a catch in his throat. The last thing he wanted to do was to hurt her.

"That's why I have to take care of all this other stuff. So I won't hurt you."

"And how long will this take?"

That was a very fair question. She'd packed herself away over the last four years. She was now ready to go on with her life. How long could he expect her to wait for him to sort out his own life?

"I'd like to be able to answer that," he said, "but to rush it would mean you might end up with someone still not ready for a relationship."

"Would you go back to Beth?"

Another good question. "You offer everything and more that Beth could offer, and you don't come with the extra baggage. I can't imagine myself going back to Beth when I might be able to have you."

"And Pam?"

"We are together for good reasons. We're being driven apart by equally good reasons. She and I both have to consider some choices. Pam's attitude has always been to do it her way or not at all. I think it only fair to her that she knows that she will have to compromise this time around or we will go our separate ways."

"And if she says she will compromise?"

He laughed. "I wouldn't believe her," he said. "She's been known to lie to get what she wants. She'd have a lot to prove."

"And then?"

"And then I'd have a very difficult decision to make."

She nodded her head. "How difficult?" she asked.

"The kind of decision that shapes the rest of your life."

"If it's that important, then I guess I can wait for it."

At that moment he wanted her so much that he felt like pulling her to him and making love to her, Miranda in the next room or not. And he knew that she might let him, but that it would be the worst possible thing that either one of them could do. What happened to the youthful Paul, he wondered, who had sex first and asked questions later?

He let go of her hand. "Go talk to Julia."

After a long, hot shower and a shave, and after putting on clean clothes and folding up the bed and straightening the room, Paul began to feel human again. He stacked all the files on the coffee table, next to his latest research, and then he began to read while Terri went to talk to Julia.

An hour later, Terri stuck her head in the door to let him know she was back. "According to Julia, she didn't see a thing," she said.

"That's not much help."

"I didn't believe her, though."

Paul looked up. He had a deep respect for women's intuition. "She was lying?"

"No, I don't think she was lying. I think she knows something about all of this. When I told her what happened to you, she seemed honestly concerned. At the same time, though, I could see a light come on inside her head, as if she might know what it was all about."

"Did you talk to anyone else?"

"I stopped in at the coffee shop."

"Was I the topic of conversation?"

"That's the funny part," she said. "I honestly don't think that Dave knew a thing about it, nor did anyone else in there."

"So you don't think this is some kind of conspiracy?"

"It doesn't look that way. Someone obviously has it in for you, and others wish you would go away, but I don't think they are working together on it."

Pointing to the stacks of paper, Paul said, "Right now we only know of four people who admit to being in Old Town when your mother disappeared. One is Ernie Crawford. The second is Walter Higgins. The last two are the Markses. Two saw your mother. The other two didn't. We've got two choices here. One is we run under the assumption that an unknown fifth person was present, or that one of these four is responsible, something that seems unlikely."

"I think we've agreed to all that already," she said.

"We could spend the rest of our lives trying to find the fifth person. I want to deal with these four first. If I can eliminate them, then we'll simply have to tell your father that an unknown person is responsible for your mom's disappearance. I think that's the best I can do."

"With so little information, how can you eliminate the four?"

"Lateral thinking," he said.

She laughed. "You sure like to go in that direction."

"Let's dig as deep as we can to see if we can find a reason why any of the four would want me dead. Twice now I could have been killed. Whatever the person does not want me to find has to be a whopper: something that big can't be hidden under a rock. Two clever people like us ought to be able to trip over something that size."

Just then the doorbell rang. Terri went to answer it, and when she returned to the den, she was followed by Deputy Leiber. He walked into the room, beaming. "Live flotsam," he said, "I can't wait to hear this. You should have been crab bait, and I want to know how you got out. Cold water, tide and current, dark night: you get my superman award." He plopped down on the sofa and pulled out a notebook. "I want every detail."

At least someone enjoyed his misfortune, Paul thought. He narrated the details of the night as the deputy furiously wrote notes. After Paul finished, Leiber had a series of questions for him.

"How did you get into the main channel of the river?"

"I kept banging into those poles stuck in the water. I wanted to get away from them."

"Why didn't you try for the shore?"

"I figured I'd just get thumped and thrown back in the river again, maybe not conscious the second time around."

"I'd have thought the water would have pushed you to the south bank of the river. How did you make it to the north bank?"

"The river makes a turn. I tried to swim to the point, hoping I'd make it to shallow water before I got swept around the bend. I couldn't think of a thing around the bend that I wanted to face."

Leiber shook his head. "You still had a lot of river to go before you got to the jetty. Having the strength to make it to shore, though, would have been tough. The cold water would have taken most of the fight out of you. My guess is we should have found your body just this side of the jetty, washed up on the sand spit there."

"I'm glad you didn't."

Leiber looked up from his notebook. "Me, too," he said. "I was hoping for another free meal."

Terri, standing in the doorway, said, "I'm starting dinner. You're welcome to stay."

"I wish I could," the deputy said, "but I've got to follow up on this report. Can you give me any description of these men that might help?"

"They came at me fast. My impression was that they were about the same size and build, and that they were a little bigger than I am. That would put them at maybe six-two and maybe two-twenty. I managed to get in a few punches, and what I hit was pretty solid. I'd say they were in pretty good shape."

"Did they say anything?"

"Not a word."

"So they must have decided to throw you in the river from the start?"

"I didn't think about that. Since they didn't discuss it in front of me, I guess maybe they did plan it in advance."

"How hard did they hit you?"

Paul looked up at the deputy, wondering what he was getting at. "Hard enough so I couldn't resist them when they threw me in."

"From the sound of both attacks, my guess is they really didn't care if they killed you or not," Leiber said.

Paul was more cautious when it came to such assumptions. Both men could be stupid or incompetent, intent on killing him but not very good when it came to the execution. "I'll ask them the next time I'm attacked."

"There won't be a next time," both Leiber and Terri said together.

Paul smiled. "I don't plan to use myself for bait again. Now, I have a few questions for you. Some of this may be privileged information, but I really would like some answers that might keep me in one piece."

"You can fill me in on this later, Paul. I need to start dinner." Terri left for the kitchen.

"I'll answer what I can," Leiber said.

"Ernie Crawford. Any illegal activities?"

"Do you mean public record or otherwise?"

"Both."

"Ernie's got a couple of busts. He's been known to board a boat at night and walk off with some electronic goodies to hock when he's short of cash. He's been caught at it twice."

"Otherwise?"

"Ernie's got some pot growing up in the hills. He's been doing that since the sixties. He doesn't try to sell it locally, and we don't have the resources to go find it."

"Does he know you know?" Paul asked.

"We've busted him enough times and found nothing, and that would make me pretty sure he knows we're on to him. Otherwise, we'd have found some pot on him."

"Does any of that come with major consequences: prison time, fines?"

"We might get him put in the county jail for six months, but that's unlikely. He'd do a little time and a lot of probation. The fines wouldn't be more than he could pay."

"So you don't think he's likely to try to take the life of someone who might be close to exposing him?"

Leiber laughed until he turned bright red and tears flowed. When he got it under control, he said, "I think you can take that as a no. The guy's afraid of his own shadow. More so, he's unlikely to do anything that might get him hard time in prison. He'd be even more afraid of that."

"What about Higgins?"

"Straight arrow."

"Nothing?"

"I don't even think you'll find a parking ticket."

"Thirty-plus years here and he's never had a brush with the law?"

"A lot of people do it, only the press doesn't write stories about them."

"Okay. What about the Markses?"

"Mr. and Mrs. Marks? Mr. Marks walks on water around here. Even if he ever did something wrong, I doubt if anyone would turn him in, including the police chief. He's the glue that holds this community together."

"And his wife?"

Leiber lifted a thumb to his mouth and tilted it on end. "Woman's got a bad habit."

"Drinks?"

"That's the rumor."

"Arrests?"

"I don't know how Ira handles it, but to the best of my knowledge she's never had a brush with the law. Of course, most folks couldn't tell you what she looks like. She stays out of Ira's light."

"She's never seen?"

"No. She'll show up at something important. She's not socially inept or anything. When you do see her, she holds her own. It's just that she's not seen that much."

"And you think it's because she drinks?"

"That's the rumor."

"It couldn't be anything else, like hard drugs?"

"In a town this size, we know how the hard stuff gets here, who sells it, and who uses it."

"And she's not one of them?"

"No."

"If you know about the drugs, why don't you do something?"

"Because in a town this size, the druggies know what we know, too, which means it's harder than hell to catch them in the act or get the hard evidence we need to put them away."

"You've been a big help," Paul said.

Max got up and started for the door, stopping to ask, "So you have it figured out?"

"Higgins," he said. "He didn't impress me as a man who could stay squeaky clean for thirty years. I wonder what his incentive is?"

Max walked out of the room, talking as he left. "You're wasting your time. You're not going to find a killer among them. My guess is a couple of drunk fishermen who decided to do Old Town a favor and run you off." He shouted into the kitchen, "You save me some leftovers, Terri. That sure does smell good." He let himself out.

A few minutes later, Terri stuck her head in the room. "Well?" she asked.

"It doesn't sound like Crawford is worth our time to look into. I am interested in Higgins, though. If you thought his daughter knew something, then maybe he is behind this. But why?"

"He's always seemed like a nice man to me. His daughter seems to be a pretty good kid. His wife is nice; she's involved in a lot of charity work and community projects. I can't think of one thing that would even suggest that Walt has secrets."

"Do you think they live beyond their means?"

"Not at all. He does okay with the bookstore, but he scrambled for scholarships just like everyone else when it came time to send his daughter to college."

"Vices?"

"Who knows what people do behind closed doors, but I think in all this time, in a town this small, a rumor would have sprung up if either of them had been into something remotely illegal."

"I still want to look into him."

"You won't find anything."

"Somebody is responsible for your mother's disappearance. Somebody threw me in the river. Somebody doesn't want me to find anything."

She shrugged. "It's not him."

"Then I'll prove you right," he said.

[15]

THE NEXT MORNING Paul was up early. He showered and shaved, straightened the room, and logged on to the Internet. He went looking for Walter Higgins. He probably had an unreasonable expectation of finding something on the net about Higgins. If Paul typed in his own name, it came up in several places: directories of college professors, as author of several essays and books, and as a newsworthy figure entangled in a bizarre story. Walter Higgins, the one in Florence, Oregon, showed up nowhere.

He typed in a search for Terri Mankin. She showed up as a teacher at the high school in Florence. He typed in Julia Higgins. She showed up as a student at the University of Oregon. He typed in Ira Marks. He showed up in two dozen places. He tried Walter Higgins again. Nothing.

The Florence Chamber of Commerce had a website for the city. Higgins's store was mentioned, but his name did not appear in the brief blurb about it. Paul wondered how a man could run a successful business for over thirty years and not have his name show up somewhere on the Internet.

Terri came in, wearing pajamas and carrying a steaming cup of coffee. Paul immediately noticed that she did not wear a bra under her pajama tops, and chastised himself for noticing.

She handed him the cup of coffee, unaware of the attention her pajamas received from him. "I heard you take a shower an hour ago. What has you up so early?"

He tapped the screen. "I'm cruising the net to see what I can find out about Walter Higgins."

"You found out he owns a store in Florence, Oregon."

"Actually, I didn't find a thing. He didn't show up on the Internet."

"That's not very surprising. With billions of people in the world, I doubt that they all will fit on the net."

"Earlier I found you."

"Really? Earlier I thought I was in bed."

He tilted his head and rolled his eyes to show he'd gotten her joke. "You showed up on the staff for the high school."

"Oh, good. That means I'm still employed."

"Don't you find it strange that he doesn't show up on the Internet?"

"Not really."

"I do. What do you know about him?"

"Me? Like all four people on your list, he's always been here."

"Where was he before he came to Florence?"

"I'm sorry," she said, "I told myself years ago that it was not my responsibility to keep track of people who existed before I was born."

"What a thing for an English teacher to say," Paul said. "We're the keepers of the dead. We keep their lights shining."

She let out a short bark of a laugh and then covered her mouth with her hand. Finally she said, "I'm sorry, Paul, but you don't teach in a high school. I'm the one who burdens my dear, sweet students with reading assignments written by old fogies who don't have a clue what real life is all about. And simply making my students read these things makes me sadistic and gleefully punitive. Your students, though, probably love the stuff."

"You're in a gem of a mood this morning," he said.

"Don't push your luck. You're the one giving me sleepless nights."

He got up from the computer and walked over to her, folding his arms around her to give her a hug. "I'm sorry," he said.

She plopped her forehead down on his chest and said, "Oh, crud, that doesn't help. You smell good, and you feel good, and that's all I can think about when I crawl in bed."

"Then crawl in my bed."

"So I can feel worse than I do now?"

"Remember, we just met a few days ago."

"Poop on you. Don't start getting logical on me now, man who is determined to get himself killed by doing stupid things in the dark of night."

"I really am on your list today."

"I'm a sexually frustrated woman."

He unwrapped his arms and then slid his hand under the pajama top until he held her breasts in his hands. "Does that help?"

"Paul, you have a perverted sense of humor, and don't you dare take your hands away."

Miranda stuck her head in the doorway and said, "Good morning, Paul. Is breakfast ready, Mama?"

"Now you can take your hands away." Terri stepped away from him and turned to Miranda, saying, "You're a wonderful little girl who just saved her mother from a huge embarrassment."

"What?" Miranda asked, not understanding at all.

"It had something to do with where I was thinking of putting my hands, sweetheart," Terri mumbled as she left with her daughter for the kitchen.

"This is not good," Paul said to himself as he went back to the computer. "This is not good at all. So why does it feel so good?"

By the time Miranda called him to breakfast, Paul decided the one way to stir up something was to go directly to the source. He would go to Higgins and ask the man about his background.

After breakfast, when Miranda had gone in to watch cartoons, he and Terri took up the same pose, one arm propping up the chin while the other was folded in front of them on the tabletop. They stared across the table at each other, sad eyes locked on sad eyes.

Finally Terri broke the silence between them. "No sex."

"Next time wear a bra."

"You shouldn't even be looking."

"Wear a bra."

"You'd still look."

"Yeah, but not as long."

"This is getting really hard," she said.

"That's not the only thing," he said.

"Don't even go there," she said.

"Let's do a mental exercise today. Let's both go back a week in time, before we met, and remember what it was like."

"You mean venture back into the world of sanity?"

"Something like that."

"And then what?"

"Try to figure out how we got here so fast."

"Are we going to talk about what we find?"

"I think we have to," he said.

She nodded in agreement. "Okay."

He sat up. "I'm going to go see Higgins today. I'm going ask him to tell me his life story."

Terri snapped. "Oh, Paul, you're just asking for trouble again. Of course, if you get yourself killed, we won't have to worry about all these feelings."

He was surprised. This was the first time he had seen her really angry. He liked it. It gave depth to her character. Pam, when angry, became cold, calculating, and cutting. Terri became more human and less of a caretaker.

"I'm going to do this in broad daylight in front of lots of people."

"I'm coming with you."

"Terri! You worry too much. Besides, if something were to happen, it would happen to both of us instead of just the one. You're better off here."

She folded both arms on the table and leaned toward him. "Read my lips: I'm going with you."

"You've suddenly become pretty assertive."

"Maybe it's time you saw all sides of my character. Maybe I won't be so romantic to you then."

"Are you trying to drive me off?"

"Hey, if someone as assertive as Pam Livingston hasn't dented your body, I'm not even likely to scratch your paint."

"Assertiveness is much more charming on you."

"Don't think you can sweet-talk me out of this."

"You can wait for me at the coffee shop."

She thought about that for a moment. "If you don't come out of the bookstore in twenty minutes, I'll come in after you."

"Call the police first, would you?"

She got up. "I've got to call the neighbor to watch Miranda and Dad."

Ten minutes later they were walking into Old Town, Paul feeling older than the town itself. He ached in a lot of different places, and the walk, instead of loosing muscles and making him feel better, just emphasized all the places he hurt.

Paul left Terri at the door of the coffee shop and then walked down to Higgins's store. When he walked in, a half a dozen people were browsing. Julia was behind the counter.

Witnesses, Paul thought. He liked the idea of lots of witnesses. He walked to the counter to talk to Julia.

She watched him approach, her face a mask giving away nothing. Her eyes, though, looked wary. "Mr. Fischer," she said, "I'm beginning to believe that you are a man of steel."

He leaned against the counter, trying his best not to wince from the pain. "That's me—leap tall buildings."

"Are the rumors true?"

"Which rumors are those?"

"Beat up and shot at on the jetty? Tossed in the river in the middle of the night?"

"A good journalist like you should know the answers to those."

"Okay. Both are true to a point," she said, her eyes roaming his body. "I don't think you took much of a beating, though. I don't see a mark."

"Just look and don't touch."

"Sore?" she asked, the first smile to break out on her face.

"My sore spots have sore spots."

"I took a class in massage therapy once. Maybe I could help you out."

"I'm sure there are lots of things you could help a man out with, but I'll have to pass. Is your dad around?"

The smile disappeared. Caution replaced it. "Why?"

"I have some questions I want to ask him."

"What kind of questions?"

"I was wondering where he came from before he moved to Florence."

Paul saw the look, the one that Terri had seen. Julia knew something she wasn't about to share. "He came from the Midwest."

"Anything more precise than that?"

She leaned over the counter and placed a hand on Paul's arm, gently rubbing him. "You seem like a nice guy, Paul. You've got everyone in town convinced that you are determined to find out what happened to Mrs. Drexler, and you have everyone convinced that you're superman. I hope you are as smart as you are determined. If you were, you would know my father had nothing to do with Mrs. Drexler's disappearance, and you would know that it wouldn't be wise to look into it any further than that."

"I don't think I've ever been threatened by someone quite as cute as you before."

"A little girl like me couldn't possibly be a threat to you."

"I don't see a little girl. I see an attractive woman determined to protect her father from something. Maybe if I knew what that something was, and if I was sure it had nothing to do with Mrs. Drexler, then maybe I might forget about it."

"Please," she said, leaning her face close to his, "leave it alone. My father doesn't even know I know."

"You're not giving me much help here."

She moved even closer, her lips only inches from his. "Trust me. Forget this, and I'll give you anything you want."

He was looking into lovely blue eyes whose pupils just noticeably enlarged. Where was Terri when he needed rescuing, he wondered? He said, "This is the kind of thing I will look back on when I'm an old man and think myself a fool. I can think of lots of things I'd like to do with you, but not one of them would bring me closer to knowing what happened to Mrs. Drexler."

With six people watching them, Julia leaned those few inches and planted a slow, smoldering kiss on his lips. Only when she pulled away did he think that maybe he should have stepped back. "The information wouldn't help you with Mrs. Drexler, but it would do serious damage to my father."

"Can I talk to him?"

"He's not in."

"I suppose he won't be in every time I try to talk to him."

"That's a good bet."

He turned and smiled to the customers, and waved a hand to Julia as he left the store. As he walked toward the coffee shop, he was sure of one thing. A daughter who would try to seduce him in front of a store full of people wasn't beyond lying for her father. He brushed aside her warning, determined to find out the mystery behind Walter Higgins.

Terri stepped out of the coffee shop, carrying two takeout cups of coffee. "You don't want to go in there. The place is packed with town folks, and every one of them never took his or her eyes off you as you walked up the street."

"I'm that interesting?"

"Right now, I think if you walked in the coffee shop, they'd flatten themselves against the wall to give you room to pass. You're developing a reputation as a hardass. Even Dave had a compliment for you."

"And what was that?"

"He said that you're not as dumb or as soft as you look."

"I just love it when he gushes like that."

They walked across the street to the empty lot next to the kite shop and sat on a log only a few feet from the water's edge. Today the sun was out, and even though it was pushing that time in the morning when the breeze usually came up and low clouds rolled in, this time the warmth and the sunshine looked like they would hold. The sky was as clear to the west as far as Paul could see.

"What did you find out from Higgins?"

"I never got past Julia."

"Did she have anything to say?"

"Yes. She said she knew her father had nothing to do with the disappearance of your mother, and she offered to let me have my way with her if I would just back off."

Terri chuckled. "You're on a roll with women," she said.

"I didn't take her offer very seriously," he said.

"You should have."

"Why? Has she got a reputation for being loose?"

"Not at all. But she has a reputation of being very protective when it comes to her father."

"I told her that in my old age I would regret turning down her offer."

Terri pulled a little away from him so she could admire his features. Her smile suggested she was quite pleased with what she saw. "You send off signals," she said.

"I what?"

"Your body. It sends off signals."

"And what does it say?"

"It says that you're available."

"Isn't that the problem?" he asked. "I'm not available."

"Maybe that's what your mind says, but it's not what your body says."

"If I could find the switch, I'd turn it off."

She leaned back so her shoulder was resting against his. "No, we don't want that."

They finished their coffee, and walked back toward the house. As they strolled, side by side, occasionally brushing against each other, he asked her, "Have you talked to your mother's friends?"

"I'm going to finish that this afternoon. So far I haven't heard anything I didn't know. What are you going to do?"

"I'm going to call Pam."

He felt her move away from him at the mention of Pam's name. Without thinking about it, he reached out his arm and pulled her back to him. She briefly leaned her head on his shoulder. "Why?" she asked.

"She's still got some connections with the D.A.'s office in Medford and with the police department. I'm going to see if she can get someone to do a background check on Higgins. First, though, I need to see if I can get his social security number."

"I think I can get that."

"How?"

"I have a friend who works at his bank."

"That will help, but are you sure they will give you his social security number?"

"I think they will trust me with it.What else are you going to do?"

"I thought I might spend some time with Miranda, maybe take her out for an ice cream cone. And then I'd like to talk to your Dad again this afternoon."

"I'm jealous," she said. "I'd like you to take me out for an ice cream cone."

"Next time."

They were nearly to the house. "Do you think you can get any more out of Dad?"

"I'm not going to pump him for information. I'd just like to spend some time with him. I always liked him, and we both know we won't be getting much more time with him."

She suddenly jerked him to a halt and threw herself into his arms, kissing him passionately on the lips. He finally had to break up the kiss to catch his breath.

"What was that all about?" he asked.

She blushed. "I'm sorry, but sometimes you're just so wonderful."

"I must be something," he said, thinking that twice in just a few minutes he had been kissed by beautiful women. "I don't know if it is wonderful or not, but whatever it is, I'll take it."

She grabbed his hand and dragged him toward the house. "We don't want you getting too full of yourself," she said, her laughter letting him know she wasn't too concerned about it.

He had time with Miranda and Professor Drexler. Miranda was charming company, absolutely comfortable and content to be with him. His time with the professor passed pleasantly, too. Paul was able to steer the conversation to their days teaching together and to keep it light.

After the professor had returned to bed, Paul called Pam, armed with the social security number Terri had gotten, along with Higgins's birth date and place of birth, a small town in the Midwest.

His conversation with Pam did not last very long. She was busy, she pointed out the second she answered the phone. She jotted down the information and said she would give it to her secretary to take care of. She only opened up when he asked her how the case was going, and, of course, everything she found out about her client made it more difficult to defend him.

He knew this was vintage Pam. Part of the complaining was to cover her should she lose the case. Part of it was to set up the miraculous win should she actually pull it off. No matter which way the trial went, publicly she would make a good showing. She was as much politician as lawyer.

Only at the end of the call did she ask about him. He gave her a brief rundown on the progress he was making trying to find out about Irene Drexler. She wouldn't let him get away with avoiding the real issue. She asked, "And you, Paul? Emotionally, where are you?"

"What answer would reassure you the most?" he asked.

"I'm not asking to be reassured. I've got a lot of plans for the future, and I want a man behind me who is one hundred percent committed to what I'm doing. Tell me one hundred percent and maybe then I'll be reassured."

He wondered, unfairly he decided immediately after thinking it, if the man in Pam's life would always have to be behind her and not beside her. "The last couple of years have been good, Pam. The two before that were interesting. Being with you is an adventure. I'm sure the future would be as interesting." His words trailed off. He wasn't sure what he wanted to say.

"But interesting may not be good enough?" she asked, helping him out.

"Maybe simply not enough. I'm feeling a lot of dissatisfaction at the moment, and I'm not sure where it's coming from."

"You'll need to work that out for yourself," she said. "I've enjoyed our time together. If you were to leave, I'd miss you. I've never had a man in my life who has challenged me the way you do. But I also have a personal agenda, unlike you, and I intend to follow it through. If you could come up with a better one for both of us, I'd be glad to listen. Right now, though, you seem content to be a college professor in a so-so school with no great goals or ambitions. That puts my agenda far ahead of yours."

If they wanted to talk professional agendas, Paul thought. But what about personal goals? What about marriage and family? What about love? All of these things seemed to get buried under Pam's need to succeed professionally, financially. He smiled to himself. Of course. She was a Baker after all. "We do have some things to discuss," he said.

"That sounds like you're about to do something rash," she said.

"Nothing rash," he said. "But we do need to talk."

"Fair enough. I'll have my secretary give you a call when she gets the information from the police."

"Thanks."

"Just remember that you will owe me one."

Yes, for Pam, life was a tally sheet. "I owe you one."

Again she was gone without so much as a good-bye.

A little later, Terri came in carrying two cups of coffee, handing him one while carefully sitting down beside him so as not to spill her own. "I just had an interesting phone call," she said.

"You and me both," he said.

"Pam?"

"Yes. Her answer to everything is that we will be fine just as long as we do everything her way."

"That is an option," Terri said.

"No. That's the problem. It's not an option. What about your phone call?"

"Darcey McGwayne. She was a friend of my mother's, although not particularly a close one. Darcey says she still remembers something my mother said to her a few days before she disappeared. Darcey said that Mom told her she had discovered something absolutely spectacular. Of course Darcey wanted to know what it was, but Mother said that is was one of those things she had to have right or she'd look a fool."

"Any idea of what the spectacular discovery was?"

"Darcey said it was a brief conversation when the two of them had run into each other in the store. She never heard anything more about it."

"Did she tell the police at the time? I don't remember seeing anything on it."

"No one ever interviewed her. She wasn't surprised, though, because she and Mom were more like casual acquaintances than friends."

"I wonder if it could have been something about Higgins?"

"I'm not sure if we'll ever know that."

"Have you talked to all her friends?" he asked.

"I still have two more to call."

"We'll need to see if she mentioned it to anyone else. Have you gone through the things she left behind?"

"Some of it. Dad says he has a few boxes in the attic with her things in them, but he can't remember them having anything of importance in them. Most of her clothes and other personal possessions he either gave away or gave to me."

"Just the same. Pull the boxes out of the attic and let's have a look. Right now we need any help that we can find."

"Okay," she said.

She leaned a little bit toward him so that her shoulder touched his. "Did Pam have anything else to say?"

"Most of what she had to say was about the case she is working on. She seems to think I'm the one with a problem, not her."

"And what do you think about that?"

"I think she's right. She's not unhappy with the way things are right now."

"I wish I could help you," she said.

He leaned over until the side of his head touched the side of hers. "You have already. You've helped bring something to the surface that I've kept suppressed. I'm not going to have a good relationship with anyone until I deal with it."

He looked over the files again, trying to find some scrap that he had missed before that would start forming a new picture. He hadn't found it yet. After dinner, Terri brought down two cardboard boxes full of papers that her mother had left behind. Paul set them aside to go through later.

Later in the evening, a phone call from Pam's secretary made the boxes seem less important. She called to inform Paul that Walter Higgins, with the given place and date of birth, had died on November 5, 1950, at the age of four, of pneumonia.

After he hung up the phone, Paul turned to Terri and said, "Walter Higgins, of Florence, Oregon, is apparently not Walter Higgins at all."

[16]

"YOU HAVE TO go to the police," Terri told him at the breakfast table the next morning.

Paul agreed that it seemed like the logical thing to do, but he had spent the night tossing and turning, struggling with what he had learned about Higgins. Terri was right. He should go to the police. They now knew that Terri's mother had made a discovery before she disappeared, and they knew that Higgins had something to hide. Logic said this tragic combination led to the death of Irene.

The struggle for Paul was with the metaphysical. Higgins seemed like a nice man. His daughter seemed like a nice young woman. Higgins was successful in the community, respected, and, in his quiet way, a contributor to local issues and causes. He didn't seem like a man who had a secret so deep and dark that he would kill someone to hide it.

That, of course, was illogical. Successful criminals were often successful because they didn't seem like people who would commit crimes. Still, Paul had his own intuitive voices at work. They said not to be hasty. If Higgins's secret was unrelated to Irene, Paul could destroy a man for no reason.

"He has to have a reason for hiding his identity," Terri said.

What Higgins had done was not an uncommon practice thirty years ago for people who needed a new identity. They would find someone born approximately the same time they were born, and one who had died not long afterward. They then would order copies of the birth certificate and use that to get a social security card. With the birth certificate and social security card, they could get just about anything else they needed as long as they didn't try to get a job that required a deep background check.

Today, in a much more computerized world, births and deaths were better cross-referenced by the feds. Someone might still risk assuming the name of a dead person, but the odds of getting caught were much higher.

Higgins had apparently become someone else, and had lived that life for over thirty years. Paul's research showed that Higgins arrived in Florence in 1968. He had worked on a fishing boat as well as working part-time in the store he would later purchase. Back then the little businesses in Old Town changed owners on a regular basis. Only a few were profitable; the majority lost money. In early 1970 Higgins bought the store. He had borrowed heavily from the bank to do it, and he had made the store work for him. It took him years to pay off the loan.

And that meant he had not come to Florence flush with cash. If he had been a criminal, he was an unsuccessful one. Paul could think of several reasons why someone might want to change his name and escape to a distant place. Higgins could have been embroiled in family problems. Maybe there was a wife he was trying to get away from. Maybe he had a brush with the law, and something out there was hanging over his head. Maybe he simply wanted a clean start someplace else. Whatever it was, Higgins had not wanted to be found. Would he kill to make sure that didn't happen? Everything Paul had learned about him said no.

"I'll go to the police for you if you are reluctant," Terri said.

He smiled at her. She was afraid that he would go out again and come back hurt, or not at all. In her mind, everything from this point on had to be handled by the police. He appreciated her concern for his safety, but he also felt that to turn any of this over to the police would make the odds less likely that he would get to the bottom of it. Whoever was behind the attacks on him might figure out that they only need to wait and the advantage was theirs. Once Drexler died, the incentive would no longer be there to pursue the mystery. Not only that, it would not be long until Paul's boys arrived in Oregon. He would have to take them someplace, and he knew he wouldn't bring them here if a threat to his life still existed.

Time was running out. Paul was still looking for a jump-start, something that would break this open. "I'll go to the police," he said.

Terri looked relieved. "I was afraid you wouldn't. I was afraid you might do something stupid like try to talk to Higgins."

"I wouldn't think of it." He pushed himself away from the table. "In fact, I think I'll go now."

"Give me a few minutes to line up babysitting, and I'll go with you."

"Who knows how long this will take, Terri. I don't think you want to be away from your dad too long."

She was suspicious. He could see it in her face. "You will be going to police, right?"

"Absolutely."

"And if I were to call the police department in a half an hour, they would tell me you were there?"

"Definitely."

"Why don't I believe you?"

He walked over to her, took her in his arms, and kissed her on the lips. He had meant it as an act to divert her attention, but then the kiss took on a life of its own, and he pulled her more tightly to him and lifted her up so that he could feel the rich curves of her lush body against him. Passion worked both ways, and suddenly he was fighting to separate himself from her, afraid that they had crossed the line and nothing could keep them from having sex on the kitchen table.

He eased her back to the floor, put his hands on her hips, and gently pushed her away until the last things touching were their lips. With a strength he wasn't sure he could muster, he finally pulled back from the kiss. "I have to go to the police now," he said, his voice so tight he was sure it came out as no more than a squeak.

Terri's breasts were heaving in front of him. When she could finally catch enough breath to speak, she could only whisper, "You definitely have to go to the police now."

Neither moved. They stood that way for several seconds, both wound tight and ready to spring at a word or even a look from the other. Miranda saved them from themselves. She walked into the kitchen and stopped between them. She first turned her head up one way to look at Paul, then the other to look up at her mother. She glanced back and forth between the two, her eyes widening. Her expression was so funny that Paul and Terri started to laugh. The tension between them shattered.

Miranda tilted her had to one side, perplexed by the odd behavior. Finally she turned to Paul and asked, "Is Mama mad at you?"

"No, honey, she's not," he said.

She turned to her mother and raised her eyebrows, asking for confirmation. "No, Miranda, I'm not mad at him."

"You sure looked like you were fighting," she said.

"No, dear, it was something else," Terri said.

Miranda flicked her eyes from Paul to Terri, and then she turned on her heel and headed back to the living room and cartoons.

"I don't think she believed us," Paul said.

"If she had walked in a few minutes earlier, there's no telling what she would be thinking."

"I think we need to be a little more careful," he said.

"A little more careful," Terri laughed. "I don't even use birth control."

"A lot more careful?"

"Definitely a lot more careful. By the way," she added, "thanks."

"For what?"

"If I had any doubt that all my body parts still worked, I don't have that doubt now."

"Me neither."

"That was obvious."

"I think I need to go to the police now."

"I think you definitely need to go to the police now."

He drove his car down to the end of the block and then worked around until he had the car stopped at the coast highway. Instead of turning left, which would take him to the police station, he turned right, traveled a short distance and then took the exit to Old Town. He stopped his car in front of the Higgins store and got out.

He knew that Terri could not have seen him come back around from the house. If she was as flustered and confused as he was now, she wouldn't remember to call the police station in half an hour. Even if she did, that would still give him the time he needed to talk to Higgins. Paul was going to let the man give him an explanation before he acted on what he knew.

The store was still closed, but he could see Julia moving around inside, straightening items on the shelves. He tapped on the front door. She looked up, walked a few steps so she could see who it was, and then broke into broad smile. She came over to the door and let him in.

"Have you reconsidered?" she asked.

"About having my way with you?" he asked.

"Exactly."

"You certainly know how to both tempt and flatter a man," he said. "On the other hand, I think you'd panic if I put a hand on you."

The smile lost a little of its sincerity. "Were you looking to collect now?" she asked. "I really do have to get the store ready for business."

"I'm not expecting to collect at all," he said. "I'd like to talk to your father."

The smile faded. "What about?"

"I think you know what it's about."

"Look, I've had Trick Questions 101 for Journalists. I spill my guts because you think you know something, or at least you say you think you know something."

"I know your father's real name is not Walter Higgins."

It was if he had kicked her in the stomach. Her confidence was suddenly gone, and she had to put out a hand on a shelf to steady herself. "That's why everyone has been so nervous. You have a reputation for digging out information, no matter how deep it is buried."

"I want to talk to your father."

She seemed to regroup, fired by a sudden anger. "I will not let you destroy him," she said, stepping toward him, defiant.

He held his ground. "If this has nothing to do with Irene Drexler, then what I know won't go any further. But I need to make sure it has nothing to do with Irene's disappearance."

Julia wasn't mollified. "I won't let you see him."

Did that confirm that Higgins had something to do with Irene's disappearance? He asked, "Do you know why he changed his name?"

She didn't need to answer. He could tell by the expression on her face. "No," she said. "I just found out recently. I thought I'd practice my investigative reporter skills on my own family. Dad never talks much about the past, about his parents. I wondered why."

"And?"

"I found what you must have found. Walter Higgins died in 1950."

"And you don't know why your father would have changed his name?"

"He says he was an only child. He says his parents died when he was a boy. He says he was raised by distant relatives who never treated him very well, and he never wants to see them again."

"Do you know where he was from?

"He gives the name of Cottonwood Falls, Kansas, on his birth certificate, but I'm not bad at investigating myself. I managed to see a yearbook from the high school in the town when he should have been in school there. I didn't find a picture of him. He passes easily as someone from the Midwest, so I would guess that he is from the Midwest."

"And what do you think he might have done to need to change his name?"

"I spent a lot of time in the computer lab at the U of O. I reviewed news stories from a half a dozen states from the time he would have been ten until he moved out here. I couldn't find anything that matched up with him."

"So you don't think what he did was criminal?"

"Not the kind of criminal that makes big headlines in newspapers."

"Maybe we both need to talk to him, then," Paul said.

Julia glanced toward the French doors. "He's having breakfast on the deck."

He put a hand in the small of her back and guided her to the doors. "After you," he said.

Paul was not sure what to expect when he confronted Higgins. With his daughter present, Higgins was not likely to be violent. On the other hand, if he was indeed responsible for Irene's death, then there was no telling what he would do. Terri's instinct to go to the police was a good one. He hoped she wasn't right, though.

Paul directed Julia to one of the chairs and he leaned against the building so he had them both in front of him. "We've come to have coffee with you," Paul said.

"This looks like a little more than a friendly cup of coffee," Higgins said.

"I'd like to keep this friendly," Paul said, "but that will depend a lot on what you have to say."

"Say about what? I told you all I know about Irene Drexler." Higgins poured two more cups of coffee, shoving one toward Julia and the other toward Paul.

Paul reached for the cup, and then said, "I've found out that Irene Drexler stumbled across a secret soon before she was killed. I've also found out that you happen to have a secret."

Higgins leaned back in his chair and sipped his coffee. He was a handsome, confident man, Paul thought, and none of this seemed to ruffle him at all. "If Irene found out my secret, she never let me know."

"That wasn't what you talked about on the night she disappeared?"

"I told you what we talked about."

"Daddy, he knows," Julia said.

Higgins shifted his attention to his daughter. He smiled slightly. "I knew that you found out," he said. "I could see it in the way you looked at me. I was surprised you never asked me about it."

"I was afraid to," she said.

"Afraid of your father?" Paul asked.

She shook her head. "Of course not. Afraid of what I might find out."

Higgins sipped his coffee again. "Just in case, I think I need to call your bluff, Mr. Fischer. What exactly is it you think you know?"

"That Walter Higgins died in 1950. That you used his birth certificate to fabricate a new life for yourself. What neither Julia nor I know, though, is why."

Higgins gazed out across the river. He focused on some distant point for some time, the features of his face shifting as different emotions seemed to run through him. At first Paul saw sadness, then anger, then whimsy. Just from these changes Paul thought he might learn to like this man. Higgins was a thinker, one who carried some great burden, and he probably had stood outside of himself a thousand times and wondered about the game he played.

"You would think," he finally said, "that it would be very hard to give up your identity, the only thing you had known for most of your life. And it was hard. What made it easier was the fact that I could reinvent myself, and I could do that in a form I wanted. I suppose you might look at me here and think that I didn't choose much of a life. That would be ironic, considering how much pleasure this life has given me."

"What was it that made you need to reinvent yourself?" Paul asked.

Higgins smiled at Julia, and then he looked at Paul. "My father."

Paul and Julia waited for him to continue, but this was a story that Higgins obviously did not want to tell. Paul gave him incentive. "If you can't convince me that this had nothing to do with Irene, I'll have to take this to the police."

"I'm surprised you haven't taken it to the police already."

"I'm not here to ruin anyone's life," Paul said, "unless that person had something to do with the disappearance of Irene Drexler."

"This has nothing to do with that."

"You'll have to convince me."

Higgins sank back in his chair. "I'd really prefer that Julia not hear this."

She shook her head no. "I have to hear it," she said.

He nodded. "I always loved good books, good literature. I'd have to sneak them into the house because my father thought all fiction a waste of time." He paused, thinking for a moment. He then turned to Paul and said, "My father was General Hiram Waterford, once second in command of the troops in Vietnam. I was sent to boarding schools and then military schools, and finally, with my father's influence, to West Point. I was an exceptional cadet who graduated with honors. Before you do a thing, I want you to check out those facts. You will see that I am telling the truth."

"I'll do that," Paul said. "That still doesn't explain why you changed your identity."

"Just before graduation, we all received out duty assignments. My father had worked behind the scenes to get me what he said was a plum. I was to be sent to Vietnam as an infantry officer. He was delighted. He called it the fast-track to promotion, combat experience."

"And you weren't interested in combat experience?"

"Do you mean was I a coward? Perhaps, but dying in Vietnam would have been a lot less painful than what I did. I loved my mother. I loved my two sisters. I even loved my father. That I would devastate him with my choice has been the most difficult part of what I have done. But I did not believe in the war. I hadn't from the day we became involved. From my military training I was convinced that it was a war we could not win the way we were fighting it, and from my political training I knew that it would not be fought any other way. The idea of being sent there to lead men to death for a cause I could not believe in was more than I could accept."

"So you became a deserter?"

"More than that," he said. "I was a graduate. I'd received my commission. I was a deserter of the highest order, and in the eyes of my father, as he has publicly announced a thousand times, I was a traitor to my country."

"So you changed your identity."

"Oh, I had help with that. Organizations existed at the time to help draft dodgers and deserters. I was a poster boy for the antiwar movement for a while, but not one they could put on display. My identity had to be wiped out completely. My father had the resources behind him to track me to the end of the earth."

"No one had a clue who you were when you came here?"

"The pictures the public saw of me were of a clean-cut, short-haired young man in a military uniform. By the time I got here I fit in with the counterculture. Jeans, old army shirts, long hair, full beard. No one noticed. Besides, so much was happening back then that I slipped out of the headlines pretty quickly. That was false security, I knew, because I was sure my father would never stop looking for me. He would demand I receive full punishment for what I did, the only honorable thing."

"He wanted you in prison."

"He wanted me executed. He said it in *Time*, he said it in the newspapers, and he said it on television."

"Have you contacted your family since?" Julia asked.

"Honey," he said, "what I did is still punishable today. The only thing that could save me would be a presidential pardon, and unfortunately I'm not good friends with this president."

"I think that would be reason enough to want to keep Irene Drexler quiet."

Higgins propped his elbow on the table and pointed a finger at Paul. "I will tell you this for the last time. Irene Drexler never indicated to me that she knew anything about my past. I came here because it was a good place to blend in. A lot of people here had things they didn't want anyone knowing about, so not many people asked many questions."

"Can you think of anyone else who might have something to hide?"

"I can name a couple of dozen, but mostly it has to do with drugs, and not one of them would risk a murder charge. It took me nearly a decade to make the store profitable. It's only been this last decade that I let myself get involved in the community. If someone has a bigger secret than mine, he's a lot better at covering it up than I am."

Paul put his empty coffee cup on the table. He looked from Higgins to Julia. Higgins didn't look like a man whose life might come apart at the seams at any second. He seemed calm, perhaps even resolved. Maybe he always expected for it to come to an end and had prepared himself. Julia was stricken. Tears streamed down her face. Paul made a decision. He knew it wasn't a wise one, but it was what gut instinct told him to do.

"I'm not going to take this to the police, at least not unless I find a connection between you and Irene. If you are telling the truth and there is no connection, then this conversation will remain here."

"I appreciate that," Higgins said. "I can't imagine, though, going through the rest of my life without this catching up to me."

"Thirty years ago for most people is just a curiosity. I don't know how the law would look at it, but it really doesn't matter much now what you did then. Do you think your father is still searching for you?"

"Both my mother and father are dead now. My sisters married military men. The Internet is a wonderful thing. It lets you keep up, even with the past. To be honest, the only life I've ever had that has been honest is the life I've had here, hiding out under an assumed name."

"Ironic," Paul said.

"Life is full of ironies," Higgins said.

Julia followed Paul back into the store. Before he could get to the front door, she pulled him by the sleeve to stop him and then threw herself into his arms. She cried, her face buried in chest. When she could finally get it together, she said, "Thank you."

"I want to believe your dad," Paul said, "but I won't scratch him off the list until I'm positive he's innocent. I really don't care what he did thirty years ago, unless it was murder Irene Drexler. That I won't forgive him."

"He's not capable of killing her," she said.

Paul knew he would not be walking away from this now if he didn't think the same thing. If Higgins could not lead other men to death, he certainly couldn't kill a woman to save himself. He had already destroyed his life once to keep from harming others. He would certainly destroy it again rather than hurt another person.

"I hope we're both right about that."

She still held him. He carefully unwrapped her arms from around him and walked to the door.

Outside, he took only a few steps before Terri suddenly stepped in front of him. "I didn't think for a minute that you were going to the police," she said.

"It's not healthy that you've gotten to know me so well in such a short time," he said.

"It's lucky for you that I have."

He turned her around and walked her away from the bookstore. "Please tell me that you didn't call the police."

"I was going to give you five more minutes in the store, and then I was going to call them."

He stopped her on the sidewalk, put a hand behind her neck, and pulled her lips to his. After the kiss, he said, "You're a tenacious woman, and I love you for it."

"And I have only one thing to say to you: Don't let me see you wrapped up in some girl's arms again."

[17]

BACK AT THE house, after he had told Terri what he had learned about Walter Higgins, she said, "Then you can eliminate him from the list."

His lips compressed and his head tilted to one side. He wanted to nod yes to her, but he couldn't. "My gut instinct tells me he's not the one. Unfortunately, I always like to back that instinct with some hard evidence. That's the researcher in me. What I do know is that your mother found out some apparently damaging information about someone, that the last person we know she saw was Walter Higgins, and that he had a very damaging secret he didn't want known. We only have his word that your mother walked out of that store alive."

"Then you need to find someone who saw her after that," Terri said.

"Right. Easy. Do we wait for them to come to us, or do we put an ad in the paper?"

"Don't be sarcastic. You've already had two people who admitted to seeing my mother after they said they hadn't. Isn't it that possible more might exist? Weren't you going to double check the alibis of people the police interviewed against times?"

She was right. He hadn't gotten to it. The police had made a list of people who were in Old Town up to early evening. They had interviewed each, and they had checked on alibis. What the police had not done, though, was to see if the alibis had actually covered the time of the disappearance of Irene. He wouldn't have expected any more from a small-town police department, inexperienced in possible murder investigations.

In some cases, there was no issue. A deckhand said he was in such and such bar at 9:30. He couldn't have been in Old Town at the time of the disappearance. In a few cases, though, the alibi put the person in a restaurant at 10:00. What Paul needed to know was how long it would take for that person to get to the restaurant from Old Town. Was there any window of opportunity for the person to have abducted Irene and still gotten to the restaurant?

"Find me the files," he said. "I'll look at them now. And do you have a map of Old Town, preferably an older one?"

She saluted him. "Yes, captain, anything you say, captain."

"Fair enough," he said. "You call me captain and I'll call you mother."

She stuck her tongue out at him. "If you had any clue what was good for you, you wouldn't need a mother."

He didn't respond. The truth was that he was touched by the fact that she had followed him and was ready to come to his rescue, if need be. Pam simply expected him to take care of himself. Even he expected to take care of himself. But he liked the idea of someone stepping in to take care of him if she thought he needed it. He might be a big boy, but even big boys sometimes hurt themselves and need comforting.

It took him nearly two hours to go through the information. Three dozen people had been in Old Town as late as 6:00 that evening. The police had done a good job of tracking down each one to find out where they had gone that evening. Most simply had gone home to family. The others had moved around a bit before landing in one place, but Paul was able to trace their routes on a map that Terri found and confirm the times they gave. Everyone checked out but one. The report simply referred to him as Billie. He had left the docks at 9:00 that night, but he hadn't shown up at a bar until 10:00. No one had, it appeared, asked him about that hour.

Terri brought him a cup of coffee. "Do you have any idea of who Billie might be?"

"Billie? Everyone knows Billie."

"I don't know Billie."

She sat down beside him so she could see the file in his lap. "He's been a town character for years. He started out as a fisherman, and then he worked in the warehouse where the fish that are bought off the fishing boats are stored. He's a guy with a heart of gold. Until he retired, kids used to flock to the docks just to hear Billie tell one of his tall tales. I've known him all my life."

"Do you think he has anything to hide?"

"Do you mean like Walt?"

"Yes."

"No. Billie was born and raised here. He's just a character."

"Would he have had any reason to lie to the police?"

She leaned back against the sofa and stretched an arm along its back, her hand gently, unconsciously stroking the back of his head. "I think there was some concern at one time by parents about his fondness for children. In time, though, I think it was pretty clear that it was children who had a fondness for him. Maybe about the time Mom disappeared the police were watching him closely. I don't know for sure; that was just something I had heard."

"So, if he saw your mother that night, he might not want to share it with the police?"

"You'd have to ask him."

"He's still around?"

"He's in a local nursing home. Diabetes sort of took his legs out from under him."

"I'm going to ask you to do me a favor," he said. "I want you to go see Billie and ask him about that night. He's not going to tell me anything, but if he remembers you, he might tell you the truth."

"The truth?"

"Yes. The truth. There's a chance that Billie didn't leave the docks at 9:00 that night, but about 9:50. He might have seen your mother walk through before he left, if she got that far."

"Why wouldn't he tell the police that?"

"Maybe he thought the police already believed he was a pervert."

"Then why didn't the police look at his alibi more closely?"

"Because maybe they thought he was fond of little children."

Her hand moved down to his neck and began to message it. He leaned his head back and closed his eyes. "I can go over there now if you will watch Dad and Miranda," she said.

He smiled to himself. If she was going to let him out of her sights, it was only going to be when he was tied down with responsibilities that wouldn't let him slip away. "Do that. If Billie did see your mother, that might clear Walt. In the meantime, I'm going to log on to the Internet and see if I can confirm the history that Higgins gave me."

Neither of them moved. He kept his eyes closed as her weight shifted and she twisted around until she was straddling his lap. Then he felt her lips on his. It was a soft kiss. Her hands gently cradled his cheeks. When the kiss stopped, she rested her forehead on his. "I can't seem to keep from touching you," she said.

Since his hands were now resting on her hips, he couldn't exactly claim that the same wasn't true of him. "I think we're going to create a mighty mess," he said. "There's a logical way of doing things, even when it comes to love, and we've not done any of it right."

"Did I hear the L word again?"

He slowly moved his hands up and down her sides, feeling the lushness of her body, with each stroke his thumbs coming to rest under her breasts. "Creationism," he said.

"What?"

"Love created in seven days. They say evolution is better in the end."

"Love evolves slowly?"

"Exactly."

"But you're a creationist."

"Against my will."

"Half of marriages end in divorce, creationism or evolution be damned."

He smiled. "It's always good to give a logical bent to the illogical."

"What are we going to do?"

"For right now, not what we both desperately want to do."

She pushed herself up from the sofa. "And I thought I was the one who would have to show resolve."

"I assure you this is killing me."

She chuckled. "It better be."

"Go before my resolve melts."

She left for the nursing home while he turned to the computer. By the time she returned an hour later, he knew that Higgins had told the truth about his past. Not only had his father disowned his son for his actions, he also insisted that if his son were ever found he should be executed as a deserter. Who said that blood was thicker than water?

Terri was beaming when she walked into the den. "Walt is off the hook." She wrapped her arms around his neck from behind and put her face next to his as she looked at the information on the computer screen.

"Billie did see your mother, then."

"Yes. He said he would admit it to me, but he wouldn't talk to the police. He's never forgiven them for hassling him those first few years. He saw Mom walk past the docks into the field that they used for parking, and then he saw her turn around and come back. From there she went to the next block over, toward the store."

"That doesn't sound like it takes Walter off the hook," he said.

"No," she said, "Mom didn't come back the way she came. She walked back up the next block, the one that leads toward the store."

"Hand me the map," he said.

She picked it up from the coffee table and dropped it in his lap, wrapping again her arms around his neck. While he looked at the map, she traced the route her mother had taken with her finger. "He said he watched her until she disappeared."

"And where was he?"

She pointed to a spot on the docks. "He was repairing a net on a fishing boat."

Paul took a pencil and lined up the spot where Billie had been and the spot where Irene would have disappeared from sight. "She couldn't have been more than a half a block from the store."

"That's what Billie said."

"And he didn't hear anything unusual?"

"I asked him. He said as soon as she disappeared, he walked from the boat to the parking lot, got in his car, and went to the bar. He guessed it might have been about a quarter till ten."

"Did you ask him if he caught another glimpse of her when he went to his car?"

She smiled and nodded her head. "Yes, I did. I did a thorough job of asking questions. He said he looked for her, but she was gone."

"Can you believe him?" Paul asked.

She laughed. "The reason kids loved Billie is that he is a simple soul. If he was lying, he couldn't hide it."

Paul went back to the map. He took a measurement using the pencil, and then he transferred the distance to the spot where Billie had last seen Irene. "Unless someone jumped out of the shadows, knocked her on the head, and dragged her off, I see only one place where she could have gone."

"To the store."

"Exactly."

"But both of the Marks say that they didn't see her that night."

"We're three for three so far. What do you want to bet that we go five for five?"

"Three for three?"

"Three people told the police they did not see your mother that night, and now we know that all three lied. With that kind of a string, I wouldn't be surprised if the Markses didn't lie, too."

"But why would they?"

That was the question, Paul thought. Finding the answer wasn't going to be as easy as it had been with the others. Marks was a powerful man in the community. He'd already made it clear he did not want to talk to Paul. He had also made it clear that Paul was to stay away from his wife. Paul wouldn't be able to come close to the Marks family unless he was loaded with ammunition against them. The police wouldn't listen to him without it. He and Terri may have run up against a stone wall they couldn't get over.

"Maybe for the same reason as the others," he said. "Maybe they didn't want the attention the police would give them if they admitted to seeing something."

"If my mother had been at their store and left, why wouldn't they want to admit that?"

"Maybe they saw what happened to her after she left."

"Then they would have called the police."

Marks certainly would have, Paul thought. That was the kind of man he was. But he had not called the police, and he claimed to be in the store that night. It did not sound as if he had seen Irene being abducted. What had he seen, though? Why wouldn't he want anyone to know that Irene had been in the store?

"I think I need to learn a lot more about the Marks family before I even begin to think about these questions. We started with four people of interest. We've ended up with five. Of those, we seem to have eliminated three. What we need to do now is to eliminate the Markses."

"And if we do that?"

"Then your mother was abducted somewhere between the store and her return home. We will be out of suspects, and the only thing I will be able to tell your father is that she was taken away by a person or persons unknown. That will be the best we can do."

"How do you plan to eliminate the Markses?"

"Right now I don't have a clue. I've already put too much time into this today. I need a break."

"And I need to fix dinner."

"Is there any way I can take you and Miranda out for dinner?"

"I do have a very responsible young teen down the block who has come in to watch dad in the past when I've had parent nights and things like that. We could leave your cell phone number with her, but only on one condition."

"What's that?"

"That you curl up on the sofa with me and watch a movie after we get back."

"No hanky panky, right?"

She smiled. "I didn't say that."

"You drive a hard bargain," he said, "but I think I can do that."

Paul took them to the restaurant just around the bend from the house. After dinner, they did curl up on the sofa in the front room to watch a movie—all three of them. Miranda burrowed her way into a nest between them and became so comfortable that she quickly fell asleep.

Terri had rented two movies, one with Miranda in mind. While the first rewound, she put Miranda to bed, checked on her father, and then returned to the living room with hot chocolate and popcorn for the second movie. By the time it ended, Paul and Terri were very much wrapped up in each other's arms, and they had both lost track of the plot some time before.

Between kisses, Paul was the one to make the suggestion. "Why don't we just do this and get it over with?"

"I thought we were doing it," she whispered breathlessly.

"It doesn't count if we still have our clothes on," he said.

He heard three breaths before she could reply, "Let's go to my room."

"Won't we need to worry about waking Miranda or your Dad?" he asked.

"Dad's out like a light and Miranda is at the other end of the hall. I have a very big bed, and I want to be comfortable and enjoy every moment of this."

She had a point. The sofa bed in the den wasn't particularly comfortable for one, it definitely wouldn't be that comfortable for two, and they were already having trouble staying on the sofa.

"Okay."

If either Miranda or the professor were going to wake up, both would have from the noise Terri and Paul made on the stairs. They tugged at each others' clothing. A shoe slid down several steps. Paul banged against the wall as Terri pulled his shirt off. She was wearing jeans, and by the time they reached the top landing, he had them unbuttoned, unzipped, and dragged down to her thighs. In her bedroom, with the lights out, more clothes were peeled away until they both stood naked in an embrace that melded the two of them together.

He could not believe how wonderful she felt, all curves and softness, such incredible softness. They had long gone past the need for preliminaries. He gently shoved her back on the bed, and she, with elbows and heels, worked her way onto the mattress. Paul followed closely behind, so close that when she stopped he entered her.

A deep, almost joyous moan escaped from one of them, although both were so absorbed that neither could have told which one made the noise. Terri came quickly, and then came quickly again, which only drove Paul deeper into passion. He was totally lost in her. The rhythm, the heat, the desire and then, far outside of himself, so distant that he nearly didn't recognize it, came a noise, and because a part of him was tuned to the rooms down the hall, afraid of waking either Miranda or the professor, he couldn't ignore the sound.

Terri tensed under him. She had heard it, too.

"That sounded like glass breaking," he said.

"I think it was the outside door in the kitchen," she said.

Reluctantly, very reluctantly, he slid off her and groped around on the floor. He found his pants but not his socks. He put on the pants and one shoe. The other was somewhere near the top of the stairs. Down below he could hear the door open and the crunch of glass as a foot stepped on it.

Terri had gotten out of bed on the other side and slipped on a robe. She picked up the phone next to the bed and dialed 911. After a moment, she put the phone back down. "The phone's dead."

The only thing Paul could think of was the famous line from Poltergeist: *They're back!* "My cell phone is in the den. Do you have any kind of a weapon up here?"

"I don't have a gun, Paul. I have a four-year-old in the house."

"Take Miranda and lock her in the bathroom with you. Don't let anyone in unless it is me or the police."

"You come with us."

"No," he whispered, a fierceness in his voice. "They want me. If I'm in there, we'll all be in danger."

"What are you going to do?"

"Try to get help."

"You will be careful."

He didn't answer. He hadn't been very good at this the first two times. He didn't expect to come out ahead the third time. If he could get downstairs and to the front door, he might be able to make it to a neighbor's house and get them to call the police.

Paul found his other shoe and put it on. He then slowly came down the stairs, careful not to make a noise—quite a contrast, he thought, to how he had just gone up them. He made it to the entryway. He had a clear path to the front door, but whispers coming from the den stopped him.

One voice said, "Damn it! He's not here."

A second voice answered, "I bet that son of a bitch is in bed with Terri."

The first voice, replied, "Then we go up and do them all."

Paul froze in place. If he slipped out now, the two would go upstairs. He didn't want to think what "do them" meant, but he knew he couldn't let the men go up. He quietly moved to the hall near the den door.

It was only open a crack, and he could see the beam of a flashlight moving around in the room. When the beam shifted back to the door, Paul timed his move, hoping it would be just right. He built up enough momentum so that when he hit the door, he struck it with a tremendous force. The door flew open about six inches and then slammed to a stop before it gave again. The two men on the other side were bowled backward as the door crashed into them.

Half open, the door hung up one of the men. Paul slid to the side and fell into the room on top of the second man. What followed was a flurry of elbows, fists, and knees pumping wildly. Paul did most of it. The man beneath him had already been stunned once, and now Paul pummeled him into near unconsciousness.

Not quite sure what happened, but aware of the threat, the other man slid on his back away from the door, pulled a gun from his waistband, and aimed at the shadows a few feet away. He fired the first shot over their heads.

At the flash of the gun, Paul threw himself off the man he was beating and rolled away. Above him, he could hear Terri scream. He scrambled to his right just in time, for the man with gun, seeing Paul in the flash of the shot, aimed and fired again.

Although Paul had moved out of the way, the flash illuminated him again. He dove once more, this time toward the flashlight on the floor he had seen when the gun went off, and again he just avoided another bullet coming his way. He rolled over the flashlight, grabbing it as he did, and came up in a sitting position. With all his strength, he hurled the flashlight in the direction of the man with the gun.

The man grunted, and Paul heard the sound of metal hitting the floor. He couldn't be sure if it was the gun or the flashlight that fell, but he had to take advantage of the confusion. He scrambled to his feet and threw his body in the direction of the man.

Stunned or not, the man was bigger and more powerful than Paul. Paul hit him chest high, but the man was able to twist away so that Paul fell to the floor. And then he dropped his own weight on Paul and the wrestling match began.

Paul did his best to fight. He tried to bring every free part of his body in contact with the man. He caught him on the jaw with an elbow. He butted the man's face with his forehead. He threw short punches into the man's ribs. Despite all of this, he was still losing the battle. The man was on top of him, and he threw one measured punch after another, each like a hammer blow to Paul's head. Paul could feel his strength slipping away, and he could feel the light in his brain beginning to dim.

A piercing scream stopped the next blow. Some small part of Paul's mind had registered the footsteps on the stairwell, had noticed the hall light go on, and had heard the front door open. The scream had jolted the man on top of him to a stop. Paul smiled. Terri had a wonderful scream, he thought, a beautiful scream, one so full of terror that it would bring all the neighbors for blocks around.

The man pushed himself off Paul and hurriedly felt around on the floor, searching for his gun. Paul wasn't worried about the gun. He could feel it under him, biting into his back. The man gave up the search, stood, and then quickly swung a leg toward Paul's head. He missed. Paul was quick enough to catch the leg in midair and send the man tumbling.

That took the fight out of him. He got back to his feet and grabbed the second man, who was only now staggering off the floor, and dragged him from the room. The two moved back into the kitchen and clumsily crashed through the open back door together, tumbling down the three steps to the yard.

Paul followed closely behind them with the gun in his hand. He let them get into the yard, and then he fired off three shots into the ground around their feet, which encouraged them to move away even faster.

He walked back through the kitchen, dropping the gun on the floor, and moved to the hallway. Terri stood in the open front door, neighbors already hurrying up the steps behind her. Paul smiled at her and crumpled into a heap on the floor.

[18]

PAUL WAS BACK in the bed in the den again, this time with all the aches and pains from before plus a few more. Everything he had used to fight back—knees, elbows, fists, and forehead—hurt. His head hurt the most. Whoever had hit him had powerful blows that had left one eye black, the other swollen shut, and both cheekbones ruby red. Considering the beating he had taken, he should have been in worse condition.

Paul didn't care. He wasn't a man to fight. He didn't think fists were a solution to anything, and he thought a man should go with his strength in a confrontation. Paul was quick. In a short sprint, he was fast. Running had always seemed the best defensive option to him, especially when outnumbered by bigger men. This one time he was proud of himself. He had leveled one of the men, and he had held his own with the other, the one with the gun. If this scenario were replayed ten times, Paul was sure he would have been killed in nine of them. Despite the odds, it felt like a victory, and it felt good. He'd done a little payback.

Terri sat cross-legged on the bed, her face in her hands. Miranda clung to her side, her face buried in her mother's robe. Paul hadn't had a chance to talk to them yet. Within minutes the police were everywhere, and Paul was in the hands of paramedics. Terri had kept it together long enough to let everyone know what had happened, and then she had hovered over the shoulders of the paramedics, Miranda clinging to her leg. Half of the Florence police force had been in and out of his room, including Max Leiber. Paul had answered a thousand questions already, but one had not been asked by anyone. What had Terri and Paul been doing when the men broke into the house? The fact that Terri was in a bathrobe and Paul shirtless and in jeans may have made the question unnecessary.

Paul asked Terri, "Are you okay?"

She pulled her hands away from her face and then seemed to notice Miranda for the first time. She wrapped the girl in her arms and stroked her hair. "I'm scared half to death, I ache for your poor face, and I'm mortified sitting here in this thin bathrobe, knowing exactly what every man is thinking when he looks at me."

"Every man is thinking: God, that Paul Fischer is a lucky guy."

Tears rolled down her cheeks. "How can you make jokes?" she asked.

"Because I'm still alive, which means I can make jokes. And that wasn't a joke. I'm sure that's exactly what they are thinking. How's your Dad?"

"The doctor's with him. The gunshots and the screaming terrified him."

"You have a lovely scream. It terrified me, too. I won't tell you what the gunshots did until I change my underwear."

She half sobbed and half laughed. "What were you thinking? You could have been killed."

"I heard them say they were coming upstairs." He left out the other part, the part about killing them all.

She rolled over and crawled to him, dragging Miranda under one arm. When she reached him, she very carefully cuddled next to him, being cautious not to touch his face. Miranda snuggled in between them. He stroked their hair, loving their closeness despite the fact that his body hurt.

"Tell me about Marks's sons," he said.

Terri moved her head so she could look at his face. "You don't think those were Seth and Abe, do you?"

"We just cleared Higgins, so I don't think he's sending anyone after us. The closer we've moved toward the Marks family, the more violent the attacks have gotten."

"How would they know?"

"I suspect we're being watched. I suspect that the people we've talked to, they've talked to as well. I don't think it would be hard for them to figure out that we've put your mother in the store that night."

"Describe the men who attacked you again," she said.

"Both around six-two or six-three. One solid as a rock. The other softer but still strong. Not a lot of endurance, so I'd guess they do some health club stuff, but no running or conditioning. Their eyes are dark, not blue. I had enough light to see the eyes behind the ski masks. I would have noticed light eyes."

"I hadn't even thought about them before," she said. "I just assumed it was a couple of guys off the boats. The general description fits them both. Abe's softer, carries more weight. Seth works out regularly. Abe will play some basketball or some handball, but only occasionally."

"What exactly is it they do?"

"They're responsible for the warehouses and the shipping of food to the stores."

"Does that keep them busy?"

"Rumor has it that Ira put them in these jobs so they wouldn't have much to do. Neither is exactly a mental giant, and both were lazy students. That happens a lot to kids when they know they have a successful business to move into after school."

"Let's see if we can get Max to maybe give them a once-over to see if they look any better than I do."

"Do you think you marked them?"

"Most of my aches are coming from the parts of my body that I slammed into them. I'd better have marked them or I'm going to join a health club."

Just barely touching him, she ran her fingers over his face. Even this caused him to wince once or twice. "We need to let the police do this now," she said. "I think you should leave, go back to Medford where it's safe."

"Nothing like being kissed and dropped," he said, mindful of Miranda's little ears nearby.

"You don't know how I wish they had waited about ten more minutes. I'm not trying to drive you away, but I know you well enough now to know you're a dog with a bone, and you won't let go of it."

"Such a lovely way to be described," he said.

"You have to let it go. Even Dad says so. He's stunned that his call for help has led to this."

"He should be stunned. What this tells me clearly is that someone murdered your mother, and now he is trying to cover his tracks. Don't you think it's time that Ira Marks faced justice?"

"You can't really believe it was Ira?"

"Why else would he sic his boys on me?"

"Let's wait and see what Max has to say after he's seen Seth and Abe."

He ran his fingers through her hair and got them entwined there, loving the way her hair filled out around her face and made her even prettier than before. "Fair enough, but I'm not going back to Medford, and I am going to talk to Ira Marks, whether he likes it or not. First, though, I'm going to soak my whole body in the bathtub. Next I'm going to insist that Max gets us an armed guard for the night, and then the three of us are going to go up to your bedroom, bar the door from the inside, and sleep together in that lovely bed of yours. I'll content myself for now by dreaming about where we were just before we were so rudely interrupted."

"Miranda and I get the tub after you," she said.

"Fair enough."

His plans took two hours in the making. That was how long it took for the police to wrap up what they were doing, for Leiber to lecture him about firing a gun inside the city limits, for a carpenter to cover the window to the kitchen door, and for the mess that had been made to be cleaned up.

Paul was patient, because he got not one armed guard, but two—one for the front of the house and one for the back. With calm restored, at least for the moment, Paul had his bath, and then while Terri and Miranda took theirs, he began going through the boxes with Irene's papers in them.

He read through a collection of papers that had been accumulated over time. Old Christmas cards, recipes, articles on childbirth and childcare, and clippings about Professor Drexler made up most of the papers that she had kept. Also included in the box were a dozen old magazines, one tagging an article about Florence, but the others showing no signs of bookmarks, so he wasn't sure why she had kept them. Nothing in his first reading of the papers offered a clue.

Before he thumbed through the magazines, he decided to give Pam a call. She would be mad at him if she heard the story on the news first.

She obviously had been asleep before she answered the phone. He didn't give her a chance to complain, explaining quickly the events of the evening.

"Paul, are you all right?"

"A little worse for wear," he said.

"You're not seriously hurt?"

"I look worse than I feel," he said.

"What are you going to do now? Come home?"

"I still haven't gotten to the bottom of this."

"And you're going to get to the bottom of it even if it kills you. I know all about the tenacity of Paul Fischer."

"I have a police officer at the front door and one at the back. The chances of it killing me at the moment are pretty slim. I also think I know who's responsible and now I want to prove it."

For a moment he thought they had been disconnected because of the silence. When Pam finally spoke, it was with a tone he had not heard before. She said, "Is she very pretty?"

"She?"

"Terri Drexler?"

"Yes. And her daughter is a doll."

"Do I need to be worried?"

"I think we need to talk."

"Which means we still have something to talk about?"

"Yes, which means we still have something to talk about."

"I love you, Paul," she said, and then disconnected the phone.

That was like her, he thought, save the best for last, for an emergency. She didn't seem to understand that he needed her love all the time, not just when she wanted to meter it out; that he needed a deeper relationship with her than he had. That he needed for them to be a family. He felt only a child could give them that feeling. How quickly, he thought, in an instant, it all became so clear. Pam would have to give him all that Terri was giving him right now if she was to have a chance to keep him. And as clear to him was the knowledge that Pam could not give that much.

The bathroom door opened and Miranda came out first, and she came over and cautiously crawled onto his lap and into his arms. "You smell wonderful," he said.

"So does Mama."

Terri followed, wrapped in the thin bathrobe that now clung to the curves of her body because of the moisture left from the bath. He took a deep breath and held it, and then he admired every step she took as she came to him. "Was that you on the phone?" she asked.

"I called Pam."

As if pre-programmed, her face took on the quizzical look it did when Pam's name was mentioned. "About?"

"I didn't want her to hear about this on the news."

"And she was concerned?"

"About lots of things."

"She knows?"

"She's worried."

Terri sat down beside him and Miranda crawled from his lap to hers. She hugged her daughter to herself, and then asked the question that needed to be answered. "What do you intend to do?"

It was a fair question, but it wasn't the right time to ask it. He wasn't sure yet what he would do. He knew where his emotions were pulling him, but he also knew what kind of man he was. He was one who liked to play fair, and already he had not played fair with Pam.

"I can give you all kinds of answers, but to be honest, I would just be guessing. This has to be sorted and it has to take time. If you will wait for me, I think I will come back to you. If I can't do that, I will let you know as soon as I can. I know that isn't a good enough answer for you, and I will understand if you say you can't wait, but I have to do this right or I will destroy two relationships instead of one."

She said nothing as she gently rocked Miranda. When she did get up from the sofa, she looked back at him and said, "Let's go to bed."

He got up and followed behind her, thinking that going to bed with her, even with Miranda there, seemed like the most natural thing in the world.

He was up early, long before Terri or Miranda stirred. He looked in on the professor, who was awake but in no need of care.

They talked for a few minutes about the night before, and the professor said the same thing to him that he had said to Terri—this was too much to appease the curiosity of an old man.

Paul told the professor what he believed. If justice can be served, it must be served.

He put on a pot of coffee in the kitchen and then he went to the bathroom to survey the damage done to him. He was surprised. Once the swelling was gone, his one eye looked normal. His cheeks weren't bad, either. He had a little more blush than usual, but in some ways it was attractive. Why was it that women got to have all the fun with makeup and not the guys, he wondered. The other eye wasn't as bad as he thought it would be. Yes, he had a bit of a mouse, but the week had taken a huge toll on him already, and it showed by the dark circles under his eyes. The mouse was nearly obscured.

Terri would feel better once she saw his face, he knew. Last night the sight of him had been the worst of the trauma for her. For him, it had been when he heard the two men talking about going upstairs and killing all of them. When he was fighting with the men in the room, even when he was overwhelmed or having bullets fired at him, he hadn't felt fear. He still felt the odds were even for him then. The idea, though, of them going after and Miranda and Terri was almost more than he could hold inside. That was why he woke so early. The anger had boiled in him in the middle of the night. It had grown into a rage, and the only thing he could do to satisfy it was to promise himself that if he got the chance, he'd kill the men before he would let them harm this family. With that decided, he crawled back in bed.

Two hours later, all of it spent staring at the ceiling and listening to the gentle breathing of the two females who clung to him in their sleep, he let the rage subside. He was, after all, a gentle man. He wouldn't kill anyone unless he had to. Instead, he would see to it that the men got put away for as long as the law allowed. Either way, whatever he had to do, they would not threaten Terri and Miranda again.

After a shower and a very careful shave, he dressed and went back to the kitchen to cook breakfast. When mother and child came down, the kitchen was filled with the aroma of hash browns, sausages, and eggs. Terri made a stack of toast, and the three of them had a feast.

"Nothing like stark terror to stimulate the appetite," Terri said. "And by the way, you're beautiful again. I didn't think it would ever happen."

"Loan me some of your makeup and see what I can do."

"No way."

"Selfish."

"Not selfish. You might start to like it and then you'd be using my makeup all the time."

During breakfast, Leiber called to tell them that the guards would be pulled at 8:00, and then he'd have a regular patrol during the day by the local police. They'd get guards again that night.

Paul asked about Marks's sons. Leiber, obviously trying to be diplomatic, said, "I think you will want to come up with something more substantial before you make any accusations against this family."

"Which means you are not going to try to interview the sons? Christ, Max, one look at them will tell you if I'm wrong," Paul said.

"Don't accuse me of not doing my job. I tried to see the two, but a funny thing happened. It seems they went out of town on business. They left early this morning."

"And no one has seen them, right? So no one can tell us if they show signs of being in a fight."

"Something like that."

"Can you have them tracked down?"

"Maybe if I call in the state police," Leiber said, "but I'm not going to do that without some proof. Your description could fit two hundred combinations of men from this area. And, considering that you never saw a face, you just don't give us enough to go on, legally or otherwise."

"Have you found out anything new?"

Leiber laughed. "We're not the N.Y.P.D."

"They don't always do so well themselves. Anything on the gun?"

"The serial number was ground off."

"Any idea where it came from?"

Again Leiber laughed. "Every other house that is broken into has a gun stolen from it. If you don't want to steal one, you can buy it from someone who did. Or you can get one at a gun show, or buy it new, or order on off the internet, or … "

"I get it," Paul said.

"Without the serial number, it doesn't matter where the gun came from," Leiber said.

"I'm sorry if I messed up any prints," Paul said. "At the time I wasn't thinking about prints."

"You didn't mess up any prints. Yours were clear. And they were the only ones. It is obvious that your attackers were wearing gloves. We didn't find any prints we shouldn't have."

"Thanks for the call," Paul said.

"You're welcome. And one more thing," Leiber said. "Stay in bed and let us do our job."

Paul hung up the phone.

"Let me guess," Terri said. "They can't locate Abe and Seth."

"If the boys are out of town, then this might be the right time to go talk to Ira again," he said.

Terri folded her napkin and placed it on the table. "Give me a few minutes to arrange for Dad and Miranda, and then we'll go see Ira together."

"Wait a minute," he said.

She came out of her chair fast, put a hand on his chest, and shoved him against the kitchen wall. He was so caught off guard that he could do little but struggle to keep his balance.

"Don't even think for a minute I'm letting you go by yourself. This involves me, too, now, and you're not going anywhere without me."

He wanted to laugh; her fierceness contrasted so much with the woman he knew. He had overlooked this strength, and now he knew he shouldn't have. She'd buried a husband, nursed a dying father, and kept them all afloat with her salary. Not only that, but she'd raised a terrific kid, and she had resisted jumping into a relationship simply because she was lonely. Here it was, laid bare for him, her incredible strength.

"Would you settle for staying in the waiting room with the cell phone to call for help if I need it?"

She eased up the pressure on his chest. "I'll think about it," she said.

He leaned down, cautiously at first, and kissed her lightly on the lips. Then he kissed her again, and again. She pulled away and mumbled, "Kisses, kisses, kisses. So many kisses."

"Too many?" he asked.

"Not in a lifetime," she said, and pressed her lips to his mouth so hard that his own lips hurt against his teeth.

A half an hour later, they were standing in front of Ira Marks's secretary, being told that they could not possibly see him today. He was far too busy. Paul and Terri shared a knowing look, and Paul brushed past the secretary, went to Marks's office door, and threw it open. It banged noisily against the wall. Marks, sitting behind his desk and pouring over columns of figures, only raised his head after he had written down his last tally.

While Terri stood in the waiting room with cell phone in hand, Paul shut the office door behind him and walked to Marks's desk. "We have sort of a precedent here," Paul said. "Everyone who was in Old Town the night Irene Drexler disappeared lied about it to the police. They've told me the truth. You lied when you said that Irene hadn't come into your store. Now it's time to tell me the truth."

Marks leaned back in his chair and locked eyes with Paul. "Get the fuck out of my office," he said.

"You know, I've been beaten up three times now. I've been shot at on two occasions. Once I was thrown in the river and left to drown. Sticks and stones may break my bones, but words aren't going to get me to move one goddamned inch."

Marks reached for his phone. "Then we'll have the cops do it for you."

Paul reached out, grabbed the phone, and hurled it across the room. It flew about five feet, snapped the phone line, and continued across the office to bounce twice before hitting the wall. "I want the truth."

"My secretary has already called the police," Marks said.

"Not likely. Terri Mankin would have broken her fingers."

Marks seemed to consider his options. Paul was between him and a dash for the door. The office was isolated from the rest of the building, probably so Marks wouldn't have to put up with noise. Yelling wasn't going to do him much good. Marks wasn't a weak man, so violence wasn't out of the question, but Paul was determined to get answers, whatever it took.

Marks leaned back in his chair and relaxed. "What is it you think I'm going to tell you?"

"I think you're going to tell me that Irene came into your store and then left. I'm not going to believe it, though. If that's what she had done, then you would have told the police that thirty years ago. She came into your store and something happened. You're going to tell me what happened."

"I would," Marks said, "but I didn't see her in the store that night."

"That's bullshit and you know it."

Marks smiled. "I took a lie detector test back then. Your records don't show that, do they?"

"What?" Paul couldn't believe what he was hearing. "You what?"

"Do you think the cops would take us at our word back then? They didn't know us from Adam, and because we were part of the Old Town crowd, they didn't trust us one bit. They insisted that I take a lie detector test. So I took it and I passed. I did not see Irene Drexler that night."

"Did anyone else take a lie detector test at the time?" Paul asked.

"How would I know?" Marks asked. "If the cops did test anyone else, then that person must have passed it, too, because no one got arrested."

"If Irene Drexler did not make it to your store, she had to disappear within a half a block of it. You didn't hear or see anything?"

Marks leaned forward on his desk and smiled even more broadly. "Not a damned thing."

That took the steam out of Paul. He decided to try a different tack. "Did you send your boys out of town this morning?" he asked.

Marks's smile disappeared. "What have my boys got to do with this?"

Paul was good at reading faces. Well, most faces. He hadn't done too well with Pam and her friends at one time, but he had since gotten better. The expression on Marks's face said clearly he could not imagine his sons involved in any of this. "Did you send them out of town?"

"I don't run their schedule. They run their own."

"Did they have a reason for leaving town this morning?"

Marks shrugged. "Probably. We've got warehouses all over the place to supply my stores. It's their job to make sure the warehouses are doing what they're supposed to do. That means regular checkups."

Now Paul's steam had petered out altogether. He couldn't think of anything else to ask. He was so sure that Marks had been lying. "I'll check on that lie detector test," he said rather lamely.

As he opened the door to leave, Marks called out to him. "You'll pay for the phone and any damage to the door, and the next time you try something like this, I'll make sure you go to jail."

Terri looked at Paul quizzically as he walked by. Without looking back, he grabbed her by the hand and pulled her along behind him. He glanced once at the secretary, who sat straight up in her chair, her face pure white and her hands folded in her lap.

"I bet there's a reason why she's sitting like that," he said.

He didn't see the smile on Terri face as she said, "I think I'll be joining you in jail."

[19]

WHEN PAUL STOPPED his car in front of the Drexler house, Max Leiber was sitting on the front step, waiting for them.

"Busted," Terri said.

They got out of the car and walked up the steps to meet the deputy. He wasn't smiling. "Word travels fast," Paul said.

"Actually," Leiber said, rising, "I was the fifth person to get a call. Let me see, that might be a new record. Five angry phone calls in less than ten minutes."

"Coffee?" Terri asked.

"Don't be nice to me, Terri. I could easily arrest both of you."

Paul walked past him and opened the front door. "No," he said. "I think the Florence police have the jurisdiction on this one."

Leiber and Terri followed him in. "Assuming you were thinking at all," Leiber asked, "what were you thinking?"

Paul went straight to the study and rifled through files until he came up with the one on Marks. Nowhere in it did anyone mention a lie detector test. Turning to Leiber, he said, "Marks said he took a lie detector test. How come it doesn't show up on the records?"

"Will you back off Marks if I can find it for you?" he asked.

"I'd have to."

"And then what?"

"I'd be out of suspects. I'd have to tell Bill that whatever happened to his wife was perpetuated by people unknown."

"Good answer," Leiber said. "I think that's an answer that everyone around here can live with, since it's the one they came up with thirty years ago. And if it will get you to back off before we have to lock you up, I'm sure someone will come up with those lie detector results, if they still exist."

"I'll make the coffee now," Terri said, leaving for the kitchen.

Leiber called after her, "Keep it hot. I'm going see if I can get those results right away."

Alone, Paul sat back on the sofa and tried to sort through it all. Was it possible that Irene never reached the store? Even now the street heading back up to the highway was dark. If she had been knocked out or grabbed around the mouth, she might not have had a chance to scream. Maybe everyone was telling the truth. Maybe he had just made a huge mistake and should be thankful he wasn't in jail.

Terri stuck her head in the doorway. "Feeling foolish?"

"No, I'm saving that for when I see the lie detector test."

"He might have been able to beat the lie detector. I've heard that some people can."

"Maybe now, but I doubt if he was as self-possessed then as he is today."

"If he did tell the truth, then my mother had to have disappeared before she got to the store."

"Exactly. A dark spot, maybe a car parked on the street. She could have walked by, and someone stepped out of the car and grabbed her, put her in the car, and drove off. It would have only taken a few seconds. They could have been out of town in minutes."

"Except for one thing."

"What's that?" he asked.

"Billie said the street was deserted. No mom and no cars."

"And we believe Billie?" Paul asked again

"I do," Terri said.

"Damn," he said, and turned back to the stack of files. He had gone through two cups of coffee and most of the files again when Leiber returned. He held a slim manila folder in his hand.

"This police department doesn't throw anything away," he said, handing the folder to Paul.

"Why wasn't I given it in the first place?" Paul asked.

"Because it has Marks's name on it. He may not have been something then, but he is something now."

"Of course. He's one of the good old boys."

"No, but he's been good to this community. You get this because it makes him look good, not bad."

The actual readout from the test was not there, but the person who had administered the test wrote a detailed analysis. His conclusion was absolute. Marks had not seen Irene Drexler that night. The last thing Paul looked at were the list of questions Marks was asked. After going through it once, he started to set aside the list, and then it hit him. He looked again. After the second time, he tossed the questions aside and began rummaging through the files again until he found one on Mary Ann Stranton. He read that again.

"I'll be damned," he said.

He had an audience but hadn't noticed. Both Leiber and Terri leaned in the doorway, watching him shuffle through the papers. "What did you find?" Terri asked.

"We've been looking at the wrong person," he said.

"That's what I told you," Leiber said.

Paul picked up the list of questions and waved them in the air. "The administrator of the lie detector test asked all the right questions but one. He asked if Irene came in the store. He asked if Marks knew what happened to her. He asked if he had seen her that night. He even asked if Marks killed her."

"And he passed all those questions with flying colors."

"Yes. But the questioner left out the most obvious question. Was Marks even in the store during the time that Irene disappeared?"

"Of course he was," Leiber said. "He said he was."

"But he wasn't in the store." Paul held up another file folder. "Mary Ann Stranton was interviewed about where she was that night. You see, Mary Ann was a part-time clerk in Marks's store. She left work at 9:00 that night. Marks gave her a ride home."

"So he left the store for a few minutes," Leiber said.

"According to her, her ride didn't leave until 10:30. Marks took her home and stayed for ... "

"Dessert?" Terri offered.

"He apparently stayed for something, but whoever has gone through these files before never picked up on it. Marks was out of the store for more than an hour and a half."

"And his time was accounted for," Leiber said.

"So the version of what happened at the store when Irene was walking toward it comes from his wife, not from him."

"So now you think Beverly is the murderer?" Leiber asked, incredulous.

"I didn't say that," Paul said. "But I would like to talk to her."

Leiber shook his head. "No!" he said. "Absolutely not. You should have gone to jail for your last little trick. Leave it alone."

"But Max," he pleaded, "look at the reports. Marks answered all the questions for the police that night. His wife didn't say a thing. We really don't have her statement."

"Forget it," Leiber said.

Paul knew he wasn't going to get his way. He also knew that the chances of him talking to Beverly Marks were nil. Still, to give up now, with one potential witness unquestioned, wasn't something he was willing to do. He had to find a way to convince Leiber.

"Then I want to talk to Mary Ann Stranton," Paul said.

"That isn't going to happen," Leiber said.

"You're not going to let me talk to her? What, does she own a chain of stores, too?"

"If you can find her, feel free to talk to her. I ran what little information we have on her. She doesn't show up anywhere. My guess is she moved away long ago."

"Okay, I give up," Paul said. When he glanced up, he could see that neither Leiber nor Terri believed him. "Go have your coffee. I'm going to put this stuff away."

After they left the room, he went back to the box with Irene's papers. He looked at each paper again, making sure that he hadn't missed something. Then he started on the magazines. Irene had said she had found out a secret about someone. Paul had assumed that it must be a male, since almost everyone in Old Town that night was a male. He hadn't considered that it might be a female.

He heard Leiber leave. Terri stuck her head in to ask if he would listen for her father while she took Miranda next door to play and she had coffee with her neighbor. He agreed, barely lifting his head from the pile of papers and magazines that surrounded him.

He finally found it in a copy of *Time*. The picture wasn't very good and he would have missed it altogether, except Irene had circled it. The story was about a group of left-wing activists who were responsible for a series of attacks, fires, and bombings that had left eleven people dead, all part of a protest against America's involvement in the Vietnam War. As the article pointed out, four of the radicals were now dead. Two were killed in an attempted bank holdup. Two more were killed when police found their hiding place. Only one of the radicals remained free, Myra Louise Estes. She had left to go to the store just before the police arrived, it appeared. Seeing the police when she returned, she dumped her groceries and took off.

Paul went to the Internet and began a new search. He ended up on a site with the FBI's most wanted list. Still active was a file on Myra Louise Estes. She had never been found, and she was still wanted for capital offenses, the kind that did not have a statute of limitation. The kind that could get the death penalty today.

Beverly Marks was publicity-shy. She only appeared in public when she could wear big, floppy hats and sunglasses, but she wasn't perfect. In the archives of the local newspaper, which were now available on the net, one picture had been taken that showed her in the background, behind her husband. The picture was ten years old. Still, with only a little imagination, a curious person might see a similarity between Beverly and Myra Louise Estes. Maybe Walter Higgins wasn't the only person to find Florence the perfect place to start a new life with a new identity.

Paul stayed on the Internet, searching for a variety of things from marriage records to maiden names to family histories. Two hours later he was absolutely sure of one thing. Beverly Meyers—Beverly Marks's maiden name—was not who she seemed. He could ask Pam to see if she could get the police in Medford to run another check, but he didn't see the point. He had enough information to know he had to talk to Beverly Marks. Now, he had to figure out a way to do that—safely.

If she was Myra Louise Estes, then Paul was sure she had unleashed her boys on him without a second thought of the consequences. She had been a hardcore radical in her day, and she had preached violence as the way to get what you wanted. Not only that, she had practiced it. At least three of the deaths credited to her group were carried out by her. She had remained on the FBI's top ten most-wanted list for five years. If Beverly Marks was Myra, she had nothing to lose by seeing Paul dead. Taken into custody, she would never see freedom again, and she might face the death penalty.

That might explain why the two sons kept coming after Paul. He wondered where Ira Marks fit into all of this. From what he had learned from records, back newspapers, and Marks's official company biography, he had met Beverly in Florence in 1968. She was waiting tables in a small café on the south side of the river. Marks used to go there for lunch when he could afford it, which wasn't very often at the time. It took nearly a year for a romance to begin, and another year before they were married. Marks had already opened his store and was making a success of it by that time.

From the description of the bride in the local newspaper, she was blonde and she had her hair cut short. She certainly did not match the description of the long, dark haired, brown-eyed Myra, except for height and weight. Paul got that from the FBI wanted information and from Beverly's description in the gushing account of their marriage in the local, weekly newspaper at the time. Chances were that Marks still didn't know whom he had married.

He found Marks's address in the phone book and located the home on the map Terri had given him. Once Marks had become successful, he built a sizable home for his family, described by the local paper as a compound. Up beyond the docks in Old Town, the Siuslaw widened to the north, some of it the mudflats that Paul noticed when he first came into town. Just around the bend though, the water was still deep and there, on the bank of the river, Marks had built his home. The spot was high enough so he did not have to worry about floodwaters, and it had a sloping yard in the back, a lush green lawn that ran down to the river and the Marks's private dock.

The perimeter of the property was surrounded by a ten-foot stucco wall, and iron gates closed off the only entrance. The article said Marks had one of the best security systems available, including a camera at the gate to identify visitors. Marks had chosen to build the two-story Spanish style home in a U shape, so that the interior courtyard was surrounded by verandas and at its center was a swimming pool.

Paul wasn't sure how he was going to get into the compound, but he knew he had to find a way, and soon. Marks would still be at work and the boys were out of town. If he could meet Beverly face to face, he was sure he would finally find out what happened to Irene.

He called next door to tell Terri that he needed to run some things back to the local library. It seemed like he had just hung up the phone when the front door opened and Terri returned.

"That was fast," he called from the den.

Terri came to the door. "Give us about a half an hour and we'll go with you. My neighbor can come over to watch Dad then."

"Terri, it will just take me a few minutes to run these things back."

"I want to go with you."

"Now you're being silly."

"I'm not being silly, Paul. I'm being very practical. After this morning, you showed me that it is very important that one of us remains very practical."

"Which means you don't trust me."

"I don't trust you," she said, nodding her head in agreement.

"Terri, ten minutes. Twenty at the most."

She wasn't smiling. "Will you promise me to go to the library and come right back?"

"I promise," he said, feeling only a slight hint of guilt as he said it.

"If you're not back in twenty minutes, I'm calling Max."

"What are you going to tell him? I'm overdue at the library?"

"I'm going to tell him that you are trying to get to Mrs. Marks."

"If I want to get to Mrs. Marks, I could call her."

"If she'd answer the phone."

She would not answer her phone. That was the first thing he tried when he decided he needed to talk to her. That was why he decided he needed to go directly to the house. "I'm going to work on Max. I'm going to see if I can get him to talk to her."

"Twenty minutes. If you're not back, I call."

"Fine," he said. He gathered up some materials and tucked them under one arm. As he walked by Terri, he kissed her on the cheek. She still did not smile at him. Already she had him figured out, only she was so new at it that she didn't know she had it right. If they spent a year together, he'd never be able to get away with anything again.

She was standing in the front window, watching him as he pulled away. He could almost imagine her beating a quick path to her car and following him. He sped up. He had no time to fool around. He drove directly to Marks's house and stopped the car in front of the iron gates. A speakerphone was built into the wall next to the gate. He got out of the car and pushed the button, expecting no answer.

A woman's voice said, "Yes?"

"This is Paul Fischer to see Mrs. Marks," he said, pushing the button a second time and bending town to talk into the speaker.

The iron gates swung open. Surprised by how easy all of this was, he got back into the car and drove along the circular drive until he stopped in front of double doors in the center of the house. As he got out of the car, one of the doors swung open, an invitation for him to enter.

He expected a maid to be on the other side of the door. He was wrong. Seth stood behind the door, and as soon as Paul walked in, he stepped out and placed the muzzle of a .45 automatic to Paul's forehead. From the other side of the doorway, Abe joined his brother with a second gun in hand. Beverly Marks entered from the living room. Paul had to smile at what he saw. Over fifty now, Beverly had let her hair go back to its natural color and she had let it grow out again. Even with her hair heavily streaked with gray, she looked like the grainy black and white photo in *Time*. Irene Drexler must have had a good eye for faces to recognize her as she had.

To Seth she said, "Put his car in the garage."

"Myra Louise Estes, I presume," Paul said.

"You disappoint me," she said. "I expected someone much less stupid."

"Stupid for coming here?" he asked.

"No, that just confirms my initial impression. I thought you were stupid when you didn't pack up and leave after the first time the boys attacked you. Bring him in the kitchen."

She turned and walked back into the living room. Paul followed along behind, the automatic shoved against the base of his spine. Abe wasn't stupid about guns. With the barrel where it was, Paul couldn't have made any kind of a move without getting a major hole in his anatomy.

As she led them into the kitchen, she asked, "What has possessed you to come here?"

"I came to Florence to find the answer to a mystery. You seem to be the one who has the answer. Where else would I go?"

"To the police," she said.

"Oh, don't worry. They'll be along soon."

"When they do arrive, no one will be around to answer the door," she said. "Should they snoop around, they won't find anyone, and even if they were able to peek into the garage, all that they would see is a car with a cover thrown over it."

"And where will we all be?" he asked. He knew that he had taken the most daring and direct approach. He knew that Terri was probably calling the police right now, and he also knew the police would arrive within minutes to try to keep him from duplicating what he had done in Marks's office. He wasn't afraid, even with a gun in his back, and he wasn't worried. He knew he held all the cards. Within a few minutes, they would know it too.

She smiled at him. It wasn't a practiced smile, he noted. In fact, it looked like it almost pained her to do it. "The only thing

right now between you and the deep blue sea is a boat ride."
She nodded to her son.

Paul was surprised that they hadn't gotten it yet. He'd forced the issue. "You don't dare do anything stupid . . ."

He never got to finish the thought. The butt of the gun slammed into the back of his head, and he was out before his body hit the floor.

[20]

WHEN HE FINALLY came to, when he finally realized the throbbing in his head was as much the throbbing of a boat motor as pain, when he finally realized he was tied up and had tape over his mouth, and when he finally realized he couldn't see because he was hidden under a tarp, Paul took the time to wonder just exactly what had gone wrong. He knew from experience that disasters usually started out sounding like pretty good ideas at the time. He also knew that intelligent people were sometimes the most gullible. He had known all of that before he had driven into the Marks's compound.

He hadn't felt himself a fool at the time. If he had tried to sneak in, one of them would have shot him and said they thought he was an intruder. By walking in the front door, in broad daylight, with the police not far behind, he thought he was doing the most logical thing. He'd have his confrontation before the police got there, he'd have the answer to the mystery of Irene Drexler, and he would force the police to look seriously at Mrs. Marks. It had seemed reasonable.

What he had apparently overlooked was that his only other experiences at tracking down mysteries had been pretty benign.

Yes, he had been roughed up. Yes, he had been threatened. Yes, of course, he had been manipulated. Yes, he had nearly been killed. But before now, no one had systematically tried to kill him. These three had. That was the mistake he had made, he knew now. He had overestimated their capacity to give up.

Suddenly he was blinded by light. When he could see again, after his eyes had adjusted to the low, silver-gray clouds overhead, he could make out Beverly Marks squatting down beside him, the corner of the tarp in her hand.

"I just thought I'd let you know," she shouted over the noise of the engine, the wind and the waves, "that we have this wonderful seagoing cruiser. Things will get rough for a little while until we make it through the jetty and over the bar, but then we'll have clear sailing to deep waters." She smiled at him. "I guess maybe you have about a half an hour more to live. I'm kind of glad. I thought we had killed you back there. This gives us a chance to talk."

He tried to say something, but, of course, the tape made that impossible. He expected her to pull the tarp back over his face, but instead she reached down and with a quick jerk, ripped the tape from his mouth. "Don't even bother to yell," she said. "Your voice won't carry beyond the boat."

Once he had recovered from the pain of facial hair being removed with the tape, he asked, "Irene Drexler?"

She laughed. "What they say about you is right. You are a tenacious searcher. What do you want to know? That she came into the store that night, that she said I looked just like that radical they were looking for, and that I killed her, beat her to death with a quart bottle of milk?"

"Is that the way it happened?"

"Not quite," she said. "I assured her I wasn't the radical at all. She said it would have been a good story if I were, a good joke. You see, she and her husband were part of the liberal university crowd who never saw what we did for what it was—terrorism. They thought it some romantic kind of noble act. If I had told her who I was, I knew she wouldn't turn me into the police. But she would have to tell someone. She felt too clever about it, having discovered me. I could see she wasn't convinced I wasn't Myra."

"Where did you kill her?" he asked.

"Right there," she said, smiling again. "She had turned her head to look at the magazines, and I picked up the milk bottle she had set down and swung it like a baseball bat and caught her right on the temple. She never saw it coming; she never made a sound. She simply collapsed on the spot. It was perfect. The bottle didn't even break, and the side of her head sort of cracked like an eggshell, but even then there was very little blood. I hardly broke the skin. I closed the store, dragged her to my car and put her in the trunk."

"That must have been difficult," Paul said.

"Are you another one of those chauvinists who think a woman can't do anything? I was fit back then, and she didn't weigh all that much."

"What did you do with her?"

"That's the really funny part," she said. "She's buried no more than two hundred yards from Drexler's house, no more than 400 yards from the store, across the river in Honeyman Park, not that far from the shore of the Siuslaw. I didn't have much time. I dragged her up next to a steep bank of sand, and then I started to scoop the sand on top of her. I got lucky. I got a slide going that buried her for me. Drexler has probably looked out at the spot from his house almost every day he was home for the last thirty years. I laugh every time I think of it. It's funny now when I think back on it, but it wasn't funny at the time. I was in a panic. I just beat Ira back to the store with enough time to clean up, and it wasn't five minutes later that a cop car cruised by.

"I'm surprised no one has found the body by now. I couldn't get it very deep with the time I had, but I put it in a natural area that's closed to the people who use the park but close to an access road."

Nuts in the beginning, nuts in the end, Paul thought. She was enjoying telling him the story. She probably took pride in the fact that she started out as a killer, and now she would get to continue it, with the bonus of dragging her boys along with her this time.

He couldn't resist another question. "Didn't the police search Honeyman Park?"

She smiled and shrugged. "The bitch disappeared in Old Town so they searched Old Town."

"Did Ira know?"

She laughed longer this time. "Ira doesn't have a clue. I hope that someday he finds out who I am. I just came here to hide out. It's a great place to hide out."

"And he suspected nothing about Irene?"

"He had his own secrets to worry about. He was so self-absorbed with the affair he was having that it never crossed his mind that I might have my own secrets."

"You didn't care if he had an affair?" he asked.

"I only married him to help me stay hidden," she said.

As long as he was going to die anyway, Paul wanted to make sure he had all the questions answered. "Why did he say he was in the store?"

"Obviously I didn't want any close contact with the police. I told him I hadn't seen Irene that night, and I wanted him to deal with the police. He did."

She really seemed pleased to be able to tell him all of this. She wanted someone to appreciate how clever she was. Having been in hiding all these years, she'd no doubt had to suppress her pride of accomplishment, he thought. "Your boys?" he asked.

She glanced up, toward the upper deck of the boat, where the controls were. "It's just like them," she said, her face softening. "It takes one of them to steer and the other one to figure out the direction. They're not stupid boys, just lazy. Their father gave up on them early."

"They know about you?"

"After the thing with Irene," she said, "I no longer felt safe in the store. I insisted to Ira that I wanted to be a housewife, have children. He didn't object much. I knew he was banging Mary Ann even then, and to have me out of the store would just give him time to bang more women. Ira is like that."

Again he asked, "The boys?"

"They're mama's boys. How else would they be? Ira was never around for them. When they became teens, I saw that they were disrespecting me the way they disrespected their father. I had to do something to let them know I wasn't just another woman, another housewife. I let them know that I'd been someone."

"You told them about your past?"

With pride she said, "You bet I did. I'd burned down buildings, blown up chemistry labs, robbed banks and killed people—and I'd gotten away with it. They learned quickly that their mama was someone to respect."

"So when I came along, it didn't take much to get them to go after me."

"Those boys," she said, pride showing on her face, "want to be just like their mama."

The boat began to rise slowly and then drop down into troughs as it worked its way between the jetty walls toward the open sea. Once past the Coast Guard tower, the rising and falling became more dramatic, and Paul could hear the change in the engine as the boys added more power to keep the boat stable.

As the boat dropped down from the next wave, Beverly lost her balance and flopped down on her butt. Paul might have laughed at another time, but he knew he had to focus on how he was going to get himself out of this. Somewhere in the back of his mind, he knew that the odds would catch up with him eventually. Deep down his subconscious was telling him it was time to kiss his ass good-bye, but his conscious was cheerfully saying, we can do it, Paul.

When she had fallen, Beverly let go of the tarp. The boat came down, twisted with the swell, and tilted to one side. The tarp fell away from much of Paul's body. Beverly seemed unconcerned. She carefully got to her feet and then, hand on the side of the boat to steady her, worked her way to the ladder that led to the upper deck. She climbed up a few steps so that her head lifted above the cabin and shouted something to the boys, the words carried away by the wind, the sound of the waves, and the noise of the engine.

With her back turned, Paul took the opportunity to kick the rest of the tarp away from his body. He lifted his head up so he could see himself. The boys had tied his feet together, and they had crossed his hands and tied them in front of him. Near his feet was an anchor, but they had yet to tie that to him. They would, though, he knew, if he gave them the chance.

As the boat fell into another trough, Paul was able to fix their location. It wasn't very good news. To his right he could see the marker light that sat on the end of the North Jetty. In another few minutes they would be over the bar and out to sea.

Paul didn't have a plan. He made plans for things like this, he told himself, when he thought he would get into things like this. If he had a future, and if he took on any more of these projects, he'd have to do a better job of planning.

For now he accepted two possibilities. One, if he stayed in the boat, they would eventually attach an anchor to his feet and throw him overboard out to sea. Even if he managed to get free of the anchor, the chances of him making it back to shore were slim. The second possibility, which was equally bleak, was to go overboard now and take his chance on the ocean. With the tide coming in and the surf pounding, odds were that he wouldn't make it, even if they didn't manage to shoot him first. Still, as remote as it seemed, the second option gave him a chance.

He spun around on his back. When the boat finally cleared the bar and the waves settled down, Beverly turned back to him. He let her take about four steps toward him before he lifted his legs and thrust out his feet to plant them firmly in her stomach. She flew backward and slammed into the ladder, and then she doubled over and fell to the deck.

He thought it would be a nice, fluid movement. He'd get to his feet and throw himself overboard. However, with his hands and feet bound, he discovered nothing was fluid. He managed to roll over on his stomach, and he managed to get up on his knees, but he couldn't get up on his feet. He had to hop on his knees to the cushioned seats that ran in a U shape around the stern of the boat. There he was able to push himself up to a standing position.

He got his hands on the railing around the boat and his knees on the cushions, and then he heard the screaming. Beverly had recovered. She threw herself at him and grabbed him around the waist, her head against his side, the whole time yelling, "Boys, help me!"

Paul couldn't pull himself over the railing with her weight dragging him back. He looked up to the control deck. Both boys were staring down at them, each with a gun in hand. He didn't have much time. Paul pulled his arms to the left, and then he swung them back to the right, his elbow catching Beverly on the side of the head. Her grip slackened.

A bullet shattered fiberglass close to Paul's shoulder. Beverly screamed, "Don't shoot, stupid, or you'll hit me!"

Paul swung again and hit her a second time. She let go, yelling, "Now shoot the son of a bitch."

Paul lunged forward, bullets flying all around him. It only took a second for him to hit the water, but it seemed like a lifetime. The water wasn't going to help him much, he knew. The boys had the boat in idle and were swinging it around, so that when he came up, Paul was off the stern. Here the water was still rough, but he was rising and falling with waves, each rise bringing him into the sights of the guns.

The boys emptied their guns, and then they reloaded and emptied them again. Paul let himself sink under water as often as he could to escape the bullets, but he had to breathe, and each time he came up, he faced the guns again.

The boys were not like their mother. They had proven to him twice before they didn't have the instinct to go for the kill. The bullets missed—except for a wild shot that hit something in the boat that brought the motor to a stop. Suddenly the boys had more important things on their mind than Paul. Not Beverly, though. While the boys hurried back to the controls of the boat, she climbed the ladder, grabbed one of the guns, and began taking aim at Paul again.

With movements better suiting a mermaid, he had been undulating his way away from the boat. A .45 made big holes at close range, but beyond twenty-five feet it was a scattergun. As hard as Beverly tried, she didn't come close to hitting Paul. It didn't help her aim, either, that the boat was now being driven by the tide back into the jetty, the waves tossing and turning it out of control.

Paul had his own worries. If he were driven back into the jetty, too, he'd never survive. If he didn't drown in the churning waves, he'd be smashed against the rocks. He needed to slip to the other side of the North Jetty and see if he could make it to the beach.

He let himself sink under the water and folded over so he could feel the rope around his feet. It took him a half a dozen tries before he got the knot loose, and then another half dozen tries to unwrap the rope from his feet.

He was cold and exhausted when he finally had his feet free, and when he looked up he was only twenty yards away from the end of the jetty, being swept by the tide directly toward the boulders. He rolled over on his back and began kicking his feet with all the strength he had left. He closed his eyes and kept kicking until he didn't have the strength to kick any more.

When he opened his eyes again, what he saw terrified him. He was being lifted in the air by a monster wave and sent flying directly toward a huge rock at the very tip of the jetty. He shut his eyes again and waited for the pain. Instead, he felt himself plunged back into deep water. The wave had swept him over the boulder and into the surf on the north side of the rocks.

It was high tide, and the waves were massive. Although the shore was no more than a hundred yards away, Paul couldn't imagine himself having the strength to swim to it with his hands tied. He glanced around, hoping against hope that help would be there.

Help came in a strange form. A seal went flying by no more than twenty feet away, riding on the crest of a wave. The seal was body surfing. Once, as a kid, Paul had tried it. With so little strength left, he couldn't imagine himself having the energy to catch a wave, but faces flashed through his mind: Terri, Miranda, his boys, Beth, Pam. . . How could he slip from earth with so much unsettled? He kicked his feet again, as hard as he could, and when it seemed like he could kick no more and he had failed, a wave embraced him, lifted him up, and shot him toward the shore.

It was a large, ponderous wave, one that he rode nearly to the beach, but it wasn't one that was going to set him down gently on the sand. When it ran out of power, it simply tumbled to a halt and dumped him. He was head over heels first, being rolled violently toward the shore, and then he was violently sucked back to the ocean. Twice he'd swallowed water, only to spit it out. He held his breath until he thought he could not hold it any longer even though his head was still under water.

He let it out and gasped one last time.

And he sucked in air as strong arms lifted his head from the surf.

Although no one would notice because he was already soaked in salt water, he cried. The next moment, an explosion nearby directed everyone's attention to the jetty.

[21]

IN THE END, Paul thought, the mother was no smarter and just as lazy as the boys. None of the three had thought to put on a life vest. When the boat was driven into the jetty and then toward the rocks on the south side, they had stayed with it instead of going into the water. Maybe they wouldn't have survived either one. When the boat finally crashed into the rocks, it exploded, killing all three.

Paul had been pulled from the surf by several people, just some of a dozen or so who were on the beach that day and saw his body being hurled to shore by the waves. Ironically, because of the pounding surf and the wind no one had heard the gunshots. No one had witnessed what had taken place on the boat. No one had been on the jetty at the time because of the waves breaking over its top.

More due to dumb luck and incompetence than anything, Beverly Marks's plan had not worked. Paul had been lucky again, and he knew it.

For two days the police grilled Paul, sure that he had somehow caused the death of the Markses. He had been put in the hospital under observation, and a police officer was assigned to his door. He had been as good as under arrest. He took the matter in his own hands. He called the FBI.

The feds swept in and took over the case. All three of the Markses were fished out of the water, all three of their bodies worse for wear. The FBI brought in their own people to do the autopsy on Mrs. Marks, and shortly afterward, in a dramatic press conference, the regional director announced that one of the most notorious radicals from the sixties had been removed from their most-wanted list.

While he was in the good graces of the FBI, if not the local authorities, Paul asked a favor. He asked them to bring in their experts to see if they could find the remains of Mrs. Drexler. It took them three days, but they did. When Paul was allowed to leave the hospital and return to the Drexler house, it was an emotional reunion. Terri and Professor Drexler had just learned that Irene's remains had been found, and they were planning a funeral service and a burial. The professor had purchased a double plot years ago in the local cemetery. He would join his wife there soon, he told Terri, but he said it with such joy that she couldn't feel sad about it.

Terri was still mad at Paul for lying about going to the library. She came to the hospital both days to tell him how mad she was, and she reminded him again once he returned to her house from the hospital, right after she had thrown her arms around his neck and bawled.

When things finally settled down, Paul shut himself in the study and made several phone calls. The last one was to Pam. Although she didn't know it, when she had called him at the hospital, she had made up his mind for him. Once she had learned that he was suffering mostly from exhaustion and exposure and nothing more serious, she decided to stay in Medford and work on her case instead of coming to see him.

Now, after several calls, he finally tracked her down at the courthouse where she had just filed some preliminary motions involving her client. She took his call on her cell phone.

"Busy?" he asked.

Breathless, she answered, "I've been on the run all day. I won't even have time for dinner. The trial starts next week, finally."

"Good. You'll be glad when it's over."

"You're telling me." As an afterthought, she asked, "How are you?"

"I'm out of the hospital, but I've been told to take it easy for a few days to let everything heal. My body's taken a real beating."

"Will you be coming home then? I mean, you have solved the mystery and all."

"Not right away," he said. "I don't think we'll get much time to talk until your trial is over, and we do need to talk."

"I don't need the added pressure right now, Paul," she said.

"That's why I've rented a cabin on one of the lakes down here. I'm picking up the boys at the first of next week. I've got the cabin for three weeks. Hopefully your trial will be done by then."

"That cabin wouldn't be very far away from the Drexler house, would it?" Pam asked.

"No, not very far," he said.

"It seems like maybe you've made a decision already."

"No," he said, "I still have a lot to think about."

"We'll talk after the trial," she said and disconnected.

He stared at his cell phone, thinking that even when they were in the middle of an emotional struggle about their relationship, Pam needed to be in control. Even if she was losing, she needed to be in control. He glanced up. Terri was standing in the doorway.

"On which lake?" she asked.

"Siltcoos," he said.

"The kids will like that. Boating, fishing, swimming—it's got a channel that runs all the way to the ocean."

"I'm sure they'll find it and explore it."

She leaned her head against the doorframe. "Will we still get to see you?" she asked.

He dropped the cell phone on the coffee table and walked to her, taking her in his arms and resting his head on her forehead. "Every day," he said. To himself, he thought, and more often than that if I can.

And then they kissed.